Don't Get
Me Wrong

Also by Marianne Kavanagh

For Once in My Life

Don't Get Me Wrong

A Novel

Marianne Kavanagh

EMILY BESTLER BOOKS

ATRIA

New York   London   Toronto   Sydney   New Delhi

ATRIA PAPERBACK
An Imprint of Simon & Schuster, Inc.
1230 Avenue of the Americas
New York, NY 10020

First Emily Bestler Books/Atria Paperback edition August 2015

EMILY BESTLER BOOKS / ATRIA PAPERBACK and colophons are trademarks of Simon & Schuster, Inc.

For information about special discounts for bulk purchases, please contact Simon & Schuster Special Sales at 1-866-506-1949 or business@simonandschuster.com.

The Simon & Schuster Speakers Bureau can bring authors to your live event. For more information or to book an event, contact the Simon & Schuster Speakers Bureau at 1-866-248-3049 or visit our website at www.simonspeakers.com.

Manufactured in the United States of America

10 9 8 7 6 5 4 3 2 1

Library of Congress Cataloging-in-Publication Data

Kavanagh, Marianne Morgan.
  Don't get me wrong : a novel / by Marianne Kavanagh. — First Emily Bestler Books/Atria paperback edition.
    pages ; cm
  I. Title.
  PR6111.A866D66 2016
  823'.92—dc23   2015024169

ISBN 978-1-4767-5533-5
ISBN 978-1-4767-5537-3 (ebook)

To Philippa

Don't Get Me Wrong

❦ 2015 ❧

The waiting room was painted off-white. There were blue plastic chairs all the way round, their backs against the walls. In one corner, two women surrounded by shopping bags, heads close together, were whispering.

It was the kind of room that made you feel you were in the wrong place.

Kim was sitting by the window. Her blond hair was sticking up in tufts.

He sat down. Hospitals are always hot. But he didn't take off his jacket in case it looked like he was assuming something. Like a welcome. "Any news?"

She shook her head.

The whispering in the corner got louder. One of the women shifted her weight and a Tesco bag fell sideways, gaping open. Harry could see pizza boxes and a liter carton of milk. He said, "Can I get you something?"

She looked up. Someone had pressed inky thumbprints beneath her eyes.

He said, "You look terrible."

"Thanks."

She wore black jeans, as usual, but her T-shirt was faded. You could just make out the stencil of a grinning face and BRIXTON LIVE! in red letters. He said, "I meant you look tired."

She didn't reply.

"Coffee?"

"What?"

"Do you want me to get you some coffee?"

"No."

After a while, he said, "Tea?"

"Harry, shut up." Her voice was so loud that one of the women in the corner looked up. "I wouldn't have rung you if I thought you were going to sit there wittering all night."

Harry said slowly, "I'm glad you did, though."

She slumped, defeated. "I thought you ought to know."

Both women were staring at them now. We have become a TV drama, thought Harry. A bit of hospital entertainment for a Sunday night. He flashed them a brilliant smile to shame them, and they dropped their eyes. One of them righted the Tesco bag and moved it closer to her chair.

For a while, no one in the room spoke at all. Harry wanted to ask more questions. He wanted to take off his jacket. He wanted to get some coffee—ideally from the kind of machine that promised a double espresso. But he was unable to move. He felt like a fly in a web, all bundled up in sticky silk.

The door opened. A woman in a blue tunic and trousers glanced round. Kim went white and sat up straight.

"Don't get up," said the woman. "I just wanted to let you know that we're all done. I'm going off duty now, so I won't see you again until tomorrow. If you're still here then."

"What's happening?" said Harry.

"Are you a relative?"

"No, he's not," said Kim.

Harry read the name badge. Dr. Annan.

"He's a friend," said Kim, after a pause.

Harry shot her a quick glance.

The doctor said, "No change. We have to let the drugs do their work."

"How long before we know?" said Kim.

"I can't tell you, I'm sorry. It's just a matter of waiting."

Update over. Harry couldn't believe that Kim was letting her go. They watched the doctor walk out of the room, and Harry's need to know more was so strong that he almost shouted out. But he had no right to demand information. He had no right to anything. He felt the two women in the corner watching him. They had been listening to every word. "It's wonderful, isn't it?" he said in a loud voice, addressing them both. "The National Health Service. Such dedicated staff."

They looked away.

"But she's good," said Kim.

"I didn't say she wasn't."

He thought she was going to argue. The old Kim would have. Dived in to deliver a lecture on the public ownership of essential services. From each according to his ability, to each according to his need. But she said nothing.

"So what now?" said Harry.

"We wait." Her eyes had no expression. "Or at least I wait. You can do what you like."

"Here?"

"You can go in if you want. It's the bed on the left."

"Are you coming?"

"Not now."

She looked so small and defenseless, sitting there in the bland chair against the blank wall. It didn't suit her. Kim was a fighter. He said, "I could go home and get some stuff for you. A change of clothes?"

She shook her head. But he understood that. If life is shit, a clean pair of jeans isn't going to help. And she'd never cared much about the way she looked anyway. It was Eva who cared, with her long hippie skirts and beads and trailing scarves. Harry swallowed. "Do you want me to ring anyone?"

"Like who?"

"Your mother?" He could almost hear her voice. *I've never been very good with illness. I find it so draining.*

"I rang her this morning. She can't come."

Harry nodded. He wouldn't have expected anything else.

"Your father?"

She looked at him as if he were stupid. "Why would I want you to ring my father?"

Because he's family. And that's what you do at a time like this. You gather people around who might help. Even if you haven't seen them for years. "What about Jake?"

Kim stood up so suddenly, the chair jumped. "Harry, if you don't shut up, I'm going to find somewhere else to sit, OK? This is not some mess that needs you to barge in and take control. I've done everything that has to be done. I rang you because I thought I should. But I don't need you. I'm fine on my own."

She was shaking.

After a while, she sat down. But she kept her head turned towards the window, although you couldn't see anything—trees, red buses, ambulances—because of the white slatted blinds.

Harry felt in his jacket pocket for his phone. "I'm going outside. I'll be back later."

If she heard, she gave no sign.

In the corridor, which smelt of warm disinfectant, Harry—in his City suit, handmade, cashmere—leant back against the wall. The hopelessness made his body feel light, his bones hollow.

· · ·

Kim felt sick. The effort of standing up to Harry had swallowed the last bit of energy she had. She wished she had something in her pocket to eat—an old packet of mints, some chocolate. But she had nothing. She didn't even have any cash in her purse. That would have been something he could have helped with. He always had money. Notes folded over in thick wads, ready to be peeled off and spent.

"That your boyfriend?" said one of the women in the corner. They were both staring at her.

Kim shook her head.

"I wouldn't say no to him," said the bigger one. Her hair was pulled back so tight that the skin on her forehead was smooth and shiny. She wore gold hoop earrings.

Both the women laughed.

"He looks like that actor off the telly," said the woman with the earrings to her friend. "The Italian one who's always smiling. You know." She turned back to Kim. "So who is he, then?"

Kim realized she was shivering. She ran her hands up and down her arms.

"You all right?"

Kim hugged her arms closer.

"It's the waiting. That's what it is. It gets to you. We've been here since three. And now they're taking blood from him." She shuddered. "I can't do blood. I've never been any good at blood."

Leave me alone. Please leave me alone. I can't think about anything but not thinking.

The door opened. A nurse in a blue uniform stood at the threshold. Kim's heart missed a beat. But the nurse looked over at the women in the corner. "You can come through now."

There was the kerfuffle of finding coats and hoisting bags onto shoulders. As they left, the woman who'd been doing all the talking looked over at Kim and nodded. "I hope it goes all right for you."

The door slammed shut. Kim was alone again.

Except, as usual, Harry was around somewhere. Harry was always around somewhere.

Kim put her head in her hands.

2006

can't see her," said Kim.

Outside in the hot July sun, all the parents stood shoulder to shoulder, laughing and talking like guests at a wedding. The women wore pink silks and cream linen, the men pale gray suits. Gold bracelets shone. Diamonds caught the light, sparks of electricity. The new graduates in their black gowns stood out like crows.

From the top of the stone steps, Kim searched the faces below. All through the ceremony, she hadn't been sure.

"She'll be here somewhere," said Izzie.

But would she? Eva was never on time for anything. Kim took a deep breath. Don't think about it. Keep your mind blank.

Next to her, Izzie started waving. Kim looked down the steps, and the crowd parted, and there beneath them was a creased-looking man with a red face supporting what seemed to be a large floral sofa.

Izzie's eyes widened.

"All right, pet?" said the red-faced man, leaning up to kiss her.

"That was lovely," said the floral sofa. "I cried all the way through."

Izzie's dad seemed half-strangled by his collar. He kept jam-

11

ming a finger behind the top button, straining his neck like a football fan who can't see the pitch.

"So you got here OK," said Kim, to break the growing silence. "From Newcastle."

"No problem at all," said Izzie's dad. "Just a bit of trouble round Alnwick."

"Mam," said Izzie, finding her voice, "where did you get that dress?"

Her mother looked down, as if pleasantly surprised by the view. "I made it. What do you think?"

"Did you bring a coat?"

The crowd swayed against them. Izzie's mum rolled sideways, gliding on castors.

"Shall we go and find a cup of tea?" said Izzie desperately.

Kim shook her head. "I can't go yet."

The noise of the crowd was getting louder.

"You're waiting for your parents?" said Izzie's dad.

Kim shook her head. That feeling of desolation was creeping up on her again, like a cold mist. She wasn't expecting her parents. Her mother wouldn't dream of traveling all the way from the South of France. And her father, living in Leicester with his new wife and small sons, didn't even know the date of her graduation. "No," she said. "For my sister."

"So how about a few photos?" said Izzie's dad, taking out a battered camera in a brown leather case.

Kim felt embarrassed. She didn't want to get involved in someone else's family mementos. Izzie had been her friend since the first year, but that didn't meant she wanted to end up in a silver frame on a telly in Newcastle. She was just shuffling sideways, taking small steps so that no one would notice, when there was a shout to her left and a small explosion, like a firework. Somebody shouted, "Watch out!" way too late, and Kim found herself sprayed at close range by a magnum of cava or prosecco or, for all she knew (this being Edinburgh), vintage champagne. She blinked and spluttered as someone said, "Oh, sorry!" and then found herself, dripping wet, in the middle of a crowd, mobbed by people anxious to help, dabbed at with tissues, urged to take off her sodden rented gown. A tall woman in a bright blue fascinator kept saying over and over again, "Poor girl. Look at her. Look at her! Like a drowned rat." And then, in the midst of it all, shaking champagne from her hair, she heard a voice she knew.

"Kim?" said Eva.

With a rush of joy, Kim looked up. There was her sister with her white-blond hair, her fine-boned face, that same, ever-present look of slight surprise. And in the exact moment that she recognized her—as the familiarity of the person she loved more than anyone else in the world brought her truly alive again, from the top of her head to the tips of her fingers—Kim realized with a jolt to her heart that Eva was not alone.

Next to Eva, smiling, was Harry.

Kim narrowed her eyes. "What the hell," she said to her sister, "is he doing here?"

• • •

The hand basins were tiny. Every time someone turned on the taps, water hit the white enamel and sprayed all over the floor. As a result, the tiles underfoot were treacherous, like ice.

"I hate him," said Kim.

"I know. You've told me. Many times." Izzie's Newcastle accent was stronger than usual. Her parents had reactivated it, like sugar on yeast.

"She should never have brought him. Not without asking me."

"What would you have said?"

"What?"

"If she'd asked you?"

Kim lifted her chin. "I would have said no."

They had just arrived at the restaurant to celebrate their new graduate status. As the others took their seats, Kim, still seething, had grabbed Izzie's hand and raced her upstairs. Rage bubbled inside her, red-hot, like molten lava. She had visions of erupting like a volcano, turning everyone around her into stone. Years ago, Eva, briefly excited by homeopathy, had said that Kim's constitutional type was Phosphorus. This meant she was like a match—quick to light, and just as quick to burn out. It didn't help, knowing this. Kim would rather have been calm and saintly like Gwyneth Paltrow.

"You know, from the outside," said Izzie, "he seems quite normal."

Izzie had great admiration for people who fitted in. She didn't quite know how you did it. She pored over magazines, making lists of magical beauty products and books on self-improvement. She listened carefully when people raved about yoga or goji berries or learning Japanese. She worried that her hair was too wild, her thighs too fat, and that no one else found bassoons funny. "You look at someone like Kate Moss," she'd say, "and she doesn't seem to follow any of the rules. But everyone loves her. So what are you supposed to do?" Kim found this strange. Let people think what they like. What else can you do but just be yourself?

"He was talking to my dad about Michael Owen," said Izzie.

Kim looked blank.

"Newcastle United. Knee injury. World Cup."

"But that's exactly what Harry does," said Kim in a burst of irritability. She was leaning against the hand dryer on the wall, while Izzie—her foot jammed against the cubicle door to keep it open—sat on the closed lid of the nearest toilet. "Finds out what you're interested in and gets you talking."

"That's not a crime, is it? Being a bit chatty?"

The main door banged back against the wall, and a roar from the restaurant below rushed in. "Oh, sorry," said a woman with bright red hair and a green dress.

"Don't mind us," said Izzie. "We're just hiding from Harry."

The woman lunged forwards, skidded on the wet floor, and crashed headlong into a cubicle. They heard a small cry of pain.

Kim tried again. "He charms people. Gets them to like him."

"You don't like him."

"I see through him."

Izzie put her head on one side. "So you're saying it's all fake?"

"You can see it in his eyes. He's not straight."

"Not straight?"

"Hiding something," said Kim impatiently.

"We all hide something."

"You don't."

"How do you know?" Izzie raised her eyebrows.

Kim shifted position. The hand dryer turned itself on. Blasted by lukewarm air, she shouted, over the noise, "He's bad for her."

"For Eva?" Izzie waited for the racket to stop. "She can look after herself."

No, she can't. You have no idea. She's not as strong as she seems on the surface.

"Some people might say she's done well for herself," said Izzie. "He's rich. He's good-looking. There isn't a woman here who'd turn him down."

He's like toilet paper stuck to the sole of her shoe.

"What's he done that makes you hate him?"

Kim's head was spitting with so much fury she couldn't think where to start.

Izzie sighed. "I know. She's your sister. No one's good enough. But if he's the one she wants, you're fighting a losing battle. You're just going to make yourself miserable."

The toilet flushed in the next cubicle.

Izzie stood up. "It's like the serenity prayer. Change what you can, put up with what you can't, and be wise enough to know the difference."

This made Kim cross. Maybe you should follow your own advice, she thought, and stop trying to change yourself into what you think other people want you to be. But then she felt guilty. Izzie was only trying to help.

Back downstairs, deafened by shrieks and crashing cutlery, they were flattened against the wall by a waiter carrying a silver tray. "Do you want to swap places?" shouted Izzie. "I could sit next to him if you like."

It wouldn't make any difference, thought Kim as she followed Izzie through the crowded restaurant. Even if he was at the other end of the table. It's that oozing self-confidence. That conviction he's right. It seeps into the air like fog. He laughs at everything I care about. He makes me feel small and insignificant—as if I'm scurrying about like a tiny black ant while he strides about like God. The very first time I met him, he blocked out the sun. What was I—thirteen? Lying in the back garden in tatty old shorts and a crop top, the grass long under my fingers, soaking up the first hot day for weeks. Christine next door said the TV weather map had turned completely orange. I could feel my skin burning, tiny prickles of heat. *Always stay out of the sun,* my mother used to say. *So aging.* My one act of teenage rebellion—sunbathing.

"Kim? This is Harry."

The world went dark. An eclipse.

Eva said, "We're going to buy ice cream. Do you want some?"

I couldn't speak. Half-asleep, dazed by heat, I couldn't say a word.

"No ice cream?" A deep voice. A posh boy voice.

I looked up. But I couldn't see his face—just shadow, like a cliff, against the glaring white light.

"Are you always this talkative?"

"Oh leave her, Harry. She just wants to enjoy the sunshine."

I put up my hand to shield my eyes. And now I could see his expression.

"Harry?"

Laughing at me. His whole face creased up, grinning from ear to ear, as if I was one huge joke.

"Harry? Come on."

Then he moved, and the sun blinded me. I sat up, and the world was washed out, like someone had bleached it. I kept staring as they sauntered back to the house. He was a head taller than Eva but thin. Nothing but bones, as Christine would say.

At the top of the concrete steps, he stopped. "So that's your baby sister."

I waited, very still.

"You know, she could look quite pretty if she smiled."

The hurt. The rage. You'd think the years would make a difference. But they don't.

He spent most weekends in our house when I was a teenager. Taking up space. There was no one to stop him. Dad had walked out. Mum was floating about in a cocktail dress and a cloud of Chanel, happy to spend the evening (the week, the weekend) with anyone who asked her. You wouldn't know Mum had been born above a chip shop in Torquay. From her voice, you'd think she'd grown up in Kensington—in one of those grand white houses with black iron railings and nannies with prams like Cinderella coaches. Mum loved Harry. *Like a young Montgomery Clift. You know, darling? All those films from the 1950s.* She said he fitted so well with Eva—tall and dark against Eva's blond fragility.

That's all that mattered to Mum. The way things looked.

So Dad had gone, and Mum had gone, but Harry was always around. I'd walk into the living room to watch TV and there he was, lying on the sofa—head one end, feet the other, taking up all the seats. If he wasn't on the sofa, he was upstairs in Eva's room. I'd be sitting at the kitchen table, my GCSE maths book open in front of me, staring at the misshapen rectangles, and I'd

hear them laughing, and then thumping sounds, like things falling down, or off, or over, and music all the time, the old 1960s
stuff Eva liked—the Mamas and the Papas, Janis Joplin, Jimi
Hendrix. The Byrds, their voices twining in and out like textiles.
Eva said one of their songs was written by King Solomon. It was
in the Bible. To every thing there is a season, and a time to every
purpose under heaven. (If something isn't working, there's no
point jumping up and down, getting all stressed. That would be
like banging your head against a brick wall.) A time to be born
and a time to die. A time to weep and a time to laugh. A time to
love, and a time to hate. A time of war and a time of peace.

A time for calculating areas and perimeters.

I drew a small mouse in pencil on the corner of the book. It
had a pointed nose, two big ears like satellite dishes, and a long
thin tail.

There was no more thumping. They must have finished having sex. I colored in the mouse's ears.

I heard the bedroom door open. Maybe it was still the Byrds.
But it might have been Bob Dylan. The noise of feet coming
down the stairs. I pulled up a piece of paper to hide the mouse.

Harry came into the kitchen. He was almost as tall as the
door frame. Black shiny curls, like a cocker spaniel. A white
shirt, half-unbuttoned, making his skin look even darker. He always wore a white shirt. Like he never left the office.

"Doing your homework?"

I didn't answer.

Harry glanced down at the table. "Maths."

This didn't seem to need an answer either.

"Eva says you find it hard. You don't like it."

I wouldn't look up.

"It's not difficult. Give me five minutes and I could explain it to you."

So superior. Because you went to a private school. The thought of sitting with Harry looking at a maths book made me feel sick. I bent over my rectangles. I listened to him clattering about, making tea, dropping a spoon in the stainless steel sink.

At the door, on the way out, he stopped. I could feel him standing there, just watching me. Then he said, "You know where I am. If you change your mind."

I drew a large black blobby nose on the mouse, pressing hard into the paper. It stared back, affronted.

I know where you are. You're always bloody here.

. . .

"So what do you do, pet?" said Izzie's mother, settling back into her chair with a billow of flowery fabric. She wasn't the only parent who'd turned up in Edinburgh in strange clothes. But she was the only one apparently swathed in curtains.

"Not much," said Eva, smiling.

"She's a musician," said Kim, "and an environmental campaigner."

They had a table tucked into the corner of the restaurant, half-hidden by a stud wall. This meant their conversation wasn't drowned out by all the celebratory whooping and cheering from the new graduates around them. But it also meant that the waitress kept forgetting they were there. That's why I feel so drunk, thought Kim as she refilled her glass. There isn't enough food to soak up all the alcohol.

"Which means," said Harry, "that she travels round the country with her guitar, tramping through muddy fields in Wellington boots."

Eva laughed.

Kim glared at him. "What would you know?"

Eva's face was always angles and shadows. But tonight, whenever she stopped smiling, you could see she had dark circles under her eyes. Kim frowned. Was something wrong? Eva was never normally ground down by anything. Sometimes she found other people puzzling. But generally she believed that life sorted itself out if you didn't stress too much about the details.

"He came with me once," said Eva. "To a community in west Wales. A little farming settlement in the woods. I said he couldn't judge until he'd experienced it."

Harry looked mournful. "They made me eat lentils."

"Vegetarianism," said Kim, "is a much more efficient way of feeding the world."

"And fermented tofu."

"It's about putting precious land to the best use."

"And hemp." Harry frowned. "Or is that what you wear?"

A duel of wits with Harry excluded everyone else. Kim knew this. But she couldn't stop herself. "You can't pretend that eating a steak is just an individual choice. It isn't. What you do affects other people."

Izzie's mother glanced down at her empty plate with an expression of alarm.

"Basically," said Harry, "Eva was born in the wrong century. She wants to turn the clock back. No TV, no cars, no modern medicine. Her ideal would be some kind of medieval village.

Getting water from a well. Milking by hand. Grubbing for potatoes in the dirt. " His expression was wide-eyed and innocent.
"Full of people with boils and bad teeth."

As if, thought Kim. Eva radiates light. She shines. Children
and old ladies gaze after her with wistful smiles. Men stare at her,
wondering whether their lives could have been different with a
woman like that at their side. Eva, in her tatty hippie clothes,
drifting along in her own thoughts, doesn't notice the effect she
has on other people. But I do. And it's my job to protect her.

"That's not what Eva thinks at all." Kim gripped the edge
of the table, feeling the starched white linen under her hands.
"She's searching for a different way of life. It's not about turning
the clock back. It's about treading lightly on the earth."

"Making walls out of mud and straw," said Harry.

"Living in balance with nature."

"Chanting. There was a lot of chanting in Wales."

"It's a big movement now," said Kim loudly, because raising
the volume seemed the only way to drown Harry out. "There
are communities all over Europe. Germany, Italy, France, Spain,
Portugal, Lithuania—"

"We had to use compost toilets. In the dark. Surrounded by
Welsh sheep."

"—and all across the world. Australia, Brazil, the US—"

"She wants to live in an ecovillage," said Harry, leaning
sideways towards Izzie's father, who was looking completely
bewildered.

"Who does? Eva or Kim?"

"You know," said Harry, "I often wonder the same thing
myself."

"It must be a lot cheaper growing your own food," said Izzie's mum. "Sometimes I go shopping and I can't believe my eyes. The prices they charge! I said to the girl in Morrisons', these days you have to rob a bank just to pay for a KitKat."

"Climate change is caused by human greed and an over-reliance on cheap oil." Kim's voice rose above the hubbub of the restaurant. Diners at other tables were looking up. One of the waiters stood rooted to the spot, transfixed. "We can't carry on making selfish decisions, or we'll run out of resources. Politicians keep talking about growth. But what they mean is rampant consumerism."

"Would anyone like dessert?" said Izzie, half-standing. "They've got steamed ginger pudding with hot toffee sauce."

"I don't know," said Harry. "Is it vegan?"

"Our current economic model," said Kim, her cheeks flushed, "is unsustainable. We have to wake up to reality before it's too late. What kind of world do we want to pass on to our children and grandchildren? Unless we get to grips with this now, we're going to run out of time."

"Kim?" said Izzie. "Shall we go and find the waitress?"

Kim screwed up her eyes. Izzie seemed strangely out of focus. "What?"

"So we can order dessert."

"It doesn't need two of us, does it?"

Izzie pushed back her chair so violently that it almost fell over. Watching her best friend thread her way through the crowded restaurant, Kim frowned, confused. Was Izzie cross? Why?

"I do worry about you all," said Izzie's mum, turning to Kim in a sudden flurry of chintz, "setting out on your own. It's all right while you're living at home. But once you're in charge of paying all the bills, how are you going to manage?"

"Izzie can stay with us in London anytime," said Kim, looking to Eva for confirmation. But her sister seemed to be avoiding her eyes. This was getting ridiculous. What was wrong with everyone?

"She might take you up on that, pet. After she's done her teacher training. Her first job could be anywhere, couldn't it?"

Kim still couldn't imagine Izzie teaching. She'd asked her once, as they left a comedy club in the early hours, shivering with cold, "Do you actually like children?"

Izzie looked confused. "Is that part of the job?"

Izzie's mother settled back into her seat. "And what about you, pet? What are your plans for the future?"

Kim was finding it hard to concentrate. To her left, Harry and Izzie's dad seemed to have struck up a conversation about growing spring greens. Eva was toying with a butter knife, watching it balance on the end of her finger, catching the light. The restaurant was getting hotter.

"I'll do anything for a bit. You know, a call center. Or bar work or something. Just to earn some money." She sensed that Harry was looking at her. She could feel his gaze resting on her like a heavy weight. "And then I thought I'd try and get a job in housing."

"Like an estate agent?"

Kim looked horrified. "No. Social policy."

Harry laughed.

"And what about you, Harry? What is it that you do?"

"He's a banker." Kim managed to make it sound like a different word entirely. "Which is why he doesn't understand that some people can't afford market rents."

Izzie was squeezing past the back of her father's chair. "She's coming. And she says the sticky ginger pudding is delicious."

"What kind of banker?" said Izzie's mother. "One of those smiley people behind the security glass?"

Harry shook his head. "In the City. An analyst. I advise investors on what stock to buy."

"He gambles," said Kim. "With other people's money."

Harry leant back in his chair, grinning. "She doesn't have a very high opinion of banking."

"Because the City gets rich at the expense of the poor."

"The City is the UK's biggest industry. It provides jobs for thousands of people."

"Rich people."

"All people. And pays tax that funds housing benefit, and unemployment benefit, and the NHS—"

"Bankers," said Kim, at full volume, "are responsible for everything that's wrong with this country. They are evil, bloodsucking parasites." She hit the table for emphasis. Her glass of Rioja upended. Everyone looked down at the huge, spreading stain, seeping into the white cotton, thought Kim, like blood.

Izzie's mother shook her head with an expression of tragic gloom. "Can you imagine the size of the laundry bills in a place like this?"

. . .

"You know, it's not even real, what he does. It's just an illusion. Smoke and mirrors. Figures on a screen. One minute you're rich, the next you're nothing. But he doesn't care. You could be on the streets with all your clothes in a paper bag and he'd still be swanning round in his Porsche, eating Michelin stars and shooting pheasants. That's what they do, you know. Kill birds that can't even fly. Their wings aren't strong enough to get them out of the bushes. But all these fat idiots in pinstripe suits come and shoot at them anyway, just so they can say, Oh, look at me, aren't I clever, I shot a pheasant. I killed a deer and put its antlers on the wall. I speared a trout. I killed a lion. And then I flew off to the Bahamas in a private jet. You know, he doesn't even care about global warming? He said we might get champagne in Birmingham if it carries on like this."

"Kim?"

"What?"

"You're drunk."

Kim and Izzie were back in the restaurant toilets. The meal celebrating their graduation was over. Kim had a vague recollection of being frog-marched away from the table while the others hunted around for coats and jackets. Clinging to the hand basin, she tried to focus. In the mirror she could see her short blond hair sticking up from her head in soft bristles, making her look like a baby chick in a high wind.

Izzie was rummaging in her bag. "You've got to stop shouting at everyone. It's like being lectured by John Prescott. It's not the time or the place. We're meant to be enjoying ourselves. And there's no point going back to my parents' hotel for a nightcap if you're going to bore us all to death with another eco sermon."

Kim leant her head against the cold white wall. What's wrong with me? I didn't mean to shout at people. And I never drink too much. Ever. It's not what I do. Eva's the one who staggers back in the early hours, slamming the front door, tripping over the mat. That's what I remember from living at home—loud singing at three a.m., broken plant pots. I used to sleep with a pillow over my head. It was the only way to get any peace. During my last two years at school, Eva had a job in a gift shop, selling essential oils and dream catchers. Wafting about in a haze of incense. But every night, she got off her head and persuaded other people to do the same.

Most people find it hard to sleep in student halls of residence. Slamming doors, shouting in the corridors. But my first few weeks in Edinburgh were bliss. I slept for the first time in months.

The door to the restaurant toilets burst open. A gaggle of teenage girls came skidding across the floor, novices on a skating rink.

Izzie found a pot of blusher and brushed her cheeks pink. "I know you hate Harry. But you're making it really hard for anyone to have a good time. Including me. Everyone's looking at us. Did you see the woman at the next table? She was laughing so much I thought she was going to burst."

Kim hung her head. I'm acting like a child, she thought. Letting my feelings get the better of me. Have I ruined everything?

When she looked up, Izzie was staring at their twin reflections side by side in the mirror. They couldn't have looked less alike. Izzie made you think of a sepia-tinted photograph of Edwardian female perfection—round and soft, with pink cheeks and a cloud of dark hair. Kim—white faced, washed out, angular—looked like a ghost.

"What?" Kim didn't like being scrutinized so closely.

"There's something you're not telling me."

"Like what?"

"He's a smug git who's going out with your sister. But that's not enough to make you hate him. There's something else."

Kim shook her head.

"It goes way back, doesn't it? What did he do? Steal your pocket money? Kill your hamster? Shred your skipping rope?"

You don't understand.

Izzie looked thoughtful. "You know, sometimes people snipe at each other to hide how they really feel."

"What do you mean?"

"I'm wondering if you secretly like Harry. If you want your sister's boyfriend for yourself."

"No." Kim looked furious.

"Are you sure?"

"I can't believe you're even saying it." It was so way off the mark, it was insulting.

Izzie shrugged. "I'm only trying to find out what's going on. Because the way I see it, you're part of the problem. He's just fishing. But you grab the bait. Every time. And then he reels you in."

Kim swallowed.

"You let him get to you. And I keep thinking, Why?

For a moment, they stood there, staring at themselves—Izzie, the picture of rosy health, Kim dusty and white, as if she'd just crawled out of an understairs cupboard.

Kim dropped her eyes.

"If I were you," said Izzie, "I'd make a real effort not to say another word to Harry for the rest of the evening. Just pretend he's not there." Izzie twisted the clasp on her bag shut. "Because everyone else quite likes him. And I know you'll say he was only doing it to show off, but I think it was really kind of him to pay the bill. Before my dad could even find his glasses. And then say that it was our graduation present, so that my parents weren't embarrassed. It must have cost a fortune. With all the wine we got through."

The teenage girls were banging out of the cubicles. One of them slipped, landed in a heap on her bottom, and burst into loud screams of laughter.

"At least she's stopped drinking," said Izzie. "Have you noticed? Eva hasn't touched a drop all night."

.   .   .

Even though it was late, the streets of Edinburgh were still crowded. The air was warm. Walking back to the hotel where Izzie's parents were staying, the six of them had arranged themselves into pairs—Eva and Harry leading the way, Kim and Izzie following, with Izzie's parents bringing up the rear.

From time to time, they all stopped to let gangs of rowdy students take over the pavement. The whole city seemed to be one huge party.

Kim felt as if she was floating on a sea of alcohol. It wasn't pleasant. She was worried she might sink. Ahead of her, Harry and Eva were arm in arm, their bodies moving to the same rhythm. He was bending right down to listen to her, their heads close together, one dark, one fair. No one knows, thought Kim, what I know. What he's really like. And I can't tell anyone, in case Eva gets hurt.

Kim closed her eyes for a second, trying to ward off the sudden rush of memories. Eva's eighteenth birthday. She'd made her friends dress up as hippies. A re-creation of 1967 and the Summer of Love. God knows what their unremarkable suburb thought of all the headbands, caftans, and brown leather sandals trailing down the high street.

But then Nunhead was good at looking the other way.

Oh, thought Kim, I hated that time of our lives. I felt like a policeman, trying to stop Eva from self-destructing. After Dad walked out, Eva just lost it for a while. Drink, drugs—anything to blot out reality. She was in her last year of school but didn't turn up half the time. Not even for exams in the end. Mum wasn't any help. She was off on her own mission of self-discovery, trying to live it up before it was all too late. So it was left to me to protect Eva. Little sister looking after big sister.

Like the night of her eighteenth birthday. May 1999. Way past closing time, but Eva still wasn't home. So I went to find her. I had to bang on the door of the pub for a long time. They'd turned it into a lock-in—a private party. Inside I pushed through a wall of bodies. Jefferson Airplane, Grace Slick, White Rabbit. Sandalwood, vanilla, patchouli, skunk.

And then I saw her, sitting on a wooden stool right at the end of the bar, a purple patchwork dress falling around her in great velvet folds—cheeks flushed, eyes glazed, like a child who's been kept up way beyond bedtime.

I couldn't stop it. Seconds before I reached her, she leant towards the bar—her bangles jangling in a crash like someone had dropped a tambourine—and lost her balance. She fell through the air, arms outstretched, smashing through empty glasses and beer bottles. Someone screamed. Or maybe it was me. And then I was on my knees in the well of split beer and broken glass on the floor. She reached out and touched my face. "Where were you?"

She had cut her hand—a bloody gash at the base of her thumb.

I was fourteen. I shouldn't even have been there.

Someone was leaning down to help her, pulling her up so she could stand. Noise and heat and people all around us. The crunch of glass beneath our feet.

"I fell off," she said wonderingly. "I fell off the stool."

Harry was holding her. He had his arm round her waist. She rested against him, tucking her head into the crook of his shoulder. He lifted her hand and turned it over. He put his mouth against her palm, sucking away the blood. It was an act of such dirty intimacy that I felt sick.

"Is it Dusty?" I thought, for a moment, that Eva was talking about her hand. But she was listening to the music. Eyes closed. Drifting off again

I glared at him. "Why didn't you stop her?"

" 'The Look of Love,' " said Eva. "Dusty Springfield."

"Stop her falling?" Harry was smiling, as if it was all a joke.

"Stop her drinking so much."

"As if I had any influence over what your sister does."

Liar, I thought. Liar, liar.

"She died, you know," said Eva. "A few weeks ago. Breast cancer."

I wanted to get Eva home. I wanted to find some antiseptic and bandage her hand. I wanted to make a cup of tea and sit with her as she sobered up. I said, "Is it time to go? Time to get back?"

She opened her eyes wide. Even in the dingy light of the bar, you could see how blue they were. "It's too early. You haven't met all my friends yet."

"I can meet them another time."

"But I don't want to go."

"You've had an accident."

Eva pouted. "Only a little one. Harry will look after me."

"Like he has already?"

"I promise," said Harry, "that from now on I won't leave her side."

"You think I trust you?"

Dusty disappeared. A new voice rose above the noise in the bar—urgent, insistent soul.

"Try a little tenderness," said Harry, grinning.

I wanted to hit him. Turning Otis Redding into a joke.

He hid behind that smile all the time. Kind Harry. Nice Harry. Charming Harry. *Romeo and Juliet. So devoted. And comes from such a good family. Old money. Eton, I think. Or Harrow. And you know, he'll always be able to support her, working in the City. Such a relief for a mother to know her daughter will be financially secure.* Everyone was taken in by it. They all loved him. I was the only one who saw through it. And because of that, he tried to poison Eva against me. After every argument about how I wanted a different kind of world, how I wanted justice and fairness and equality, he'd mock me, belittle me, make me sound stupid.

"Has she always been like this?"

Sunday morning. Eva's door wasn't quite shut. I stood outside on the landing, listening to the whispers, imagining them in bed together.

"Ssshhh, Harry. She'll hear."

"She's a complete fantasist."

"It's just the way she is."

"She's insane."

It hurt so much. Not just what he said, but hearing Eva laugh. Because it meant she was on his side.

I found out the truth one Friday night. We were in a pub in New Cross. A whole load of us from school. Damaris, of course. And the usual gang of nerdy boys with thin wrists and soft stubble. None of us eighteen yet, so we shouldn't have been drinking at all. But the landlord turned a blind eye if we stuck to beer. That's what comes of going to the local neighborhood school. You blend into your surroundings. You become invisible.

And I looked up, and there was Harry. Sitting at a little table right in the corner. With someone who wasn't Eva. A girl with long black hair.

Of course you can have a drink with a friend. Why not?

And then he leant forward and kissed her very slowly on the mouth.

It was like an electric shock.

"Kim? Are you OK?" Damaris must have seen my face.

I felt sick. I wanted to rush over and scream at him. But I was too dizzy to move.

He should have seen me when they left. He walked right past our table. But he had his arm round her waist and was looking down into her face, laughing. He didn't have eyes for anyone else but her.

The next day, I shut myself in my room. I didn't come out once. Eva said, through the door, "Kim, are you all right?"

I couldn't face her. "I'm studying."

She said, "Harry and I are going to see a band tonight. Do you want to come?"

I felt like curdled milk—sour and rotten. Guilty, as if I was the one doing the cheating.

And so it went on. Southeast London is huge. It sprawls for miles. But somehow I kept seeing Harry and the girl with black hair all the time. Whenever I was out, there they were. It was like fate was rubbing my nose in it.

She was very pretty. Dark brown skin, gold earrings, red lipstick. When she looked up at Harry, it was like they were sharing a secret.

I wanted to tell Eva.

But I couldn't bring myself to do it. Because Eva loved him.

I said to Damaris, "If you knew that someone was being cheated on, would you tell them?"

"Who?"

I shook my head. "I can't say."

Damaris thought about this. "I read somewhere that you tell just to make yourself feel better. You don't do it for the person you're telling. Because they'd rather not know. So I don't think you should, no."

So I didn't. Eva was too fragile for reality. It pushed her too close to the edge.

And so we'd spend evenings together in our parentless house in Nunhead—Eva, Harry, and I—with all the secrets hanging between us, and I would look at him with hatred, and he would look back, questioning, his eyes amused. Sometimes he'd say, "Got a boyfriend yet, Kim?"

Back then, I didn't have the words. So I just glared at him.

He smiled. "I could give you a few pointers. A bit of advice on what boys like."

"Oh leave her alone, Harry," Eva would say, pushing his shoulder.

He opened his eyes wide. "Just trying to be helpful. It's a big, scary world out there."

I would sit there, hot and confused, looking at his shiny curls and dark skin and huge white smile, and think of him with the girl with long black hair.

And I wanted to curl up and die.

• • •

It was seven a.m. Already, even at this hour of the morning, the heat was rising up from the pavement. The sun glanced off a silver necklace, the buckle of a leather briefcase, bright blond hair. Once, in a crush of City workers, Harry thought he saw Kim. He knew she was back in London now, her Edinburgh life packed away. But then the woman stopped to let him pass, giving him a quick flirtatious look from under her lashes, and he realized his mistake. Kim, fists clenched, frowning furiously, would have elbowed him out of the way.

People look for patterns all the time, thought Harry. It's a natural impulse. Because patterns save time. You try to recognize what you already know so that you don't have to analyze every piece of information that comes your way. Otherwise life would be exhausting. You'd be living in a blur of constant panic.

But sometimes, he thought, pushed forward in a surge of commuters, patterns break down. Here the sequence is just as you expected. But here it falls apart. Why? Human error? A calculated change? Or just some random occurrence that no one could possibly have predicted? As Donald Rumsfeld once said, there are known knowns. There are known unknowns. And there are also unknown unknowns.

Sometimes, when it all cracks apart, you find the secret that no one wants you to see.

Harry liked the early mornings, walking to the office from the tube. You had your head to yourself, before the day filled it with rubbish. They called him the Iceman at the bank. They said he never panicked. He never rushed or shouted or swore. It wasn't intentional, this coolness. It was just the way he'd learned to behave. Look relaxed. Look calm. Smile. Keep the sludge of insecurity secret. Don't show anyone what you really feel.

Life's a lot easier if you keep emotion out of it.

"You're not like the others," Syed said to him once. "You don't talk down to anyone."

"How could I? I'm at the bottom looking up."

Syed laughed. But Harry wasn't joking. He'd worked his way through the ranks, from desk assistant to a trial position with the health care team. By the time he was twenty-four, he'd been promoted to associate and was on the same footing as the university graduates. But he never felt secure. It could all disappear in an instant. He felt like an imposter, waiting to be found out.

Syed tapped the side of his nose. "You stick with me, my friend, and we will rise together. We're a team."

"Ant and Dec."

"Batman and Robin."

"Itchy and Scratchy."

"The thing about me," said Syed, "is that I was born lucky. Money loves me. I can't fail."

Syed was a trader. He didn't see the point of the analysis that went on in Harry's part of the bank. It made him uneasy. Trading, he said, was about gut feeling. The market was a wild animal that could suddenly turn and rip you to shreds. "Trust your instincts. When she's not happy, you feel it."

Harry liked the picture. But he preferred to rely on spreadsheets.

Sometimes, when Syed was drunk, he became almost angry. "How many analysts does it take to change a lightbulb?"

"I don't know. How many analysts does it take to change a lightbulb?"

"Who knows? They're all in the dark."

Harry smiled. "Very funny."

"You know fuck all, you lot." It was Friday night, and the bar was heaving with bankers. Syed, his eyes half-closed, had already drunk two bottles of champagne and was beginning to slur his words. "You didn't even exist before Big Bang. But then the US arrived. And now we can't move for analysts." Syed leant forward, his breath hot on Harry's face. "It's meaningless. Charts and graphs and models and forecasts. You just make it up as you go along. Come up with a little theory and find the facts to fit."

"So you don't want facts."

"No."

"You don't want investment advice based on a sound analysis of a company's prospects?"

"Couldn't give a fuck." Syed shrugged. "I don't care what a company does. I don't care what it makes. I don't care whether it's run by Mickey Mouse or Mother Teresa. The only thing I care about is when to sell. When to buy. And how to make myself a fuck of a lot of money."

Harry laughed. "You're the evil face of capitalism."

But Syed wasn't listening. He had caught sight of a very pretty woman in a tight blue dress at the end of the bar.

Harry smiled at the memory. Maybe Syed is right, he thought, as the lift reached his floor and he walked past the banks of desks to reach his own. We like to pretend we can predict the market with computer models and analysis of variables and risk. But maybe it's all an illusion. Maybe we're not in control at all.

Harry caught sight of the headline on his screen. Shit.

He was still staring, lost in thought, when the phone rang. It took him a moment to pick up.

"You're on. Fifteen minutes."

"What about Phillip?"

"Not in."

The phone went dead.

Harry stared. He looked across at his boss's desk. Empty.

Nothing stopped Phillip coming to work. Except a car accident, maybe. He always drove too fast.

Harry closed his eyes. This can't be happening. This can't be happening.

Ten minutes later, head buzzing with panic, Harry was striding across the trading floor. All around him were equity traders and salesmen, row upon row of them. You could feel it in the air, the anticipation before the market opened, like prematch nerves. Harry concentrated on putting one foot in front of the other. He reached the lectern. His collar felt so tight he could hardly breathe. He panicked, briefly, about whether he'd remembered to shave.

And now his face, his magnified face, was on drop-down screens across the trading floor—simultaneously across the bank's offices in London and Frankfurt and Milan and Paris and Madrid—and he could see his huge mouth opening and shutting as if he was a contestant on *The X Factor*, and he could hear himself (a junior analyst, still wet behind the ears, what did he know, what did he know about anything?) giving his considered opinion that although the new drug had failed level-two FDA testing, the company was way ahead of the competition and had two more attempts to pass the trial—so on balance, despite an initial panic, the stock would perform as predicted. His throat was dry.

But, strangely, Harry-on-the-screen looked quite relaxed. You wouldn't know that real-life Harry, Harry from Essex, badly educated Harry—Harry from an indifferent school where no one had ever aspired to anything much except, perhaps, getting away with it—was so frightened his stomach was somewhere on the floor.

And then it was over, and Harry was walking back through the trading floor, and his shirt was sticking to the sweat on his back, and no one was staring at him in horror, or shouting after him, or even looking at him at all, because their eyes were back on the constantly changing data, flicking from screen to screen, tracking minuscule movements like cats watching mice in the dark.

I did it. *I did it.* And who knows? I might get lucky. Maybe the stock will do exactly what I said. He was suddenly, gloriously, happy. Maybe, he thought, grinning from ear to ear, it's like *Ocean's Eleven*—one massive confidence trick. It doesn't matter what you say, just how you say it. Act like you know what you're talking about and you can get away with anything.

But back at his desk, the doubts set in. He'd made the wrong call. There was no way he should have sounded so confident. How did he know what the shares were going to do? He checked his emails. There was one from Syed. *And the Oscar goes to . . .*

Harry smiled. He had forgotten that Syed would be listening to him. Reveling in the drama, probably. Trading was a game to Syed. He loved it—the gossip, the backstabbing, the extravagant excesses (including one memorable lunch bill for £10,000). An East End boy from a Bengali family that could trace its London roots back to the 1770s, Syed took everything to extremes. He was a fitness fanatic. He rarely slept. He even managed to find time for traditional City vices like gambling and strip clubs.

No one at home had any idea what he got up to. Especially not his mother.

"I always think you should tell your mother as little as possible. On a need-to-know basis. As in, she doesn't need to know."

"So you're one person at home and someone completely different at work."

"Isn't everybody?"

No, thought Harry. According to Eva, I'm consistently unreadable all the time.

Melanie, one of the secretaries, stopped behind his desk. "Coffee?"

"I'll get you one. I need a walk anyway."

For Syed, thought Harry, as he headed for the coffee machine, the City is like *Star Wars*. A cosmic battle. He sits there on the trading floor in front of all the live screens—Bloomberg, instant messaging, information updated second by second—and it's everything he could possibly want. It's competition, danger, money, power, and the best interactive digital game anyone has ever invented.

Maybe that's why he's so good, thought Harry, watching the jet of coffee squirt into his cup. I work with graduates from Harvard, Yale, Oxford, Cambridge. But none of them has Syed's nose for the market. He sniffs out change before it even happens. He smells it in the air.

Harry put a white Styrofoam cup on Melanie's desk. "What happened to Phillip?"

Melanie looked up, surprised. "I thought you knew." She hesitated. Then her forefinger traced the air across her neck from ear to ear.

It was only when Harry glanced across to Phillip's desk that he realized it had been stripped. There was nothing there—no papers, no pens, no files, no photographs. It was as if he had never existed.

That's how it works in the City. Maximum gain. Zero security.

· · ·

Kim went white. "He can't do this."

They were sitting in the kitchen of the ramshackle house in Nunhead. It was a room that had seen better days—last decorated in 1991 when their father, in one of his odd bursts of enthusiasm, had bought several tins of yellow paint from a street market in Peckham. It made you feel, said their mother wearily, as if you'd been drowned in a vat of custard.

Open on the table was a creased piece of white A4. The paper had been handled so often it was going thin and wispy at the edges.

"I didn't show it to you before now," said Eva, "because you were doing exams."

> *Dear Eva,*
>
> *I have just come off the phone after speaking to your mother in Nice, and she requested that I write to you.*
>
> *As you know, Kim will graduate from university this summer. This means that neither you nor she is any longer in full-time education. As such, you are now adults and responsible for making your own financial arrangements.*
>
> *This letter is to give you notice that I intend to sell the house in Nunhead as soon as you can make alternative arrangements.*
>
> *Jia tells me that it can be difficult to find affordable property to rent in London. I am, therefore, prepared to set the end of this year, that is 31 December 2006, as an appropriate date by which I will expect you to have vacated the property.*
>
> *Best wishes,*
> *Dad*

Kim's eyes were big with shock. "He's making us homeless."

"We'll never be homeless," said Eva. "As long as Christine's next door."

Christine, who took in all south London's waifs and strays. "What if we refuse to go?"

"It's his house. He can sell if he wants to."

"What about Mum? Isn't it hers as well?"

Eva shook her head. "He bought her out when they divorced. She used the money to buy the flat in France."

"But why's he doing it?"

"I don't know. Maybe he thinks we don't need it anymore."

"But we do."

"We've been lucky in a way. He could have sold it years ago." Eva always defended their father. It wasn't just that she was trying to be fair. She didn't want to hate him.

"I don't feel very lucky."

"I know, but look at it from his point of view. He's got a new family to support."

"Oh yes," said Kim. "The lovely Jia."

"I wonder what she's like."

"I don't."

"Really? Ever?"

"Why would I?" She broke up a family. She stole our father. I try not to think about her.

"Don't be too hard on her." Eva sounded weary. "From the sound of it, she persuaded him to let us stay on for longer than he wanted us to."

You're too reasonable. It's irritating. "So what are we going to do?"

Eva leant across the table and took her hand. "Harry said he'd help."

Kim snatched her hand back. "No."

"Just as a friend."

"I'd rather starve."

Eva, who normally treated Kim's furious dislike of Harry as a huge joke, looked defeated.

"We can manage," said Kim. "We'll find somewhere. I'll get a job. Maybe you could look for something part-time as well as your teaching—"

"I sent a reply," said Eva, "asking him to reconsider."

Kim was surprised. Eva wasn't usually so assertive. "What did he say?"

Eva's expression was unreadable. She held out another folded sheet of A4.

> Dear Eva,
>
> May I offer my congratulations.
>
> I do not feel that your news should alter the decision I have already communicated to you in my previous letter.
>
> You have sufficient time to find alternative accommodation. I believe that I am under no obligation to offer financial assistance as you have made an independent, adult choice to keep the baby.
>
> Yours ever,
> Dad

The letter fell to the floor.

"I always knew he'd make a good grandfather." Eva's smile was sad.

Kim was too stunned to breathe.

"It was your finals," said Eva when the silence got scarily

long. "I thought I shouldn't tell you about the house. Or this. In case it freaked you out." She bent down, picked up the letter, and folded it back into the envelope, smoothing it carefully so that it lay quite flat.

"So you're—"

"Fourteen weeks."

Kim swallowed.

"It was a relief, in the end, when I found out. I thought I'd got some terrible disease that was making me throw up every day."

"So was it—?"

"Planned?" Eva shook her head. "No. But I'm OK with it now. It seems a good thing to do when you're twenty-five. Have a baby."

Kim's whole body felt heavy, as if someone had filled her with wet cement. So that's why Eva's so calm about the house being sold. She'll move in with Harry.

"What did Mum say?"

Eva pulled a face. "That my pelvic floor would never be the same again."

You can't believe how much I suffered having babies.

They sat at the wooden table, pitted and pockmarked from years of family meals and teenage experiments with henna and leg wax and burning incense, and looked at each other.

"So I'm going to be an auntie."

"Auntie Kim."

"I'll be brilliant."

"I know you will."

Kim tried a smile. It was a bit wobbly, but it was better than nothing. "So when's it due?"

"The New Year. A January baby."

"Boy or girl?"

"No idea."

"Can you feel it?"

"Not yet. They say you don't always, the first time round. Another month maybe."

They used to call it the quickening, when the baby first starts to move. The thought of Eva having a child was so huge that Kim had to take a deep breath to calm herself. This wasn't supposed to happen. Eva shouldn't be tied down like this. Eva should be free. Sitting by a campfire, the light red and gold on her face. Traveling, her guitar slung over her shoulder, weighed down by nothing more than an old canvas bag.

After a while, Eva said, "So you'll let Harry find somewhere for us?"

Kim looked at her in horror. "For all of us?"

Eva frowned. "For the two of us. You and me. You don't want to live with Harry, do you?" When Kim still looked puzzled, she said, "Kimmy, Harry and I aren't together."

I know. He's been cheating on you for years. I saw him once with that girl with red hair who's been all over the magazines. "What do you mean?"

"We're not a couple."

Kim felt the pressure of all the words she couldn't say. "But you're always together."

Eva smiled. "How would you know? You've been away for three years."

"He hasn't been living here?"

"He's my friend. My best friend."

Not me. Harry. Treats my sister like dirt and ends up with her devotion.

"This is my baby. My decision. Nothing to do with him."

Kim was hot with confusion. "So he's not the father?"

Eva's face was calm. "I'm not going to say who the father is. Not even to you. I promised myself I wouldn't."

"You can say whether or not it's Harry."

"All right," said Eva. "OK. It's not Harry. Of course it's not Harry."

Do I believe her? Or is she just saying that to shut me up? "Is that true?"

"You see? You won't stop. It's not fair, Kim. You're not trying to understand. You'll go on and on and on until you get what you want. So it's better if I don't say anything at all."

After a while, Kim said, "Why won't you say?"

Eva shook her head.

"Because you won't? Or you can't?"

"You're not listening."

A rush of fury—or possibly grief that was being screwed down so tightly that an explosion was inevitable—made Kim say, in a very loud voice, "But we don't have any money."

Which, roughly translated, meant: If this is Harry's baby, he should pay for it.

Eva looked over to the window. Outside, the leaves of the sycamore tree were bright green. "We'll manage."

"How?" said Kim in a small voice.

"We always do," said Eva.

· · ·

Harry rolled out of bed and killed the alarm. He always woke before it went off. But last night he hadn't slept much anyway. A July heat wave. Thirty-six degrees at Gatwick. The senior vice presidents had already disappeared to Tuscany or Provence, spending their days dozing in hammocks, or half-asleep under olive trees, or swimming in private infinity pools. But the bank's less important employees carried on as usual, emerging late in the evening from the ice-cold fridge of air-conditioning to the dark, smelly sweat bath of London's streets.

At night, in these record-breaking temperatures, there was a frenzied party atmosphere. Everyone spilled out onto the pavements from the bars and cafés. You stayed up until the heat left the brickwork, until the early hours brought air that felt, by comparison, soft and new. And only then did you head for home, with the carnival still alive around you, through crowds laughing and singing and shouting.

Which made getting up even harder, thought Harry, looking out of the window. He yawned. This high up, in the clouds, you couldn't see much. Mist, or perhaps pollution, meant the city was still shrouded in gloom. But he knew the great, wide river was down there somewhere. Although even the Thames had lost its cool. It wasn't so much gray and aloof as boiled to a kind of khaki.

When Harry got back from the shower, there was a message on his phone. *R u free Sat lunch? At my brother's.*

He had a mental picture of Titania with her long legs and carefully tousled blond hair. Titania, named after the queen of the fairies. ("I can forgive my mother for loving Shakespeare. But what was wrong with Rosalind? Or Miranda?") An English rose, complete with thorns, she survived in the male-dominated world of investment banking by behaving with the brisk detachment of a boarding school headmistress. She treated most of the traders as silly little boys. In retaliation, they called her the Iron Lady.

Syed was terrified of her. "She'd have me for breakfast."

"She wouldn't want you for breakfast."

"That makes it worse." Syed shot him a sideways glance. "And how do you know what she likes for breakfast?"

"I'm telling you nothing."

"Very wise. It would be all over the bank by lunchtime."

"You have no discretion, do you?" said Harry, grinning.

"None at all," said Syed with satisfaction.

Titania usually wore silk shirts in soft blush colors like oyster and pink, fastened to a point just above her cleavage. Fund managers fantasized about missing buttons.

Harry, in the cool, sleek modernism of his recently renovated flat—white walls, full-length mirrors, white blinds over the floor-to-ceiling windows—looked again at her message. He texted back, *Sorry, no. Busy.*

The last time they'd had dinner (two Michelin stars, an extraordinary wine list, and a chef so keen on deconstruction that it was amazing any food ended up on the plate at all), Titania had said casually, over coffee, "What do you do at weekends?"

"What do you mean?"

"All the times you're busy."

He shrugged. "Working."

She flashed him an icy glance from her gray-blue eyes. "Harry, this is me you're talking to. I know you work at weekends. We all do. But when you're not working, what do you do?"

"What's brought this on?"

"I just don't feel I know you any better than I did a year ago."

He picked up a coffee spoon and turned it round between his fingers. "What do you want to know?"

"Anything. Everything. Where you were born, where you went to school, brothers and sisters, parents . . ."

"Childhood illnesses? Phobias? Dead pets?"

"I'm serious."

"I've had a very boring life. There's nothing to tell."

"Try me."

Harry smiled. But the light had gone from his eyes. It was a relationship with no commitment. He had always made that clear. "There's no mystery. What you see is what you get."

"But that's the point, isn't it, Harry?" She gave him the kind of direct stare that would have had Syed backing off in terror. "There isn't that much of you on show."

The conversation replayed in his head as he got dressed. He liked Titania. She was beautiful, funny, clever. He didn't want to lose her.

Damage limitation, he thought. Weekend in Paris? Flowers? Her favorite restaurant? He picked up his phone and texted, *Friday night Sauterelle at the Royal Exchange?*

I might be busy.

Harry laughed.

.   .   .

Kim, late for her interview, leapt onto the bus. She pressed her Oyster card against the yellow reader. Nothing happened. She tried again. The bus driver, hands on the wheel, stared straight ahead.

"I put five pounds on it just now," said Kim.

Rain lashed against the windows.

"Try again," said the driver.

Behind her, the squashed queue of wet people with useless umbrellas was getting impatient. Kim pushed her card against the reader. She rubbed it round and round in circles. Nothing registered. There was no cheery little bleep.

"You have to get off."

"I put money on it just now. A few minutes ago. At the newsagent." Kim fumbled in her pocket. "Here's the receipt. Look. Five pounds."

"It makes no difference. It's not on the card. You have to get off."

Kim walked forward into the body of the bus and sat down. Behind her the queue, released, surged forward. Commuters distributed themselves onto damp seats. But the bus doors stayed open.

"You have to get off," said the bus driver for the third time.

"Are you talking to me?"

Some of the passengers groaned.

"I'm talking to you. You haven't paid. You have to get off."

"But I have paid. I showed you the receipt."

The bus driver turned off the engine. Someone at the back shouted, "Get off!" A young man with a red beard frowned at her. Kim glared back.

"You got no cash, love?" said an elderly woman in a tweed coat.

"I've got cash. But I'm not paying full fare. There's five pounds on my Oyster."

"Some of us have got to get to work, though," said a young woman with eyebrows plucked into such fine arcs she looked astonished.

Kim stared straight ahead.

"Are you getting off or what?" shouted the bus driver.

"Look, I'll pay for you," said a man in a suit with a nose stud. "Sit down."

"But I—"

"Sit down!" said Kim in a voice of such ringing authority that the man cringed backwards as if she'd hit him.

"Oh thank you," said a woman, breathless, running onto the bus through the open doors in the mistaken belief that the driver had waited for her.

No one spoke.

The driver swore unintelligibly. The engine labored into life. There was a small cheer from the less stressed commuters. Steam covered the windows so thickly you could have been floating in a cloud.

The young man with the red beard leant forward. "You know, I normally use a bicycle. But the chain broke."

"I'm so sorry," said Kim, "but I really don't want to talk to you."

"No," said the young man. "Right."

The bus grumbled on towards Brixton.

• • •

"Is Wales always this bloody cold?"

Harry grinned. "Didn't bring your thermals?"

"Did I, fuck. I came here for the fine dining. Not hanging around in a howling wind freezing my bollocks off."

If someone had tried to come up with a cartoon version of a posh English banker, they would probably have drawn Giles. He was tall but fleshy, as if way too fond of strawberry jam, sweet tea, and port. Cold weather and excitement made his cheeks burn red, like someone had slapped him. In his late twenties, he already had the beginnings of a paunch, a bald spot on his crown, and a face that was beginning to droop into jowls at the jawline. Despite this disappointing appearance, Giles was brimming with confidence. He took center stage wherever he went. In a crowded bar you could hear his voice booming out across the banter and bravado.

Years ago, Harry had found people like Giles intimidating. It was the way they slotted into positions of power and privilege as if born to rule. But these days it didn't bother him. He had learned how to play the game.

They were in north Wales, guests of a multinational health care company that had invited a select group of City analysts to see their new research laboratories. The two-day visit, planned for the summer to make the most of the breathtaking scenery, included luxury accommodation in a five-star hotel and the chance to try traditional country sports like clay-pigeon shooting. So far, thunder and lightning had limited the time they could spend outdoors. Luckily, no one really cared. The meal the night before—oysters, white truffles, champagne, chocolate fondant with gold leaf—had drifted on into shots of single malt by the fire. Harry dimly remembered getting to bed around four a.m.

The best thing about trips like this, he thought, is telling Kim about them afterwards. She's so appalled by the decadence, extravagance, and overindulgence that she goes pale with fury and splutters. It's always entertaining to see her lost for words.

Giles prodded Harry in the ribs. "I think you might be in there."

In where? Harry followed Giles's gaze. Emily, the only female analyst on the trip, was being helped by a very attentive coach to position the shotgun into the hollow of her shoulder. She gave a little toss of her red hair, as if she knew she was being watched.

"She keeps giving you the eye," said Giles in his Etonian drawl.

"I think you're imagining it."

"Wish I were. Wouldn't mind getting in there myself."

Harry smiled. "I'm spoken for."

"Oh, yes, I forgot. The terrifying Titania. The Iron Lady. No one ever calls her Titty, I notice."

"I think they might regret it if they did."

Giles roared with laughter. "I tell you, Harry, if you ever get tired of her, you let me know. I'll be over like a shot."

"Pull!" shouted Emily in a loud, clear voice. The target arched out of the skeet into the murky gray sky, and she fired.

"Score!" shouted Giles, an explosion of excitement.

• • •

"Kim? Can you hear me? I'm by the pool. At Jean-Marc's house. Such a beautiful old villa. Up in the hills. Lemons, figs, oleander. But I don't know how good the reception is."

"I can hear you perfectly."

"I've booked my flights. Three weeks' time. Nice to Paris, Paris to London. I get in at two in the afternoon, September sixth. But of course, I don't expect you to meet me at the airport. I can easily carry my own bags."

"No, I can be there."

"Such a shame you don't drive. But I don't think the Heathrow Express will be that exhausting, will it?"

"I could book a cab. Although it's quite—"

"Only if you're sure. It's probably not that much more expensive if there's two of us. Or three, if Eva comes."

"She might be teaching."

"Teaching?"

"Guitar."

"How extraordinary."

"She's been taking on more pupils because it's going to be harder to get around from now on. She can't really travel round Europe as she used to."

"And that's exactly why I'm coming. To give Eva some moral support. Of course, she's not going to be the only single parent in the world. But this can't be easy for her. So I don't want to put either of you to any trouble."

"It's fine. Really. You can have my room. I would offer you the box room, but it's full of junk. A lot of it's yours—"

"I was thinking of booking into a hotel. But then of course I wouldn't be able to spend so much time with my daughters."

"Really, Mum, it's no problem. I can share with Eva for a few days."

"In the big room? My old room?"

"The one at the front."

"Such a lovely bright room. So important to make the most of whatever sunshine there is in England. Because you know I do suffer from SAD. Seasonal affective disorder. That's why I went to the South of France, really. For the sunshine."

"Are you saying you want Eva to move out of her room?"

"Oh, good heavens, no! She's pregnant. I wouldn't want to inconvenience her in any way. How's she feeling at the moment?"

"She gets heartburn."

"Oh, I remember that. With both of you. Although of course it's the birth itself that causes the long-term problems. Especially if the baby's late. Like you were. And how's she sleeping at the moment?"

"Fine, I think—"

"I only ask because the mattress in the big room is quite soft. I remember that. Fine for me, obviously. But she might find a firmer mattress suits her better as she gets bigger."

"Are you saying that you'd like to have Eva's room, and Eva should move into my room, and I should sleep on the sofa?"

"Why—do you think that's a good idea? It hadn't even occurred to me. But I'm completely happy if you think that might be the best solution."

. . .

What I don't understand, thought Kim, at the top of the loft ladder—peering into an attic full of the accumulated junk of twenty-five years' worth of family chaos—is how Harry managed to get himself so mixed up in our lives. None of my friends have their sisters' attachments coming round for Sunday lunch, turning up at birthdays, hanging round on bank holidays, and inviting themselves round for Christmas. He doesn't ask. He just assumes. A family friend. Like a creepy uncle.

I never liked it. Even before I found out he was cheating on Eva. Like the time he turned up just as we were going to Brighton for the day. Kim, holding on to the aluminum ladder, stared into space. It was the summer I was seventeen. Eva was going to her Welsh commune for a month, teaching guitar workshops, and this was our last special day before she went, before I lost her for the whole of August. I stood there in my straw hat and blue sundress and said, What's he doing here? We had the picnic all packed, with Mr. Kipling fondant fancies, and cloudy lemonade, and salt and vinegar crisps, all silly stuff reminding us of our childhood, and it was going to be just me and Eva on the pebble beach, in the Lanes, on the pier. Just the two of us throwing chips at the seagulls. And then, suddenly, there was Harry in a white T-shirt that showed off the muscles in his arms, looking at me as if this was some kind of huge joke. She said, Don't stress, he can drive us there. And I said, But we were going on the *train*. A special offer on the *train*. And she said, But the car will be quicker. And I said, But why's he coming? Why's he here? And she just smiled and said, We'll have a good time.

And I remember thinking, No, this is the way it works: you'll have a good time, he'll have a good time, and I'll just sit there getting in the way. Like I always do. Sitting on the big gray pebbles watching you and him cavorting in the waves.

I'd spent years trying to make sense of it. Once Eva was sitting in the garden playing her guitar, pretending to be Mama Cass (which she really could do, pretty much, because she had the same kind of voice), and I went and sat next to her on the grass, pulling at those stiff stalks that stick up all over the place and never break, just bend. When she'd stopped singing, and was letting her fingers walk over the strings, trying out new sounds, I said, "Why does Harry spend so much time at our house?"

It was probably that same summer as the Brighton trip. Or maybe the year before, when I was doing my GCSEs.

She said, "Why? Don't you like it?"

Even then, we weren't always straight with each other. I don't know why. Maybe in case the truth was too frightening. "I just wondered."

She smiled and picked out the tune of "It's Getting Better."

I said, "Doesn't he have a home of his own?"

"Have you asked him?"

Me? Why would I ask him anything? "No."

"Maybe you should."

Why? Why can't you tell me?

But Eva had a way of sliding off anything she didn't want to talk about. There wasn't any point in haranguing her when that happened. You could go on and on asking questions forever and she'd just smile.

The worst time was my birthday. My eighteenth birthday. Saturday morning. February 2003. We were sitting there in the kitchen, Christine and Damaris from next door, Eva and me. Mum wasn't there. We hadn't seen her for days. She'd gone off to have dinner at the Ritz and never came back.

And then the doorbell rang, and Eva smiled, the way she does, and I thought, OK, so this is some kind of surprise she's cooked up for today, and I was so excited I could hardly breathe, and then suddenly, filling the doorway, there was Harry. Grinning from ear to ear. And the atmosphere changed because Damaris looked down, all flustered, and Christine started fussing about whether he'd had breakfast, and Eva was all shiny, like she always is when he's around. And he handed me a tiny blue box with a white ribbon. Everything was in slow motion. Time became all long and pulled out, like a slippery silk scarf. On the box, it said TIFFANY & CO, and inside were diamond earrings. In the shape of flowers. Daisies.

Christine said, Well, Harry, in a voice that was almost disapproving, like she thought he'd spent half his yearly salary (because she didn't know he was always throwing money around on flash holidays and restaurants). Damaris was making silly, girly, fluttery noises, which she never did, because she had her head screwed on and was going to be a doctor. And Eva said, Shall I help you put them in?

It's hard putting earrings in for someone else. You can't find the holes, and it takes ages, and it's like waiting for water to boil when the gas isn't even alight. I sat there, in my old jeans and Bikini Kill T-shirt, and the longer it went on, the more I wanted to cry, because it was all ruined, everything was ruined. He was making some kind of point, but I didn't know what it was. Except that it was big and male and squashed me flat so I couldn't breathe.

Then Eva stood back and said, They're beautiful, they're so beautiful.

And I looked up, and Harry was staring at me. I hated it. I felt myself going bright red. And for a moment, I thought he was going to come out with one of his horrible remarks, one of those lazy laughing digs at my feminist reading group, or being antinuclear, or trying to wake people up to climate change, and I tensed, waiting, just waiting for that big grin before he put the knife in, that big grin that said, Lighten up, Kim, lost your sense of humor, can't you take a joke?

But he didn't smile. He just looked at me. And he said, in a quiet voice, Happy birthday.

And I had a really funny feeling that I'd done something wrong. And this made me mad, because all I'd done so far was get up, get dressed, open a card from my dad with a check in it, and tear the sparkly paper off presents from Eva and Damaris and Christine. What did he want me to do? Burst into tears and say, Oh, Harry, Harry, diamond earrings, you shouldn't have, just what I always wanted?

And we just stared at each other. And then he looked away.

I never wear them. Ever. They're in a drawer in my bedside table, still in their Tiffany box. I try not to see them even when I'm looking straight at them. Because they make me sad. And I don't know why.

"What are you doing up there?"

Eva was looking up from the landing beneath, her blue dressing gown tied over the bump. Eighteen weeks.

"I thought I ought to make a start at clearing out the loft."

"Really?" Eva leant against the wall, looking exhausted. "I don't think anyone's been in there for years. There's probably even some of Dad's stuff up there."

Which will go straight in the bin.

"And Harry's."

"There's Harry's stuff up here?"

Eva nodded.

"Why?"

"Oh, you know," she said vaguely. "Boxing gloves."

"What?"

"Boxing gloves."

"I have no idea what you're talking about."

Eva yawned and rubbed her eyes. "You know. Right hook. Jab. Uppercut. Do you want a cup of tea?"

And she wandered off downstairs to brew up raspberry leaf or chamomile or whatever pregnancy-friendly health-food stuff she was drinking, and I stood there on the aluminum ladder— half in the loft, half out—and thought, Boxing? No. Not Harry. Harry doesn't fight people.

He just hurts them by laughing at them.

• • • •

"And then I got to the box on the form that said, *Why do you want to be a teacher?* And I thought, But I don't. I don't want to be a teacher." Izzie looked up in distress.

It was a Saturday afternoon in late August. Every so often, the foundations of the Nunhead house shook as cars with speakers the size of dog kennels boomed their way past. The air was flat and useless, as if someone had sucked all the goodness out of it. Izzie had just arrived from Newcastle. She quite often dressed in a slightly haphazard way, like someone decorating a cake who starts off with chocolate buttons and decides halfway through that lattice icing would look much better. Kim suspected her mind was usually on other things. But today, her choices seemed even more random than usual. Izzie was wearing small brown ankle boots, a long red taffeta skirt, a man's black waistcoat with silver buttons, and a double row of pearls. Her wild brown hair was piled on top of her head and secured with a pencil. The overall effect, strangely, was demure and conservative, like Edith Wharton at her country estate.

Kim, who only ever wore black jeans and a T-shirt, was deeply impressed.

"So I don't know what to do," said Izzie, on the brink of tears. "I thought I had it all worked out. And now it's unraveling. Like a piece of bad knitting."

Kim took a deep breath. This called for clear thinking. "OK, let's start with the negatives. You don't want to teach. What else do you definitely not want to do?"

"Live with my parents."

Kim opened her mouth to speak and shut it again.

"It doesn't stop. Ever since I told them I'd changed my mind. 'You don't have to teach forever, pet. But it's a useful skill to fall back on. Because you know life's not easy these days. There are bills to pay. There's gas and electric and water. And then you've got your Council Tax. Not to mention food. Have you seen the prices? Your father and I love having you here. Of course we do. But once we're gone, how are you going to manage?'"

It was as if Izzie's mother was sitting in the room.

"It's not funny," said Izzie.

Kim wiped the smile off her face. "So you don't want to be a teacher. And you don't want to live with your parents. Is there anything you do want to do?"

Izzie hesitated.

"What?" said Kim.

"Live in London."

Kim's face lit up. "With me?"

"I could look after Eva's baby. In return for a free room."

Kim frowned. "I might not be living with Eva."

"Why?"

"I'm not that keen on living somewhere that Harry's paying for."

Izzie opened her eyes wide. "He's going to pay for it? A whole flat?"

Kim nodded.

"What's that if it isn't a guilty conscience?"

As usual, whenever conversation turned to Harry, Kim felt herself squirming and coiling, like a worm exposed to sunlight. She said, to change the subject, "So what are you going to do? If you're not going to teach?"

Izzie shrugged. "Earn some money."

"Doing what?"

"Stacking shelves?"

Kim looked gloomy. "I think you need a master's to do that these days."

"Oh," said Izzie, shocked. "You didn't get it? The research job?"

"I still haven't heard anything." Kim bit her lip. "I'm trying not to think about it. But it was perfect. A national charity campaigning against homelessness."

"Which, given your personal circumstances," said Izzie, "sounds ideal."

·   ·   ·

Whenever she and Harry were alone together without Eva, Kim felt embarrassed. They were like two politicians meeting in a corridor in Brussels, desperately in need of a translator.

On this particular Sunday afternoon, Eva was upstairs asleep when Kim got back from the supermarket. Eva often disappeared to her room these days. "It's all these baby cells multiplying and growing," she'd say. "It's exhausting." Kim wandered into the kitchen, carrying her plastic carrier bags, to find Harry sitting at the table. It shouldn't have surprised her. He still treated the Nunhead house as his second home. But her heart banged unpleasantly at the sight of him. One moment she was thinking about nothing very much—the crunch of Cox's apples, how Condoleezza Rice found time to play the piano. The next she was on red alert, marshalling her thoughts into a defensive position, turning herself into a fiercely guarded fortress with archers on the turrets and boiling oil at the ready.

Harry had the local paper open on the table in front of him. "So where should it be?"

"What?"

"Eva's new flat."

Kim put the shopping on the working surface by the kettle. "Ask Eva."

"I have asked Eva. She said to ask you."

Kim frowned. "Why?"

"Because she wants to be near you. Obviously."

Kim turned her back and took out an economy jar of store-brand instant coffee. "Izzie and I are looking round New Cross."

"Very edgy."

"Edgy?"

"On trend."

"You have no idea," said Kim, swinging round to face him, "what you're talking about."

Harry laughed.

"We're looking round New Cross because that's all we can afford."

"I could help."

"No."

"Just no?"

Kim narrowed her eyes. "I don't want your help."

Harry sat back in his chair. "Look at it this way. I work in the City and make an obscene amount of money. You've just got a short-term charity job that will pay you almost nothing. If I make a small contribution towards your rent, it's a redistribution of wealth. Social justice in action. The triumph of New Labour."

"It's not funny."

"I'm not joking."

Kim glared at him. "You're Eva's friend. If you want to pay for her flat, that's fine." It's your bloody baby. "But you're not my friend. I don't want any money from you."

Harry put his hand on his heart as if she'd wounded him. "Not your friend?"

"No."

Harry looked down at the table. After a while, he said, "Eva's the only family I've got."

For a moment, fleetingly, Kim wondered what he meant.

"She looked after me when I needed her. So I want to look after her."

Oh, thought Kim. A new little game. Harry's soft and caring side. Showing just enough emotion to bring me to heel. But I won't play. I can tell, just from looking at your face, that you're hiding what you really think. "I'm not stopping you looking after her."

Harry waited.

"But I don't want you to look after me."

There was something in his eyes she couldn't read. It was like standing in a lit doorway trying to make out the shadows in a darkened room.

Harry gave an exaggerated sigh. "So we're back to where we started. I'm going to rent a flat for Eva. Where should it be?"

"Somewhere surrounded by trees."

"Why?"

Kim shrugged as if his question was incredibly stupid. "Because she likes them."

She looked down at Harry with what she hoped was a slightly patronizing expression. But somehow it all went wrong. He stared back, and there was a long and embarrassing pause. Her superiority dissolved into a kind of panic.

Oh, I wish he'd just leave me alone, she thought, turning away to unpack the shopping.

.   .   .

The brick wall was covered with graffiti—great circular shapes, like commas, in blue and white, covering fat red letters that spelt out STUK. It had been the same for years, thought Harry. But getting more and more faded. Maybe the artist didn't use his spray cans under the arches anymore.

Tommy's Gym was hidden on the outskirts of Brixton beneath the suburban railway line that ran into Victoria Station. It wasn't a secret. All the locals knew it was there. But if you were a stranger to the area, you'd be unlikely to run across it by mistake. From the street, it looked like some kind of shabby warehouse. The windows, with wire-mesh glass, were so high up that you couldn't see inside at all. In the old days, when Harry first came with Killian, the Dubliner with dreadlocks, you had to knock to be let in. Now you punched in a code. Five nine eight one. Easy to remember. Eva's birthday.

Sweat, leather, rubber, dust—to Harry, Tommy's Gym smelt like home. Ever since that first afternoon—when he'd been handed a skipping rope by a man with gold teeth and skin so minutely tattooed that he shone a kind of luminous blue— Harry knew he belonged. He'd arrived a thin, angry eighteen-year-old. Now, at the age of twenty-six, he was fit, muscular, and in control. He loved everything about boxing—the footwork, the speed of punches, the tactics, the adrenaline. In the ring, his black hair in wet curls, his heart pumping blood, Harry felt on top of the world. Later, he'd find the bruises—black bashes up his forearms, purple patches on his ribs. But at the time, in the thick of it—landing a sequence of jab, cross, uppercut—he felt properly alive.

You don't get much time off as a banker. Especially when you're an associate with ambition. But Harry tried to make it to the gym as often as he could. Leon, who owned it, let him train whenever he wanted—early in the morning before he went to work, or late at night when most of the City slept.

It might have made more sense to find a gym near his flat.

Or somewhere in Nunhead. But Harry never did. Boxing was Tommy's Gym. This was where he wanted to be.

Leon liked Harry. It wasn't just because Harry paid his membership subs on time. Or even because he'd been coming for so long that he seemed like part of the family. Leon liked Harry because Harry knew by instinct who needed help.

It was easy to get into trouble in this part of southeast London. You could go down the wrong road and end up with all your exits barred. Boxing gave you discipline. It showed you another way.

But it was hard to take the first step. Harry, watchful, seemed to know when to say nothing and when to intervene. It wasn't much. Just the odd word. But a thirteen-year-old with a shaved head and hard eyes might look up and see the expression of friendly interest on Harry's face and feel, somehow, that he was in the right place. He'd start training hard. He'd work on his core fitness, his coordination, his stamina. Heart racing, stopping to draw breath, he'd look across the gym and see Harry smiling encouragement. Much later, in the ring, landing a sequence of punches, he'd glance past his opponent and see Harry frowning with concentration, following his every move.

He would watch Harry box—see the intensity of his expression, the accuracy of his blows. He would measure Harry with his eyes. He would see someone determined. Calm. Able to take care of himself.

Not the violence he was used to, maybe. But a fighter nonetheless.

Harry, straightening up, the tight muscles of his shoulders

and arms hidden under an old hoodie, would pick up his sports bag. And he'd look over and nod.

Nothing much, you might say.

But to that boy, that thirteen-year-old, it was everything.

. . .

"Of course she had a thing about cats."

"What kind of thing?"

"It might be better to ask," said her mother, "what kind of cats."

No wonder you moved to the South of France, thought Kim. Nunhead really wasn't the right setting. The thin September sun, fighting its way through the window above the sink, showed up the chipped yellow paint, the scratched stainless steel, the scuffed lino. But then the light fell on Grace. She turned her face towards the sun like a film star sensing the camera. You could see the sheen of her skin, the intense blue of her eyes. Her white-blond hair was a dazzling halo.

"Lions," said Grace. She was sitting right on the edge of her chair as if trying to minimize all contact with south London dirt. "Hundreds of them. Wandering round her house. Huge great African lions."

"Why?"

"She was making a film. Called *Roar*. Took years and years and went wildly over budget. One of the cameramen nearly got killed."

"Is that what turned you off her?"

Grace frowned.

"You changed your name. You called yourself Tippi for years. And then suddenly you didn't."

Grace straightened up. "You're imagining things."

No, thought Kim wearily. I'm remembering things. You wore a green suit and fur coat because of *The Birds*. We had a kitten called Forio because of the horse in *Marnie*. You were obsessed with Tippi Hedren. You were obsessed with Hitchcock blondes. Eva was named after Eva Marie Saint. I was named after Kim Novak. (I should be grateful. We could have been Janet and Doris.)

You met a man on a plane once. Around the time Dad walked out. I remember standing in the kitchen, looking down the hall to where he stood, this stranger in a black cashmere coat, framed by the front door. You leant down and whispered, "Not a word!" Then you said, in a loud voice, "And this is my little sister! People say we look so alike!"

You slipped into fiction so easily. If you got bored with reality, you just played a different part. And you were so good at it. People were often surprised to find you in a tatty London suburb. It was like finding bone china in IKEA. But they just assumed you were eccentric. Or had somehow lost the family fortune.

That sharp ascent through the English social ranks wasn't enough, though. You outgrew the British class system. You looked across to Europe, and then to the US. Becoming Grace Kelly was a stroke of genius. She was the one, after all, who ended up a princess.

"So what are we going to do?" said Grace.

Kim forced herself back to the present. "About what?"

Grace stared at her, wide-eyed. "I thought we were having a council of war."

You pretend to care. But you don't. Eva's baby is just another drama. You've never really enjoyed being a mother. Eva used to say, They married too young, that's all. They had children before they'd grown up themselves. Which is why, one day, they woke up and looked at each other and thought, Is this all there is? Am I with the right person in the right life? And it frightened them so much they had to rush off and start again before it was all too late. So Dad left and moved in with Jia. And Mum moved to the South of France.

"Your father hasn't helped the situation. Putting the house on the market. But then what can you expect?" Grace shrugged. "He was always so selfish."

"There's been an offer already."

"Well, there would be, wouldn't there? London property always sells. Although I won't see a penny of it, of course."

"Izzie and I are looking for a flat together."

Grace frowned. "You're not living with Eva? Well, of course I understand that. Babies aren't to everybody's taste. All those wet nappies. And the crying. Half the time, there's nothing wrong with them at all. They just want attention." She shot Kim a sideways glance. "So go on, then."

"What?"

Grace looked impatient. "Is it Harry's?"

"I don't know."

"Hasn't she said?"

"Not to me."

The last conversation had been the worst. Kim, her back to

Eva as she washed up the supper dishes, had tried to suggest that it wasn't fair on the baby to keep its parentage secret. Surely everyone has the right to know who their father is. And what if there's some kind of genetic disease that needs specialist treatment? Alcoholism? Depression? When she turned round, Eva was looking at her rather sadly. Kim, she said, I know you want everything neat and tidy. But life isn't like that. It's messy and unpredictable and out of control. This is best for me and the baby. I want you to accept that. And Kim, silenced by the expression in Eva's eyes, felt ashamed.

"I thought sisters were supposed to tell each other everything."

So did I.

"It seems the most likely explanation. That's why she's decided to keep it. At least Harry's doing the honorable thing and paying for her living expenses. God knows we need more men like him, willing to take responsibility for their actions."

It could be anyone. A one-night stand. Someone married with children. The father of one of her guitar pupils. In her head, Kim saw a disparate group of men turning to face her, like suspects in a police lineup.

And then she saw Harry, smiling.

Grace clasped her hands together, like an angel praying. "They're so right for each other, don't you think? I love the way Harry laughs. Finds everything so amusing. And making a fortune in the City." She sighed. "We'll just have to hope they get together once the baby's born. Set up home somewhere sweet and unpretentious. Like Chelsea."

Oh, thought Kim, flooded by silent rage, go back to Nice. Go and stalk some more faded socialites living on memories of past glamour. Because you're not doing any good here. But I can't say it out loud. Because I look at your face—at your fine cheekbones and your blue eyes and your white-blond hair—and all I see is Eva.

"I hope she's not expecting me to rush back when it's born. I'm not really the grandmother type. And I don't have any ties to London anymore."

Apart from two daughters who live here.

"It's so shockingly rude these days. No courtesy. No one says good morning or holds the door open for you. So different from the Côte d'Azur. Although they do try to take advantage even there, you know. You have to be very firm. A gentleman came up to me on the Promenade des Anglais the other day and said, Would you do me the great honor of having lunch with me, madame, and I said no thank you, and he said, But I will be devastated if you don't accept, *accablé de chagrin*, and I said, '*Monsieur, je suis trop pressée.*' Too busy. Perhaps I shouldn't have let him down so gently. I should have said, That's an outrageous suggestion. You're a perfect stranger. I don't go off and have lunch with just anybody."

That's not what I remember.

"But it's all gone from London, you know, that old-fashioned courtesy. No manners at all. Men spitting in the street. Young women lolling about, drunk, with their skirts up to their armpits. Although, from what I hear, it's no better in the country. All those four-by-fours and sex parties. People with titles behaving outrageously. Only the other day I heard about a politician hosting S and M in his gazebo."

* * *

There was something about Eva's pregnancy that pushed hostilities between Kim and Harry to the next level.

"What are you doing?"

It was Sunday afternoon. Kim had wandered into the kitchen to find Harry leaning back against the sink and Eva sitting at the kitchen table. Both were holding bottles of beer.

Harry looked surprised. "Talking to Eva?"

"You're drinking beer!"

"I know. It's allowed. I'm over eighteen."

"Not you! Eva! She shouldn't be drinking!"

Eva's eyes were big with alarm. "Kim—"

Kim ignored her. "It's bad for her health. Bad for the baby."

"Kim—"

"You know," said Harry, "some people don't agree. There are experts who believe that the odd glass of wine does no harm at all."

"Which experts?"

Harry looked vague. "I don't know. I'm sure I read it somewhere."

"You read it somewhere. Or maybe saw it on the telly? Well my information is a little more reliable. I went with Eva to her prenatal appointment last week, and the midwife reminded her that you must not drink in pregnancy."

"Kim—"

"At all. Ever. Not the odd glass. Not the occasional treat. Not even a bottle of beer."

"All I can say," said Harry, "is thank God you're here."

Kim stared at him with disbelief. "It's not funny! Why can't you just admit for once that you've got it wrong? Is that so hard?"

Eva bowed her head. Her shoulders were shaking. Oh no, thought Kim, I didn't mean to make her cry. I never meant to make her cry. But Harry's behaving like a child. Being completely irresponsible.

"You're always so emotional," said Harry. "Are you sure it's good for you?"

Eva looked up, her face awash with tears. "Kim, please stop."

"I'm not angry with you. It's Harry who . . ." Kim trailed off. Eva wasn't crying. Eva was laughing.

"Kimmy, I'm sorry," said Eva. She took a deep breath, trying to calm herself down. "You're absolutely right about drinking and pregnancy. And I'm very grateful that you're so fierce and roaring like a lion to protect me." She smiled. "But there's no need. I was getting really fed up with orange juice, and lemonade, and elderflower cordial with fizzy water, and Harry said, Why don't you try something different? So that's what I'm doing. This beer hasn't got any alcohol in it. We thought we might try some alcohol-free wine, too. There's some that's meant to taste like champagne."

Kim felt herself growing hotter. "Why didn't you tell me?"

"I did try."

Kim stared at the floor.

When Kim eventually did look up, Eva and Harry were both peering at her like anxious parents whose toddler has just had a tantrum. Kim wanted to say, Why do you always do this? Why do you always gang up on me? But that would just have made her sound whiny and immature.

Harry said, "Sorry. You were only trying to look after her."

But this, for all she knew, was yet another trap—a big pit in the jungle, loosely covered with branches, just waiting for her to fall in. She so badly wanted to shout at him for laughing at her.

But all I've got left in this situation, she thought miserably, are the last thin shreds of my dignity.

A few weeks later, it happened again. When Kim found out that Eva was intending to visit Sieben Linden—an ecovillage in Germany—at the end of November, she was appalled. "But you'll be huge!"

"It's my last chance. After that, I'll have the baby. And getting around will be so much harder."

"You'll be eight months pregnant! No one travels when they're eight months pregnant!"

Harry said, "I'll go with her."

"And you're medically qualified, are you? What help would you be in an emergency?"

"They have doctors in Germany," said Eva, in a small voice.

"That's not the point! It's not worth the risk!"

They all stared at each other—Eva flushed and miserable, Harry uncomfortable, Kim outraged.

Eva said, slowly, "If it makes you really unhappy, I won't go."

Kim, every muscle tense, just stood there. Why couldn't they *see*? Why couldn't they *see* how dangerous it was?

As the weeks passed, the precarious triangle of Kim-Eva-Harry became two versus one—Eva and Harry united against Kim. Alone in her room, staring at the scuffed carpet, Kim found herself biting her knuckles in an effort not to cry. She wanted to be happy for her sister. A new start, a new life. But instead, she felt lonely and afraid.

She began to snipe at Harry in ways that even she found absurd.

"I suppose you go to strip clubs."

Harry frowned.

"Lap dancing? Exclusive gentlemen's evenings?"

"What's brought this on?"

It was Thursday night. Harry was taking Eva out for a pizza and a film at the Peckham multiplex.

Kim folded her arms. "I keep reading about what goes on in the City."

"Times have changed."

"So you've never been to a strip club."

"Do we have to talk about this now?"

"I just want to know what you think."

"No you don't. You want to tell me what I think. You want me to say that it's something I'd pay to see."

They stared at each other. For a sudden, terrible moment, Kim was unable to look away.

Eva, wearing a floaty blue dress printed with tiny white flowers, wafted into the living room. "What would you pay to see?"

Harry's expression was unreadable. "A woman stripping off."

Eva looked confused. "I thought we were going to see *The Queen*."

•   •   •

It was waiting for him when he got back from work. Stiff white card with a fine silver line all round the edge. Curly black writing:

"Mr. and Mrs. John White request the honor of your presence at the marriage of their daughter, Emma Rose, to Mr. Martin Palmer..." Harry stood there in the entrance lobby, still holding the invitation, staring into space. After a while, he put it back in the envelope, very carefully, as if it was important to keep it safe. It had been redirected twice, in handwriting he didn't recognize. An invitation that had gone all round England, from address to address, trying to find him. And now had caught up with him in the hallway of a tall block of flats overlooking the Thames.

For a moment, he toyed with the idea of sweeping up to the church in his silver-gray Porsche. Wearing shades, perhaps. Unfolding himself from the driver's seat just slowly enough for an audience of guests to stare, openmouthed, at the impeccable cut of his handmade suit.

But then he thought, with a hollow feeling in the pit of his stomach, I don't think even a Porsche would get me noticed. Not by Mr. and Mrs. John White.

The last time he'd seen Emma Rose she'd been about eight. He remembered her as small and pink with a mass of frizzy curls. She'd never liked him much. She sensed him as a threat. Which he was, in a way. A permanent reminder of what Mr. and Mrs. John White could do to a child who didn't fit in.

He'd blocked most of it out. But he remembered the beginning. One day, it was just him and his mum. Then John White was at the breakfast table. Harry was five, maybe six. He watched carefully. John White liked the fat on bacon, listening to radio news bulletins (on the hour, every hour), and his clean socks paired by being folded over twice. His skin was colorless, like the gins he enjoyed before dinner, and the buttons of his shirt strained across his stomach. He expected total obedience, right from the start. "You do right by me, Harry, and I'll do right by you."

It was a lie, of course.

As he got older, Harry slowly realized that this had been a match based on compromise. His mother was young and pretty. But she had a child. And she was tired of worrying about money. John White was middle-aged, charmless, and a bully. But he could provide financial security. And he accepted Harry as part of the package.

It could have worked. Compromises sometimes do. But John White got greedy. Once he had the young and pretty wife under his control, he broke the contract. Looking after another man's son was irritating. Especially as the boy had a mind of his own.

"Don't, Harry, don't." His mother's voice in his ear, urgent, desperate. "Don't cross him. He's got a terrible temper."

A year after they married, Emma Rose arrived. John White was besotted. His chest swelled with pride. Every visitor to the house was told about Emma Rose's extraordinary abilities. She did everything early—talking, walking, counting, reading. She was brilliant at ballet, superlative at gymnastics, gifted at music. To her credit, little Emma Rose was intelligent enough to realize that she wasn't the superstar her father imagined. No one could be that perfect. But she didn't know how to open his eyes to reality. And she didn't have a mother who was brave enough to fight for a little girl's right to be ordinary.

So Emma Rose, terrified of falling short of her father's expectations, and exhausted by the constant pressure to be the best, became wary and mean. Sometimes the only way to stay on top was to sabotage the competition. She cut off the ribbons from other girls' ballet shoes. She hid violin bows and descant recorders. She stole homework and tore up letters home about auditions and after-school clubs.

Sadly, the one thing Emma Rose was extremely good at was making sure she was never found out. In public, Emma Rose's halo never dimmed.

Harry's great mistake was to point out the obvious.

"What's this?" he said, flicking through her maths book. "Five out of ten?"

Emma Rose tried to snatch it back. Teasing her, Harry held it high in the air. Emma Rose screamed. Harry felt the slap to the back of his skull before his head, just above his right eye, hit the edge of the table. Stunned, winded, he lay on the kitchen floor.

"You pick on someone your own size!" shouted John White.

"Try not to provoke him, Harry," whispered his mother that night as she pressed a cold flannel to his forehead in the dark.

Harry had never met his real father. His mother was able to tell him very little, except that they had both been very young, it had been a holiday romance in the summer of 1979 (on a French campsite, with families from all over Europe), and they had said good-bye before his mother had even known that Harry was on the way.

"What did he look like?"

"Like you."

"What was his name?"

"Everyone called him Zee. But it was just a nickname."

"Where did he live?"

She looked sad. "I never asked."

Dark skin, brown eyes, black hair. Tall. Quite thin. Always smiling. She remembered that he spoke good French and good English. (He sang along to Donna Summer and the Bee Gees.) But who knows? He might have spoken other languages too. Harry thought about all the places his father (the man he had never met) might live now—Italy, Germany, Spain, Morocco, Israel, Turkey, Brazil—and the world in his head got bigger and wider, and harder to navigate, and more impossible to understand. He felt lost and hopeless. And then he would look down at his hands, at his own strong hands, and he would think, I am what I am. Someone once said, you don't need to know where you're from. You just need to know where you're going.

But it made him vulnerable, not knowing. And angry. As his mother shrank back further, and Emma Rose took up center stage, Harry began to feel resentful. He had done nothing wrong. But he was treated like a temporary lodger who never paid rent. John White belittled him, goaded him, laughed at him. He hit him round the head so that his ears rang. He pushed him against walls so hard that Harry was permanently covered in bruises. Once, because Harry held his gaze a fraction too long, he kicked him down the stairs. Harry landed at the bottom in a crumpled heap, breaking his collarbone.

By the time Harry was fourteen, there was an evil, simmering atmosphere in the house.

And then came the day that John White opened his mouth to sneer and saw his stepson clench his fists.

"I'm sorry," said his mother. "He says we can't go on like this. It's him or you."

Harry found his own foster parents. He advertised in the local paper. He remembered that, years later. But he had blanked out everything in between.

His foster parents were evangelical Christians in their fifties. They were kind and well-meaning. But the day Harry finished school, he packed a bag and left. He never saw them again. (He never saw Mr. and Mrs. John White again either. Over time, he accepted what his mother had done. But he never forgave her.) He got a train to London and sat in the vast, plush reception area of the bank for two days before he got an interview. He used the time well. He listened to snippets of conversation. He studied mannerisms. He saw how people dressed. In his head, he began to see how he could adapt, transform, fit in. The old Harry was dead. His new life had begun.

Eventually, amused by Harry's persistence, the head of equities gave in. On the third morning, he sent down his chief of staff to give Harry a cursory interview. It didn't take long to discover there was more to Harry than his rather mediocre qualifications. Harry had a logical mind and a natural aptitude for maths. He was interested in business and how companies worked. He was open and straightforward, easy to talk to. But, much more important than any of this, he was hungry. Very, very hungry. This was a young man with something to prove.

The bank offered him a job as a desk assistant. Harry, who didn't know one end of London from the other, stuck a pin in a map and rented a room in Crystal Palace. It had brown lino, a sash window that rattled, and a bed with a mattress so thin that it felt like lying on cardboard. If ever he came back from work early enough to need to find somewhere to eat, he went to the small Greek restaurant round the corner. Their specialties were stuffed vine leaves and phyllo pastry filled with feta cheese.

One summer evening, he met Eva at a bus stop in Camberwell. The bottom had fallen out of her patchwork velvet rucksack, and her possessions were scattered all over the dirty gray pavement. Harry rescued a silver chain from the metal grille in the gutter. He held it up in triumph and she laughed.

A few weeks later, sitting at the kitchen table in Nunhead as the darkness began to lift outside and the first glimmerings of light turned shifting shapes into bushes and shrubs, Harry said, "How come you're always so happy?"

They had been up all night, talking, drinking tea. She made him feel safe. He could tell her anything. And nothing he said would go any further. She'd promised. They stay with me, she said. All your secrets stay with me. I won't ever talk about anything you tell me. To anyone.

"I get sad sometimes. Especially when it rains."

But this wasn't what Harry meant. "Your parents don't give a shit. But you don't hate them. You never say a bad word about either of them."

Eva thought about this. "Because it wouldn't change anything."

"Wouldn't it?"

She shook her head.

Harry looked down at the table. "Sometimes I can't sleep at night because I'm so angry."

Eva looked at him, her eyes full of sympathy.

"I start thinking, and it feels like I'm going to explode."

"You have to let it go."

"How?"

"I don't know. Imagine it floating away."

Harry looked unconvinced.

Eva said, "You can't control what other people do. The only thing you can control is how you think about it."

"Let them get away with it?" He touched the scar above his right eye.

"Let them live their life. You live your own."

Harry was silent.

Eva looked sad. "Maybe it's because I'm not very brave. I don't like facing up to things. So if something really bad happens, I try not to think about it. Or I get drunk, or stoned. Go somewhere in my mind where it doesn't matter. I just think, Do I really care about this? Is it that important?"

"Even when other people fuck up?"

"Especially then. Sometimes people are just strange. They have their reasons for doing things, but they bury them really deep. Or they shut their eyes to what they're doing, because it's sad, or it makes them feel lonely or afraid. So nothing makes sense on the surface. Not even to them. And if things are that hard to understand, you just have to let them go."

"You can really do that?"

"You can try." Eva smiled. "Live and let live."

"Make love, not war."

"Turn on, tune in, drop out."

Harry laughed. "You're such a hippie."

She liked talking about the Summer of Love. Nineteen

sixty-seven. A hundred thousand people converging on San Francisco, all trying to find something different. Fed up with conformity. Fed up with a society focused on money. It started with the Monterey Pop Festival—Janis Joplin, Jefferson Airplane, Jimi Hendrix, the Mamas and the Papas. The Byrds. It was the first time Otis Redding had played to an audience full of white people. Then, after the festival, a whole long summer spent listening to music, creating art, talking politics, taking drugs. Middle-class America was terrified. What did they want? Why were they doing it? What did it all mean?

Sometimes, talking to Eva, Harry had the uncomfortable feeling that he would have been one of the mystified onlookers. Maybe it's easier to reject something if you've always had it, thought Harry. I want money. I want the respect it brings. I want to make so much money that I feel safe and powerful forever.

Eva reached out across the table and touched his hand. "You know Killian? The one from Dublin with the dreadlocks? He goes to a gym. A boxing club. He says it helps."

"Helps what?"

"When he's angry. Centers his energy. Maybe you should go along and see what you think."

At night, when I lie there full of rage, I have fantasies of hitting John White. Breaking his nose. Smashing the bone. Blood all over his fat, sneering face.

Eva said gently, "You've had a bad time, Harry. I'm not surprised you feel a bit lost sometimes."

For a moment, he couldn't speak. It was all locked away in his mind. But he could feel the pressure of it, like a cupboard crammed full of old coats that someone has forced shut. Sometimes the effort of keeping it closed exhausted him. "I wouldn't know anyone."

"So? You'd get to know them."

"Will you come with me?"

"You're such a baby," she said, her eyes laughing at him.

He looked down at their hands on the table, the fingers intertwined. Outside, the first eerie calls of birdsong echoed, as if the world were a huge, empty space that could never be filled. It was a lonely sound. But when I'm with Eva, thought Harry, I know that everything's going to be OK. I know I'm in a much kinder place than I ever thought possible. "We'll always be together, won't we?"

"You've only just met me."

"I don't care. I'm going to know you forever."

"Forever's a long time."

They sat, smiling at each other. He said, "I should go."

"Come back later and meet my little sister."

"What's her name?"

"Kim."

"I could buy her an ice cream."

"She's thirteen."

"Roll her a joint?"

Eva laughed. "She's not like me. She has plans. She's going to change the world."

"How?"

"I don't know. Take power. Go into politics. Start a revolution. You watch. One day she'll be famous."

At the door, he turned back to look at her. The early morning sun, glancing through the window, made her hair shine gold. He said, "See you later."

She smiled at him in a way that made it hard to breathe.

. . .

Kim had spent hours working out what to wear for her first day in the new job. After three years as a student, most of her clothes had holes in them. For the interview, she'd borrowed a coat from Damaris and had kept it tightly buttoned, sweating, the whole way through. But that wasn't going to work on a regular basis.

"Borrow something of mine," said Eva.

An Indian dress with tiny little mirrors sewn onto the bodice? A floor-length skirt in red velvet? Jeans with butterflies and daisies dancing up and down the flares?

In the end, Kim settled on a navy-blue velvet pinafore that Izzie had bought in the Mind shop in East Dulwich because she thought it might make a nice cushion.

"Does it make me look pregnant?" she said, standing in front of the full-length mirror.

"No," said Eva, whose bump was now sticking out alarmingly. "This is what pregnant looks like."

But on the way there, an elderly man on crutches tried to give her his seat on the bus.

The offices of the housing charity were in Vauxhall, just south of the Thames.

"Site of the old pleasure gardens," said Jake. His hair was thick and fair, sticking out like straw on a thatched cottage. "Mentioned by Pepys and visited by thousands. For two hundred years. Concerts, fireworks, tightrope walkers, hot-air balloons. They had a reenactment of the Battle of Waterloo in 1817. Finally closed in 1859." He sat down in a large gray office chair that rolled backwards with a sigh. "But I expect you knew that."

Kim, who had lived in London all her life but had never heard of the Vauxhall pleasure gardens, stared back, tongue-tied.

"You'll be shadowing me for a week. So that you can see what we do. Watching my every move." Jake pulled his face into an expression of mock alarm, like someone who's just seen a putrefied corpse. "Stalking me."

Kim swallowed. "I hope I won't be too much trouble."

He looked at her. "You will be. Lots of trouble. But that's the only way to learn."

He's weird, thought Kim. She suddenly wished she was in a normal open-plan office with lots of people and healthy potted plants and a water cooler. She wasn't sure being stuck in a cubbyhole with Jake was such a good idea.

"So where were you working before?"

"I wasn't," said Kim. "I've just finished my degree."

Jake leant back in his chair. He had chunky thighs, like a rugby player. Or maybe it was just the baggy jeans. "In what?"

"Social policy."

"Interesting." He picked up a sheaf of papers and banged them together to make a neat block. "Where?"

"Edinburgh."

He raised his eyebrows, but she had no idea why. "So that's your desk, facing mine. I can set you up with a password and log you into the system." He had a slightly nasal voice, as if he had a permanent cold. "Our priority in the next few weeks is the

London Homelessness Report. Cross-checking all the figures in advance of the media launch. But they probably told you that at the interview."

She nodded.

"And you're on a six-month contract, apparently. A sort of paid internship. Although I wouldn't worry about that too much. You'll probably be renewed. We're currently in a state of chaos. New CEO. Got rid of the entire staff and brought in her own team. New faces. New IT system. No one has a clue what's going on. Apart from me."

Jake was momentarily distracted by something on his screen, so she sat down at her new desk and busied herself opening the nearest drawer. It was empty apart from two pencils and what looked like the wizened remains of a mummified apple core. When she looked up, he was staring at her. "Why housing?"

"Sorry?"

"What made you want to work in housing?"

He had an intense gaze. His eyes were pale blue.

"Social injustice. You can't do anything unless you have somewhere to live." Despite herself, she felt a lump in her throat. It kept happening these days. There were just two months before they had to move. She and Izzie had already paid the deposit on a smelly bedsit in New Cross with alarming stains on the carpet and black mold growing round the shower. The kitchen was two electric rings in the corner of the living room, so they wouldn't be eating anything more complicated than stew. The only consolation was that it was less than ten minutes on the bus from Eva's tiny new flat overlooking Peckham Rye. So I'll always be able to babysit, thought Kim. Whenever she needs me.

"That sounds heartfelt. Have you and your boyfriend just split up?"

This was totally inappropriate. So she ignored it. But something about his camp rudeness was making her start to relax. "How long have you worked here?"

"Five years this Christmas."

"So you like it."

"Well, I wouldn't stay if I didn't, would I?"

This annoyed her. "I don't know. You might need the money. Or be too lazy to look for something else."

"You don't hold back, do you?" He smiled. His front teeth were crooked. It was endearing in a way she didn't quite understand. "So go on, then. If we're going to work together, tell me all about yourself."

"You first."

"Twenty-eight, born in Aylesbury, Bristol University, came to London, worked for Lambeth Council, got the job here, live in Stockwell, like cats, play the trombone, spend my weekends as a volunteer restoring windmills."

Eva likes a 1960s song about windmills, thought Kim. Something to do with circles and your mind.

"Where are they?"

"What?"

"The windmills?"

"All over Britain. All three types—post, tower, smock. Your turn."

Kim thought for a moment. "Twenty-one. Born in London. Graduated last summer. About to move to New Cross. I like independent publishers, KT Tunstall, and Guinness. And my sister's having a baby."

"Which explains the maternity dress. Unless you're having one, too."

Kim opened her mouth to protest and shut it again.

"So where does she live, this sister?"

"Peckham Rye."

"The nice bit?"

Kim nodded.

"With a nice husband?"

"No."

He raised his eyebrows. "Do tell."

"Her boyfriend's paying for the flat."

"But not living in it?"

Kim shook her head.

"How very modern," said Jake.

To her great astonishment—staring at this odd, awkward man with straw hair and thick thighs—Kim found herself awash with desire.

．．．

Harry came out of the gym and stood there for a moment, re-adjusting his eyes to the shadows. The city was now in the grip of a dull, gray winter. That's why Londoners act so completely out of character when the sun starts shining in March, thought Harry. They're so relieved that life has gone back into color that they forget about being aloof and aggressive and start bouncing about like spring lambs.

It took him a while to realize that there was someone else outside with him, leaning against the wall, huddled into a hoodie. Ethan was about seven or eight, but so small and skinny he could have been much younger. He'd been coming to the kids' class at the gym for about six months. He never looked you in the eyes if he could help it. Just a quick glance in your direction sometimes, checking you out.

"Waiting for someone?"

Ethan nodded. Or it might have been an involuntary shiver.

Harry put down his sports bag and leant back against the wall as if he, too, had all the time in the world. He took out his mobile and pretended to check his messages. He didn't want to leave until he knew Ethan was safe. There were no other kids around. They usually stayed inside until they were picked up. What was he doing out here on the street? You could tell just by the way he was standing that he was nervous.

Above them, a suburban train rattled to Victoria.

On the other side of the road, a gray car came to a stop. Ethan tensed so suddenly that his body seemed to bounce back against the wall. Harry made himself stay very still. He looked up. A young woman, laughing, got out of the car, waved, and turned off towards the station. The car ground off at speed.

Ethan slumped back against the brickwork.

It was getting darker. It was as if someone had turned down the dimmer switch. The gym door opened. A huge man, about six foot four, two hundred and thirty pounds, swung out, nodded at them both, and disappeared into the gloom.

Across the road, a car slowed down, then sped up again. Ethan cringed even more deeply into his hoodie.

An arc of lights swept round the corner, temporarily blinding them. A battered blue Toyota drove up on the wrong side of the road and stopped right in front of them. There was no one in the car but the driver. She reached back over the seat to the passenger door behind and pushed it open. Harry looked at Ethan. In the light from the car, Ethan's face was happy, flooded with relief.

What's going on? Why was he so frightened? Who did he think might be in the car?

Harry said, "See you next week."

For a moment, their eyes met. Then Ethan ducked into the car, slamming the door, and Harry watched it speed off, veering out into the oncoming traffic.

It doesn't take much, Harry thought, to remember how it feels to be small and terrified.

He bent down and picked up his sports bag. But I'm grown up now, he thought with a surge of joy. And I know how to fight.

· · ·

Alisha looked nervous. "Unfortunately, due to a sudden unforeseen emergency situation, our CEO can't be with us in person today."

Jake frowned.

"So she's asked me to introduce you to Jake and"—Alisha studied her notes—"personally welcome you aboard as the newest members of the team at this exciting stage of the charity's future development going forward."

They were five of them sitting in a tight circle of chairs by the fire escape. The offices were on the top floor of a concrete block next to the main road. One of the double-glazed windows behind them had rivulets of condensation running down between the sheets of glass. The thin brown carpet beneath their feet was blackened with what looked like burn marks, and the leaves of the office palm were yellow brown, like old bananas. But this is a charity, thought Kim. You wouldn't want to waste money on inessentials.

"So, as a team-building exercise, Louisa would like us to go round and introduce ourselves, and say what made us want to work here." Alisha looked up, her eyes anxious. "And then we have to come up with an interesting fact about ourselves."

Kim felt hot and awkward. She wasn't sure that anything in her life counted as interesting. You're the only person I know, Izzie had said recently, who copes with stress in her life by working even harder.

"So I'll start, shall I? My name's Alisha, and I'm Louisa's executive personal assistant."

"Why?" said Jake.

Alisha blinked. She had very smooth brown skin, gold-rimmed spectacles, and bright red lipstick.

"You're meant to say why you wanted to work here," said Jake.

Alisha seemed to shrink back into her chair.

"Perhaps we should move on," said Jake, "and come back to you in a minute."

To Alisha's left was a thin man with bushy gray hair. His face was scored with deep lines, as if he'd spent most of his life in a desert. "I'm Brian. New IT support manager. Step up from the last job. My interesting fact is that I once had a cup of tea with Keira Knightley."

Alisha burst back into life. "How come?"

"I was an extra on *Pride and Prejudice*."

"No," breathed Alisha.

Kim, aware that Jake was watching her, frowned as if she was unimpressed by name-dropping.

"You can see me in one of the crowd scenes. Breeches and a red waistcoat."

"I loved her in *Pirates of the Caribbean*," said Alisha. "I kept hoping she'd end up with Johnny Depp."

Jake looked at his watch. "Perhaps we ought to move on?"

"I'm Steve," said the large man sitting next to Brian. He had a film of sweat across his forehead. "Communications manager."

"And why did you want to work here?"

Jake's taken over, thought Kim. He must be one of those people who like meetings.

"It seemed like something I could get my teeth into. A good opportunity. Career progression—"

"So, Kim," said Jake, cutting him off. "Over to you."

Everyone was looking at her. She took a deep breath. "I'm Kim. Research assistant. I wanted to work here because I believe it's wrong that people should be homeless in Britain in 2006. A home is not just a roof over your head. It's the place where you feel safe and secure, where you can put down roots and feel part of your community. I want to make a difference. I want to stick up for people who don't have a voice."

She was conscious of everyone staring at her. Oh no, she thought, her heart sinking. I've done it again. Misjudged the mood. Played *Hamlet* when everyone wanted *Wallace & Gromit*.

"And the interesting fact?" said Jake.

Kim looked at him, her expression desperate.

Jake smiled. "We'll come back to you when you're ready. I'm Jake. Head of research. I joined the charity some years ago. But these are exciting times. With Louisa as CEO, we're going to change the way we view homelessness in this country."

What a brilliant answer, thought Kim, wishing she'd said something similar.

"And what's your interesting fact?" said Alisha.

"Catherine Zeta-Jones," said Jake casually, "is my cousin."

After the meeting had broken up and the others had gone back to their desks, Kim said, with some surprise, "I had no idea."

"What?"

"That you were related to Catherine Zeta-Jones."

Jake shot her quick glance from his pale blue eyes. "Oh," he said, "were we supposed to be telling the truth?"

.   .   .

Sitting in the stalls at the Royal Opera House—the first night of a new production of Bizet's *Carmen*—Harry checked his phone was on vibrate. It was too early, obviously. A month too early. But these days he didn't want to be out of contact. She hadn't asked for him to be at the birth. But he wanted to be on hand, in case.

In case of what? He didn't know. Which made it worse. Sometimes the thought of Eva facing a danger he didn't understand made him light-headed with fear.

He glanced sideways. This particular client—a fund manager who regularly gave him a lot of business and always voted him best analyst in the Extel and *Institutional Investor* surveys—

liked culture. So Harry had done his homework. Over drinks beforehand, they'd discussed Tomma Abts winning the Turner Prize and the forthcoming production of *Giselle* at the Coliseum. Should they book tickets for Gilbert and George at the Tate in February? I will be whoever you want me to be, thought Harry. I will discuss Italian sopranos, prima ballerinas, and career retrospectives. I will be as educated, cultivated, and sophisticated as you are.

"You are a complete fraud," Eva had said, her eyes full of affection.

"You could think of it another way. I'm like your best-ever reflection in a mirror. Making you feel good about yourself. Giving you hope. Who knows? I might be the invisible angel of the City. The little ray of sunshine that keeps people going."

"You? A little ray of sunshine?"

"Some people quite like me, you know," said Harry, pretending to be offended.

In the seat next to him, his client settled back with an air of excited anticipation. "I think we might be in for a treat, you know."

"I'm looking forward to hearing Anna Caterina Antonacci," said Harry. "Such an incredibly versatile voice."

"Power, passion, and sensuality."

As the lights went down, Harry curled his fingers round his phone.

. . .

"That's it, then," said Jake. "Checked, referenced, and legaled. In print and online. The London Homelessness Report."

"Ready for the media launch."

"Which our esteemed patron will deliver next month."

Kim leant back in her chair. "Will we be allowed to go?"

"To the House of Commons? You bet."

"I've never been to the House of Commons. I mean, not inside it."

Jake smiled. "It's not as grand as you'd think. Just big rooms with nice stone windows. And you have to queue for hours to get past security."

"I don't look like a terrorist, do I?"

"Nobody looks like a terrorist," said Jake. "That's the point."

He stopped smiling. For a moment, neither could look away.

Jake turned back to his screen. "Right. Enough. Let's close up and get out of here."

It was eight o'clock. The offices were deserted. Kim, keeping her voice light, said, "Do you have time for a drink?"

"A drink?" Jake was looking at his keyboard.

"If you're not busy."

"Don't you have to get back to that hugely pregnant sister of yours?"

"She's fine. She's got a friend over for supper." She's got Harry over for supper. "I don't live with her, anyway. I live with Izzie."

"Ah, yes," said Jake. "The one with the secret love life."

"Well, I don't know she's got a secret love life. She's just never at home." Home? Who am I kidding? It's a smelly bedsit.

"I bet he's gorgeous," said Jake, peering round the screen. "Brad Pitt meets Will Smith."

Kim laughed.

"What about you?" His voice rose out of the darkness somewhere behind the monitor.

"What?"

"Do you have a secret love life?"

She heard the sound of a drawer shutting. After a while, she said, "I don't have any kind of love life."

Jake pushed back his chair so that he sat in the pool of light from the desk lamp. "I find that hard to believe."

"It's true."

"Someone pretty like you."

Her heart gave a little skip of delight. People called her tough. People called her uncompromising. No one had ever called her pretty. "I find most men very boring."

After a long pause, during which they both carefully examined each other's expression, Jake said, "Including me?"

"Oh no," said Kim, in a clear voice, "I don't find you boring at all."

.   .   .

"You sit down here now, Eva," said Christine. "There's plenty of room."

This was a lie. It was always a lie. There was never any room in Christine's kitchen. She had four children and nine grandchildren, as well as cousins, second cousins, and family friends all over southeast London, and she believed it was her duty to feed them all. Jamaican food, of course—jerk chicken, rice and peas, saltfish with cabbage. But she was equally at home with roast beef, sweet and sour pork, spaghetti bolognese, and Thai curry.

Christine was always at the stove. She moved the pans around from ring to ring like a juggler spinning plates, admonishing those that failed to boil and congratulating those that were simmering just nicely. She coaxed her food. She urged it to excel. She did the same with people. Stand in Christine's kitchen long enough and you found yourself with goals you didn't even know existed. Work in a shop? No, you want to own a shop. Own a shop? No, you want a nationwide chain. A nationwide chain? What's wrong with you? There's a whole world out there. All you need is hard work and determination. Haven't you heard of Lady Scotland? Andrea Levy? Sir Trevor McDonald?

So far, Christine had produced an IT consultant, a teacher, a social worker, and a junior doctor. If everything went to plan, she had in the pipeline a barrister, a bishop, and the first black prime minister. She excused the smallest grandchildren. But the youngest member of the family, just six months old, had hands big enough for a concert pianist.

"So how are you, Eva? Ready for that baby to be born?"

"Oh yes," said Eva, with feeling. It was hard to believe that someone so slight was managing to carry such an enormous bump. The huge mound of her stomach stuck out at right angles. It looked as if only willpower was keeping her upright. "Nature's very clever. Towards the end, you don't even worry about the pain. You're so desperate for the baby to come out that you'd hang upside down from the ceiling if someone told you to."

The noise in the kitchen was incredible. It was the afternoon of Christmas Eve and Christine was minding some of her grandchildren while she peeled potatoes, made bread sauce, and stuffed the turkey for lunch the next day. While she clattered about with pans and knives, a small boy was racing a fire engine with a high-pitched siren round the table legs, a baby in a high chair was banging the fridge door with a metal spoon, and someone in the hallway was playing the recorder. By the back door, apparently oblivious to the pandemonium, sat Lewis, reading the paper. Once, years ago, Kim had asked Damaris—her best friend at school and Christine's youngest—whether her dad minded living in a house that was always packed full of people. Damaris, frowning, had said she didn't think he even noticed.

Kim had never heard Lewis speak. He was, as Christine always said, a man of few words. But when Damaris got her letter accepting her into medical school, and Kim had danced her round the kitchen shouting, "You did it! You did it!," he had looked up from his paper and smiled.

"So are you girls ready for Christmas?"

We would never have managed without Christine, thought Kim. In the early days after Dad left, when Mum was out somewhere drinking cocktails, Christine would appear at the front door—small, round, and fierce, glasses falling down her nose—and somehow, with a few disapproving tuts, would usher us from our cold and empty house to the chaos of family life next door. After supper, Damaris and I would be packed upstairs to do our homework, and Eva would stay at the kitchen table, gradually thawing in the warmth of Christine's concern.

Eva pulled a face. "Not really. I can't face the crowds."

The baby threw the spoon to the floor. It's not shopping we can't face, thought Kim, bending down to pick it up. It's Christmas itself. It will be the first one we won't be spending next door to Christine. Although Eva's flat in Peckham Rye looked quite festive with its red tinsel and white fairy lights.

"And when's your mother coming?"

Kim and Eva looked at each other.

"She isn't," said Kim. "It'll just be us."

Christine had never once criticized Grace, not even in the early days when she realized that Kim and Eva had been left alone with no food in the house. But Kim could see now, from the tightening round her mouth, that Christine was struggling to understand. "She's not coming home for Christmas?"

The small boy, to everyone's intense relief, picked up his flashing fire engine and ran down the hall to the front room.

"She's been invited to spend it with friends."

One friend, to be more specific. A widower called Jean-Marc. Who lived in a villa with olive and lemon and oleander trees.

"So come here tomorrow," said Christine, "on Christmas Day. There's plenty of room."

"We've already bought the turkey," said Kim hastily. This wasn't completely true. But she'd remembered, on her way home from work, to buy a small chicken, a bag of potatoes, and a box of mince pies. And there was no way—even though it was a genuine invitation, and somehow everyone always fitted in—that she and Eva wanted to make Christine's guests even more squashed than usual.

Christine peered at them both over the top of her glasses. "But she'll be here for the baby?"

"Oh yes," said Kim, even though she knew her mother wouldn't be here for the birth either.

I'm not good with babies, darling. They're just so—unpleasant.

There was a ring on the doorbell.

"That will be Damaris," said Christine proudly. "Back from the hospital."

They listened to a hubbub of voices in the hall. Kim, who'd been standing in the kitchen doorway, turned round with a smile. And found herself face-to-face with Harry.

"Merry Christmas," he said, leaning down to kiss her.

She dodged.

"Harry!" said Christine, waving a wooden spoon at him. "You get more handsome every time I see you."

"Here," he said, handing her a bottle in a twist of red tissue paper. "Something for tomorrow."

"What do you think, Eva? Isn't he a good-looking man?"

"If I didn't know you better," said Harry, "I might think you were trying to get us together."

"I wouldn't dare. You young people will make up your own minds."

Harry grinned. "That's not what you really think."

"What I think is that no one understands what's going on with you two."

"I'm amazed they've allowed you the day off," said Kim, anxious to change the subject. "Doesn't the stock market grind to a halt without you?"

"Built any flats recently?"

"We're a campaigning charity," said Kim coldly. "We get central government to commit funds nationally to the crisis of homelessness."

"Give me five minutes," said Harry, "and I could raise all the money you need for the next five years."

Kim, pink with fury, was opening her mouth to retaliate when Eva said, "Have you heard, Harry? Kim's got a new boyfriend."

The baby threw the spoon on the floor again.

Oh, Eva, wailed Kim inside. You weren't supposed to tell anyone. "He's not a boyfriend."

"Really?" said Harry, bending down to pick up the spoon. "What's his name?"

"Jake," said Eva.

"You must bring him here," said Christine, "so we can meet him."

"And how long have you been together?"

"It's not—"

"She met him at work," said Eva.

"Ah," said Harry. "Isn't that nice? You must have so much in common. And where does he live, this Jack?"

"Jake," said Kim.

"He's a lot older than her," said Eva. "A grown-up boyfriend."

"How much older?" said Harry.

"Ten years at least."

"It's early days," said Kim desperately. "And it might not work out. So I don't think we should talk about it anymore."

"I know," said Harry, "why don't we have a party on New Year's Eve? Your last day in the house. We could invite Jock over."

"Jake," said Kim.

"I might be having a baby," said Eva.

"Really?" said Harry.

They both laughed.

"You ignore them," said Christine, catching sight of Kim's expression. "They're being very silly."

It's how they always are, thought Kim gloomily. They talk to each other in a way that excludes everyone else.

"Talking of which," said Eva, "I ought to be getting back before it gets dark and the pavements get icy. I get really worried about falling over these days."

"I'm not surprised," said Harry.

"You wait. Come New Year I'll be as light as a feather."

"I'll take you home. I've got the car."

"Would that be the Porsche? Because I only ever accept lifts in Porsches." Eva gave him the kind of luminous smile that had elderly men reminiscing about long-forgotten love affairs. "Kim? Are you coming?"

"I'm going to stay and see Damaris."

"I could come back and get you," said Harry.

"Haven't you got to go somewhere for Christmas?"

Harry grinned. "I know you're desperate for me to stay in London. But I just can't, I'm afraid."

For one tiny moment, Kim wondered where he was going. But she squashed her curiosity. She didn't want to think about Harry any more than she had to.

When Harry and Eva had gone, Christine lifted the baby out of the high chair and cuddled him close, putting her cheek onto the little soft head. "I don't know if you're right, Kim. It seems to me they're just good friends. And if it was Harry's child, I think she would have said."

Kim shrugged. She felt tired and cross. "Who knows?"

"Young men these days," said Christine sadly. "They don't seem to want to stay around when the babies come along."

Much later, on the bus back to Peckham Rye, Kim thought about her father in Leicester with his glamorous new wife.

Or they stay around while it suits them, she thought bitterly, and bugger off when they get a better offer.

.   .   .

Harry looked again at the list in front of him. "The Musigny," he said.

The waiter bowed and backed away.

Titania gave him a long look. "I bet you could tell me everything about it."

"Domaine Jacques Prieur. Grand cru. Pinot grape. Classic year."

"And you are expecting?"

"Black fruit and immense length."

Titania laughed. "I bet you could give me a list of all the vineyards in Burgundy."

Harry smiled. "You're right. I could."

It was Christmas Day. He and Titania were getting quietly drunk in an exclusive five-star hotel in the Cotswolds. He kept thinking about Eva and Kim in the flat in Peckham Rye. Come for Christmas, Eva had said. I can't, said Harry. Why? said Eva. You know why, said Harry.

"Not many people can do it," said Titania.

The hotel had a reputation for good food and superb wine. Harry had booked a room with a king-sized four-poster bed. Driving up in the gray Porsche—with Titania, smelling of expensive scent, curled up on the front seat next to him—he kept reminding himself that not having a family Christmas had its compensations.

"It's a real skill," said Titania, "I admire it."

Harry forced himself back to the present. "Admire what?"

"If you don't know about something, you find out about it. Become an expert."

Harry narrowed his eyes. "That sounds like a criticism."

"Not at all. It's just the way you operate."

"So why am I feeling uneasy?"

Titania stroked the end of her fork, pricking her finger on the sharp silver tines. "I just wonder sometimes if it's like an actor learning his lines."

"What do you mean?"

"Playing a part."

"What part?"

Her gaze was clear and direct. "Do you even like red wine?"

There was a sudden shift in atmosphere. Harry said carefully, "Is there something wrong?"

"No."

They sat in silence, listening to the murmur of conversation around them. At the next table, a very fat man with greasy gray hair let out a guffaw of laughter that trailed off into prolonged coughing. Someone, somewhere, clinked a water glass, and the sound rang out in the subdued hush of serious dining like a tiny, fairylike bell. When Titania eventually looked up, Harry's heart sank.

"I'm not sure it's working for me anymore, Harry."

"You don't mean that."

"I do."

He felt incredibly sad. Lovely, kind, clever Titania. "Are you sure?"

She nodded.

After a long time, he said, "Is there anything I can say to change your mind?"

She looked irritated. "Oh come on, Harry."

He felt ashamed. For something to do, he straightened the cutlery in front of him. When he looked up, he was shocked to see that Titania had tears in her eyes. He reached out across the table. But she shook her head. She said, "I've often wondered if there's someone else."

He said nothing.

"Someone you can't have?"

"Titania—"

"It's OK. It's none of my business. I just wanted to know."

He looked at her sadly.

"You keep hoping, don't you? Even when there's no chance at all." With a furtive flourish of white linen, Titania dabbed at her eyes with a restaurant napkin. Then she sat up straight, squaring her shoulders. "Now, where's that bloody burgundy? I need a drink."

.   .   .

All of the men dancing on the table had their trousers round their ankles. Because of this, they kept falling over. Some of the women had stripped down to their bras and one of them had fastened her ponytail with a black bow tie. A blue velvet cummerbund was hanging from the chandelier. Over by the window, an overweight young man with wet red lips was shaking another bottle of champagne. That had been the theme of the dinner party—spraying Dom Pérignon at anything that moved. Harry—tired, depressed, and stone-cold sober—dodged as a stray stiletto flew past his ear, followed by a bread roll and a lump of Stilton. There was a crash as liqueur glasses fell to the floor.

"Party, party, party!" yelled Syed.

Someone picked up a fire extinguisher.

"What's the time?" shouted a busty blonde with green glittery eye shadow.

It was ten minutes to midnight. Very soon, thought Harry, we'll hear Big Ben. And then there's going to be a lot of kissing.

"Party, party, party," shouted Syed again, leaning across towards him, losing his balance, and collapsing onto the tablecloth.

Harry pulled him upright. "Are you OK?"

"Do you know," said Syed, with an air of surprise, "I think I might have drunk too much."

"Impossible."

"Are you coming to the club?"

Harry shook his head.

"Why?"

"I don't like bribing women with fifty-pound notes to take their knickers off."

"I know. Extortionate." Syed looked suddenly gloomy. "Did I ever tell you about my brother-in-law?"

"No," said Harry.

"He's a shit."

"Oh."

"He's lost all his money."

"Not only a shit, but a stupid shit."

"And you know what?"

"What?"

"My mother wants me to give it to him."

"Beat him up?"

"No," shouted Syed. "No, no! She wants me to fucking give him all the fucking money he's fucking lost."

"From what I've heard of your mother," said Harry, "you'd better do what she says."

Syed's mouth puckered as if he was going to cry. "But I haven't got it."

"You haven't got the money?"

Syed shook his head.

Harry sighed. "I'll find it for you."

"Thank you, my friend," said Syed, nodding seriously. "But you don't have it either."

"How do you know?"

"He has lost more money in the last six months than I have made in my entire life."

Harry frowned. "That's not possible."

"Oh yes, my friend, it's possible. Because he just did it. My fuckwit of a brother-in-law just fucking did it."

"He's a gambler?"

"He's a businessman, Harry. Which is much, much worse. Respectable gambling. And my mother"—Syed's lower lip trembled—"my mother thinks I can make it all go away."

"Tell her. Tell her no one's got that kind of money. Not even you."

Syed looked mournful. "She wouldn't believe me."

"Five minutes!" shouted the busty blonde.

"It's the family honor," said Syed. "If it wasn't family, I'd say, Go fuck yourself. You got yourself in this fucking mess. Now you fucking get yourself out of it. But it's my sister's fucking husband. So I can't."

Someone threw open the sash window. A blast of cold air hit them. Outside in the street, they heard the sounds of revelers making their way towards Trafalgar Square.

Harry said, "I'm going away."

Syed frowned. "What?"

"I'm going away. In the New Year."

"Two minutes!"

"Where are you going?"

"I don't know."

"On holiday? A Caribbean island? Barbados?"

"I haven't decided."

"So why are you going?"

"Because she doesn't love me."

Syed narrowed his eyes, trying to focus.

"She doesn't love me. And she's never going to love me. And I can't do it anymore. I can't do it."

Syed, swaying, blinked. "Titania?"

TEN, NINE, EIGHT, SEVEN, SIX, FIVE, FOUR—

Harry shut his eyes.

THREE, TWO—

In his hand, the phone vibrated.

HAPPY NEW YEAR!

≈ 2007 ≈

Cheryl Cole. Flower of Newcastle. A rose tattoo on her bottom. I wanted one, too, but they only managed the outline before they ran out of ink. I've been living in London six months now. In a bedsit in New Cross. It's not that bad. I've got a boyfriend. He's very polite. He says thank you after sex. Just like on motorways when it's all one lane because of construction, and you're thinking, If this goes on for much longer I'm going to top myself, and then suddenly it stops and there's a big sign saying, 'Thank You for Your Patience.' And he's good with compliments. Whenever we go out, he says, 'You look nice, pet.' And I think, I know. *That's the point.* How could I not look nice? I've spent three hours getting ready. If you spend three hours on anything, it looks quite nice. A painting, the inside of your car, the toilet. I'd like a bit more passion. You know, 'You are the most beautiful woman I've ever seen.' Like Leonardo DiCaprio in *Titanic*. Men the way you'd like them to be. That's why women look so depressed when they come out of the cinema. They look at the boyfriend and reality hits them in the face. So he says, 'You look nice, pet,' and all I can think is how long it takes to be a woman. I mean, not biologically, obviously. You start getting black holes of hormonal despair when you're about ten these days. Writing suicide notes in crayon. No, I mean how long it takes just to look normal. Normal enough not to excite negative comment over the frozen pizzas in Sainsbury's. 'Look over there! Why's that man in a wig spending so long choosing a margherita?' I know. I know. You look at me and you think, Well obviously, she only took five minutes. But I didn't. I probably took more time putting myself together for tonight than a transvestite at Halloween. I mean, it's called 'makeup' for a reason. You make yourself up. If you want to look like a normal woman, you have to become a work of fiction. And that's not the worst of it. We're all supposed to look natural. Beautiful, without even trying. Like Lily Allen, or a dove, or one of those really surprised-looking women in the Garnier adverts. And my heart sinks. Because what that means, really, is putting on makeup to disguise the fact you've put on makeup. A bit like Tony Blair smiling about Iraq to hide the fact he's smiling about Iraq. And I think, This is ridiculous. It's going to take too long. By the time I've got ready to come onstage, you'll all have given up and gone home. Which would have saved a lot of time all around. Thank you very much, ladies and gentlemen. You've been a lovely audience. I've been Izzie from Newcastle."

· · ·

"So it was all because of George Clooney?"

Damaris looked offended. "No."

"You just said you decided to become a doctor because of box sets of *ER*."

"I didn't say it was because of George Clooney."

"Eriq La Salle?"

Damaris shook her head.

"Who, then?"

Damaris bit her lip. "Noah Wyle?"

"Of course," said Kim. "The super-intelligent, super-rich, super-repressed John Carter."

"Are you saying I only fancy men with trust funds?"

"I don't know," said Kim. "Do you?"

Damaris laughed. It lit up her face. You could see her perfect white teeth. Kim liked imagining Damaris as a GP. You'll make people better just by smiling at them, she thought. They'll come into the surgery feeling ill and tired, weighed down by the gas bill and rising damp and why the car won't start, and you'll be sitting there with your stethoscope and your slim fingers, your eyes full of sympathy, and suddenly life won't seem so bad after all.

But you didn't see Damaris smile much. Or hear her laugh. She took her training very seriously. The habit of hard work begun in childhood was so strong that she rarely stopped to look around and see how far she'd come. Damaris had always pushed herself. Christine may have been chivvying in the background, but it was Damaris who set the pace. At school, she and Kim had been labeled the Nerds. While their friends were out partying, they sat side by side in the library, putting in the hours. Kim needed the structure. Damaris needed the grades. Something of that seriousness had hung around their conversations ever since. Whenever you get together, Eva would say, you're like a couple of old professors in tweed jackets, smelling of ancient books and tobacco.

Sometimes I worry, thought Kim, that we've forgotten how to have fun.

"So go on, then," said Damaris. "Tell me about Jake."

"There's nothing to tell."

It was a Thursday evening at the end of February. Outside the night was frosty and calm, twinkling with startling whiteness. Peckham Rye looked like something out of Narnia. But inside the flat, decorated with small blue Babygros hung over the radiators, it was cozy and warm. Eva had gone to her postnatal yoga class. It's not vanity, she said. I just want to be able to get enough stomach muscles back to make it possible to get out of bed.

Damaris had come to help with babysitting. "If you're not going to tell me anything interesting about Jake, I might as well go home."

"Oh, please don't go," said Kim. "There might be a medical emergency."

"What kind of medical emergency?"

"I don't know. Babies do all sorts of strange things."

"I haven't done pediatrics yet. You probably know more than I do."

Which was probably true. Kim had pretty much moved in after the birth. Otis, still in the frowning blur of newborn discomfort, hated being apart from Eva. But Kim was a good substitute. In the evenings, while Eva had a bath, she sat with him on her lap, singing him Otis Redding songs and telling him interesting facts about London housing shortages.

"It's the first time I've seen you since Christmas," said Damaris, "so you don't have to tell me much. Anything would do. Hobbies? Dietary habits? Political leanings?"

But Kim couldn't talk about Jake. Not yet. She hadn't worked out what she felt herself. All she knew for certain was that she'd never met anyone like him. He was a mass of contradictions. On the one hand, he was eccentric, self-absorbed, and sentimental, blunt to the point of rudeness. On the other, he was clever, kind, and well-read, and anxious to share his encyclopedic knowledge with anyone who needed it.

Sometimes he just seemed weird. He was drawn to anything quirky—dogs that looked like Yoda, the African horned melon, Borat, an evaluation of Empedocles. Once, on the bus, he had a long conversation with someone wearing a witch's hat made entirely from black bin liners and chatted away animatedly about heat-resistant plastics. But this strangeness also made Kim laugh. He loved the absurd—typos in newspaper headlines, pompous CEOs. He marveled every time at the signs on two identical staircases at Angel tube, one saying UP and the other DOWN. "Who worked out which was which?" he said, his eyes bright with laughter. "Who made the ultimate decision?"

But more important—much more important than any of this—he made her feel desirable. He made her feel beautiful. He made her feel significant. Whenever he looked at her with that intense expression in his pale blue eyes, she knew that she had his complete attention. No one else mattered. There had been other boyfriends. At Edinburgh, she'd had an on-off relationship for nearly a year with Rob, a geography student obsessed with Black Sabbath and the Vaselines. But this was different. The first time Jake kissed her—when she felt his awkwardness fall away, like a heavy coat slipping from his shoulders—Kim felt for the first time the dizzying excitement of a lover's gratitude. Jake was amazed that she liked him. He seemed humbled by her interest. He said he was the luckiest man in the world. And Kim—who hated swaggering, overconfident masculinity—found this completely disarming. She was made to understand, for the first time in her life, that being pale and scruffy, with no interest in clothes, makeup, or jewelry, was highly erotic. Jake admired her hands, her eyes, her shoulders, her waist. He said she should be an artist's model because she was so perfectly in proportion. It was ridiculous, of course, this extravagant praise. She didn't take any of it seriously. But she liked it. She liked feeling, for once, that she had looks worth talking about.

What made this all the more exciting was that you would never have cast Jake as a romantic hero. You wouldn't have looked at him and seen Clark Gable's Rhett Butler, or Russell Crowe's Maximus, or Daniel Craig's James Bond. But somehow, in her company, he was transformed. Kim wandered around in a state of secret astonishment, marveling at her hidden powers.

She was surprised to discover that Jake had a very hairy chest. It seemed rampantly sexual on someone so fey. Like finding Harry Potter with a condom in his pocket.

At first, she was wary. She couldn't quite trust his adoration. Something about having Eva as an elder sister—fine, fair, ethereal Eva—had made her lose confidence. She felt plain by comparison. Her mother's perpetual criticism hadn't helped. *Obviously you take after your father rather than me. Square shoulders. And such a determined chin. If only you put a bit of effort into your appearance. A touch of makeup, a good haircut, and you'd be almost presentable. You owe it to other people to make the best of yourself. All of us have a duty to make the world a more beautiful place.*

Kim watched anxiously the first time Jake met her sister.

Would he realize his mistake? Faced with the real thing, would he turn round, see Kim properly for the first time, and back off in horror? Kim could see that Eva and Jake liked each other. Eva was, after all—in her own way—almost as eccentric as he was. But, strangely, within minutes of their first meeting, Kim could see that Jake didn't gaze at Eva in the way that most men did. He didn't stare at her with desperate longing, his mouth open and his tongue hanging out.

Much later, lying in Jake's bed, collapsed over his solid hairiness, Kim steeled herself to ask the question. "So what did you think of my sister?"

Jake frowned. "She's quite nervous, isn't she? Not very sure of herself."

"What else?"

"You won't like it if I say what I think. You never do."

"I want to know," said Kim in a small voice, bracing herself for the worst.

"She's really white. Do you think she might be anemic?"

Jake's flat in Stockwell was a strange and unnerving place—a junk shop of bits and pieces randomly displayed, with no logic or order. Every surface was covered with postcards, knives, Matchbox cars, medical instruments, opera glasses, briar-wood pipes, Chinese incense burners, melon ballers, hoof picks, and decorative teaspoons. His book collection was similarly wide-ranging—Kafka, the Koran, C. S. Lewis, Toni Morrison, *Zen and the Art of Motorcycle Maintenance.*

The first time she visited, Kim tried to clear a bit of space on a chair for her coat and bag. But she disturbed so much dust that she didn't bother after that. It seemed to make more sense to follow Jake's lead and just place anything you were likely to need urgently on top of everything else.

"Kim?"

Kim snapped back to the present—a cold February evening in the flat on Peckham Rye.

"If I ask you questions about him, will you answer?"

"I don't know," said Kim. "It depends what they are."

Damaris laughed. "OK, something safe. Is it a problem working together?"

"Not really. He's very disciplined. It's like he's got different compartments in his head. At work, I'm just his research assistant."

"And what about you?"

Sometimes I find myself lusting after him at the photocopier. It's something about his thighs. "I think it's OK because we've got our own little office. So we don't have to pretend to other people that there's nothing going on."

Damaris put her head on one side. "You really like him, don't you?"

Kim felt herself getting flustered. "Why don't you come round the next time you've got a few days off? I'll ask him to supper. And then you can meet him properly."

"Here? Or in New Cross?"

Kim's smile faded. When she'd moved in with Eva and Otis, she'd left Izzie behind in the decaying bedsit. "I'm not sure."

Damaris raised her eyebrows.

Kim, always sensitive to criticism, bristled. "What?"

"I was just thinking about all the scruples you used to have about living in a flat that Harry had paid for."

"Eva needs me. That's what's important."

"And Izzie's OK with that?"

Kim looked guilty. "I don't know. I haven't seen her for ages. And when we do meet, she's always in such a rush." Last time, she thought, we met in a pub in Holborn. Izzie had just finished her cleaning shift round the corner—a block of offices with palm trees in the foyer. She had half a lager and a packet of crisps, and then said she had to be somewhere. She left in such a hurry that she forgot her notebook, which seemed to be full of random lists of people and world events.

"Off to meet her secret lover."

Kim frowned. Izzie definitely had a secret. But she didn't look like someone in the throes of a full-blown love affair. Most of the time, she just looked terrified.

"What about your landlord? The man who earns more in five minutes than you could earn in five years?"

Kim shrugged. "He doesn't come round much."

"Doesn't he?" Damaris looked surprised.

Or maybe he chooses his moments, thought Kim. Maybe he comes to see Eva and Otis when he knows I'm not here.

"He's at Mum's all the time," said Damaris. "Whenever I call round, he's sitting at the kitchen table having a cup of tea."

Kim tried to look as if this was something she already knew. But inside she was seething. Was Harry trying to take over Christine, too?

"She's always loved Harry," said Damaris. "She thinks he should be the next governor of the Bank of England."

• • •

"Most stand-ups talk about sex. Have you noticed? It always gets a laugh. For female comics, it's an easy laugh. The kind of nervous laugh you get when people have had a shock. Or your granddad says something racist. Because most men in the audience are surprised that women have an opinion about sex at all. They don't think it ever crosses our minds. Because we're too busy thinking about shoes. As for two women having sex with each other, well, how would that work? I promise you I had that conversation once. It's like the man who goes on holiday to Paris and stands there by the Eiffel Tower thinking, How do two French people talk to each other if neither understands a word of English? There's a man in the front row down there looking really shifty. You've been thinking that for years, haven't you, pet? So sex gets a laugh because it's like food—enjoyable, but with negative side effects. Like going out for a curry. You pile everything in, chew it, swallow it, sit there belching, burping and farting, and finally end up on the toilet. Overall, as an experience, you might rate it at ninety percent, but not because of the gassy parts. The reason we all laugh at sex is because we're frightened of it. It makes us feel insecure. Because you never really know, do you, whether you're doing it right. However long you've spent secretly watching porn. You can't pass a test like you do with driving. (Although that might be quite good. You could practice your emergency stops.) And when you have sex with someone else—rather than just with yourself—you're meant to make sure the other person has a good time. So while you're eating your chicken korma, you're watching to see if he's enjoying his vindaloo. The problem is, he might not tell you the truth. Because people never do in relationships, do they? So you might say, 'Are you enjoying that, pet?' and he'll look at you with his eyes watering and say, 'Yes.' Or he'll make a big song and dance about ordering everything on the menu—papadums, prawn curry, stuffed paratha—and then, when it comes, he's finished before you've even started. They say in women's magazines that sex is all about communication. I'm not so sure. I think sex is all about keeping secrets. You have to look as if you're being carried away on a wave of passion. But inside you're thinking, Do I even like curry?"

.   .   .

Grace sounded furious. "Really, Kim, I do think you could be trying a bit harder. It's all very well saying you can't interfere, but just leaving them to go their own way isn't helping, is it? Have you thought about poor little Otis?"

Sometimes when her mother was ranting down the phone from the South of France, Kim had fantasies of pretending the flat was on fire, or there was a burst water main, or a tiger had escaped from London Zoo and was roaming Peckham Rye looking for lunch. Of course, being an independent twenty-two-year-old with a job and a shared bedsit in New Cross (even if she wasn't living there and was, instead, spending the majority of her time in a flat paid for by Harry), it should have been easy to say to her mother, Look, I'm not enjoying this conversation, it's not getting us anywhere, and I think the time has come for us to talk to each other in a more rational and grown-up manner. Instead, because Grace always made her feel about five years old, Kim gripped the receiver tightly and prayed for it all to be over as quickly as possible. "Otis is fine, Mum."

"Poor little Otis is not fine. He doesn't have a father. I know it's very modern to pretend that women can manage all on their own, but there's nothing wrong with a bit of financial support. I should know. The *years* I had to manage on a pittance."

"But Harry is—"

"If I can't be there myself, and I can't—I simply can't—I am relying on you to get this situation under control. As I've said before, they clearly adore each other. They have a child together. There really is no reason why this whole unsatisfactory situation shouldn't be cleared up as quickly as possible. All it needs, Kim, is a little imagination. A little finesse. A little creative thought. And I should have imagined, if only for your sister's sake, that you would have wanted to put just a tiny bit of effort into thinking how this could be achieved."

"But, Mum, I can't—"

"There's no such word as 'can't.' That's just negative thinking. All the great men in the world had dreams that people said were impossible. Martin Luther King. Laurence Olivier. Marlon Brando. Hitchcock himself. Focus on the goal, and go for it. If I were in London, I'd do it myself. I'd ring Harry. I'd say to him, Look, this has to stop. We can't all carry on like this. Enough is enough. But my hands are tied. I'm here, with Jean-Marc, in a Mediterranean villa miles from England. There's nothing I can do. So it has to be you, Kim. It has to be you."

"But—"

"You can't just sit around hoping this nightmare situation will resolve itself. Because what you'll discover, as you get older, is that men are very shallow. They lose interest. Something to do with testosterone. Believe me, I've seen it happen many times.

One minute they're excited, and the next it's all disappeared. So act now before it's too late. If you don't, you'll wake up one day and find he's got a job in New York or decided he's in love with another woman. That's what happens. Men are like kites. You think you've got them under control, and then suddenly they've flown off and there's no way you're ever going to catch them. Kim? Kim? Are you listening?"

• • •

Jake, with his wide-ranging knowledge on a huge number of subjects, was able to explain anything she didn't understand. It could be Mayan art, Miles Davis, or the offside rule—Jake had the facts at his fingertips.

He liked teaching her. Now that they were finally living together in Jake's flat, he seemed less diffident. You could almost say, thought Kim, that he's quite domineering.

But then, she thought, I have so much to learn.

One evening in September, Kim was watching the TV news. Long queues had formed outside branches of Northern Rock all over the UK. Since hearing about an emergency loan from the Bank of England, customers were frightened the bank was going under. They wanted their money back.

"So should they be worried?" said Kim. Jake was sitting on a hard dining room chair, texting. Sometimes, up against a publication deadline, he wore a silver earpiece so that he never missed a call. It gave him a slightly robotic air, like a bouncer or a Cyberman.

"What?" he said, thumbs busy.

"All those people queuing for their money."

Jake gave his usual secretive smile. "Not according to the chairman of the Treasury Select Committee."

"And is he right?"

"The British Bankers' Association says that Northern Rock is sound."

Kim, feeling increasingly like a small child whose ice lolly is melting, said, "But why is it happening?"

Jake looked thoughtful. "I'm not sure how much you know."

"Nothing, really."

Jake nodded. "It's the global money markets."

Kim waited for more.

"The international perspective," said Jake. "Quite complicated, really."

"Oh," said Kim.

• • • •

"Sometimes I worry my standards are too high."

Damaris looked exhausted. She'd had a new haircut, a close crop that showed off the beautiful shape of her head. But it had also left her looking naked and defenseless. Christine was even more anxious than usual. When Kim called round to the house in Nunhead for a cup of tea—ending up staying for roast chicken and a trifle—Christine kept asking if she thought Damaris was working too hard.

"I think medics have to."

Christine shook her head. "She's nothing but bones. When are you next seeing her? I've made her bread pudding and ginger cake."

Kim had a horrible suspicion that Christine's food parcels

ended up in a communal kitchen at the hospital, torn open by anyone who happened to be passing and reduced to a pile of crumbs in a single night shift.

It was Sunday afternoon, and they were sitting on a patch of grass in the ornamental gardens on Peckham Rye. All around them was a random jumble of Londoners—mothers with buggies, dog walkers, joggers, a man dressed in white practicing Tai Chi, and an elderly woman in Wellington boots and a woolly hat chatting to herself while she picked up litter. Kim was always faintly astonished to find formal avenues and pergolas in the middle of a wild expanse of common land in southeast London. But then Peckham Rye was full of secrets. The poet William Blake saw angels there.

"There's nothing wrong with high standards."

Damaris looked woebegone. "But it's almost like I feel someone has to be perfect before I'll even go out for a drink with him. And perfect people don't exist."

Jake's pretty perfect, thought Kim, leaning back on her hands, feeling the warmth of the late September sun on her face. Busy, obviously. Sometimes I feel I have to make an appointment to see him. But this is what happens when you choose a partner whose career is a vocation. "What about that tall one? The one I met in the pub on your friend's birthday?"

Damaris pulled a face. "He's got hairy earlobes. I keep wondering if all his other smooth bits are hairy, too. And nobody wants pictures like that in their head."

"You just haven't met the right person yet."

"Or maybe I have and I didn't realize it. You know, some people end up with boys they were at school with."

Kim pulled a face. "Not the boys we were at school with."

"Just imagine—your ideal man right under your nose but you're too stupid to see it." Damaris sighed and lay down, closing her eyes. "There's only one solution. Lonely hearts online."

"Or you could go to the South of France," said Kim, "and trail up and down the promenade looking for anyone who looks rich enough to take you out to lunch."

Damaris laughed. Kim lay down next to her, and for a while they were silent, listening to the sounds of Sunday on the Rye. Damaris said, "What about Eva?"

"What about her?"

"Is she going out with anyone?"

Kim frowned. "She doesn't seem to need anyone. She's got a lot of friends, but no one special. She says she's got Otis now. He's the love of her life."

"Do you think she misses Harry?"

Kim felt a little tug of guilt. It seemed all wrong, Eva and Otis in a flat in south London, Harry on the other side of the world in an apartment in Manhattan. He'd been gone for six months now. A snap decision, Eva had said. A good career move. But sometimes Kim wondered if it was all her fault. Perhaps, in the end, all her carping and criticism had driven him away. And while she was still convinced that Eva was too good for Harry, did she really have the right to control her sister's life? "She never mentions him."

Damaris turned her head and opened her eyes. "Really?"

Kim nodded.

"I always thought they'd end up together."

I know, thought Kim. We all did.

Damaris turned back to the sun. "This is fatal, lying here. I'm going to end up falling asleep."

"I think you're allowed to, the hours you work."

Damaris smiled. "Why don't we go and visit him in New York? See what he's getting up to?"

Kim screwed up her eyes very tight. No, she thought. I don't want to do that at all.

. . .

"One minute you're enjoying Saturday night with your girlfriend—someone you've known for years, and you've always had a laugh, told each other everything, felt exactly the same way about *Eat, Pray, Love*, and talked about whether you can ever be truly comfortable in a thong. And then suddenly there he is. Her new boyfriend. He's what my nan would call a gowk. A dork. A complete idiot. You know what I mean, don't you, pet? The woman in the front row. I bet your best friend's going out with someone just like that. She is? The woman sitting next to you? But you hadn't told her. Ah. Oh dear. You're in for a fun night. So she introduces you to this man, and he's not even good-looking—hair sticking out all over his head and mad, staring eyes like a trendy owl—and you're meant to simper and say, Oh, how nice to meet you. But inside you're thinking, He looks like Gollum in a wig. Have you no standards? The weeks pass. He's still there on a Saturday night. But it gets worse. Now she's ringing you all times of the day and night so she can go on and on about how wonderful he is. And you think, My friend has turned into an alien. Then it hits you. She thinks he's the One. Oh shit. You can't let that happen. You just can't. So you do what anyone does in a crisis. You google it. And there it is. 'Twenty ways to get rid of your best friend's boyfriend.' One to five are quite straightforward. Lying about her past. Herpes. That kind of thing. But number six is extraordinary. And you think, Why not? Why not have a go? All you need is a chopstick and a maraschino cherry . . ."

. . .

At ten months, Otis had a huge enthusiasm for food. He always grabbed the spoon. Because of this, mealtimes usually ended up in a sticky chaos of puréed carrot and mashed banana halfway up the walls.

But Otis never looked round and cuddly, like other babies. He had long limbs, like a sprinter.

"I suppose he's going to be tall like your father," said Grace to Eva on one of her brief, unwilling visits from the South of France. "He was always banging into chandeliers."

No one mentioned Harry's height.

Otis had light brown skin, dark hair, and serious brown eyes. He seemed to analyze every new experience with the same thoughtful care. You could sit him on the floor with a toy he hadn't seen before, and he would turn it round and round in his hands, looking at it from different angles before testing its capabilities on the carpet. He seemed to experience the world as interesting but excessive. Loud noises, extreme weather, and extravagant displays of affection all made him frown, like an elderly colonel who catches sight of a young woman in a very short skirt and isn't sure whether to complain or applaud.

He very rarely cried. Most of the time, if there was something he wanted, he just looked at Eva. They talked with their eyes.

"How did you know he was thirsty?" said Kim.

"I don't know. I just did."

The atmosphere in the flat in Peckham Rye was calm and purposeful. Sunlight flooded through the great big windows. Kim, now living with Jake in the appalling chaos of his junk-shop flat, would visit at weekends and feel as if she'd blundered into a country church halfway through a service. She was welcome, of course. But she didn't quite fit in. She was the idiot in the wrong pew with the hymn book upside down.

But she loved spending time with her nephew. One Saturday afternoon in October, while Eva went out shopping, Kim and Izzie took Otis to a children's party—the first birthday of his little friend Ruby. In the street outside, they hesitated. Noise rushed out from behind the closed front door like a howling wind—screaming, crying, bashing and banging, squeaking toys, singing frogs, and battery-operated sirens. Ushered in by a harassed woman with a dribble of sick on her shoulder, they stood in the hallway, stunned. It was like all seven floors of a West End toy shop crammed into one tiny space.

Otis, still in his buggy, stared. When he looked up, Kim burst out laughing. You could see it, written all over his face. WTF?

"I didn't realize babies were so funny," said Kim later as she and Izzie waited at the bus stop. Kim was heading for Stockwell. Izzie was going back to the dingy bedsit in New Cross. Kim, as usual, felt guilty. Izzie had been lured to London under false pretenses. She had imagined *Friends*—Rachel and Monica in Manhattan. What she'd got instead was solitude in south London.

"I don't think all babies are funny," said Izzie. "I think Otis is a star."

Kim beamed. "Eva always says that babies are complete souls. You guide them through life, but you can't change their characters. I used to think it was all hippie nonsense." Or, she thought, a way of making sure that no one spent too much time thinking about Otis's father. "But now I wonder if she's right. Otis has always been analytical. It's just the way he's made." She was about to explain that she thought Otis was probably very musical, too, which explained his sensitivity to anything being played out of tune, when she realized that Izzie was staring into the middle distance with an expression of extreme anxiety. For a moment, she wondered if Izzie was transfixed by the Rottweiler with a studded collar that was leering at them from the opposite side of the road. But Izzie wasn't looking at anything in particular. She was lost in thought. "I've got something to tell you."

Kim was shocked. "You're pregnant?"

Izzie looked at her as if she was insane. "Pregnant?"

No secret lover, then.

"I wasn't sure if it would work out. But it sort of has. After a lot of trial and error. And failing miserably quite a few times."

Kim waited.

Izzie took a deep breath. "I'm doing stand-up."

"What?"

"Stand-up comedy."

Kim frowned. "You can't be."

Izzie looked defeated.

"You mean, doing an act? Onstage? Making people laugh?" Kim couldn't believe her ears. "When? Where?"

"You just sign up," said Izzie. "It's going on all over London. I used to watch it all the time. And go through all the clips on YouTube. And one day I just went along and did it. And people quite liked it. So I did some more. So that's what I've been doing. Cleaning during the day and performing at night. With more and more people in the audience. And that's why I'm telling you. Because I'm doing ten minutes in Deptford next Saturday. A nice fifty-seater above the pub. And I wondered if you'd come. If you'd come along and watch me."

A rush of thoughts battled for first place in Kim's head. This was impossible! Izzie hated people looking at her! She was always worried about her thighs! She would never perform in public! She never told jokes either! Why didn't I know? I've been a terrible friend! On top of all this, like a fat ugly toad, was the angry thought that Izzie, by keeping her in the dark, had been lying to her.

"I mean, not if you're busy, obviously. Just if you're free. If you haven't already got plans."

Kim swallowed. "On Saturday night?"

Izzie nodded, her eyes lit up. "It's all new material. Nothing I've performed before. The kind of stuff I really want to do. More political. I've been going over it again and again. And I'd really like to know what you think. I want to see if it makes you laugh."

Kim still had the glassy expression of someone who'd just sat on a patch of thistles.

"Only if you'd like to," said Izzie in a small voice.

Kim pulled herself together. "Of course I would. I'd love to come."

"Really?"

"Can I bring Jake?"

Izzie blinked. "That would be lovely."

.   .   .

It was a Sunday towards the end of November when Eva dropped her bombshell. "I'm going to do a bit of traveling."

Kim looked up. "Traveling?"

"In the New Year."

They were lolling at opposite ends of the sofa in the flat in Peckham Rye, watching TV. Otis was fast asleep in his cot in Eva's room. Kim leant forward, grabbed the remote, and turned the volume down.

"What do you mean?"

Eva looked nervous. "Just that, really. It's something I've wanted to do for a long time. Visit a few ecovillages as a volunteer. Start off in Sieben Linden in Germany, and then go to Denmark and Lithuania. If all goes well, I should be able to hook up with some of the musicians I met in Wales years ago, and then we'll head off to Spain, Portugal, and Italy for the summer."

"And Otis?" Kim's voice was icy.

"It's the time to do it, really. Before Otis starts nursery school. And there will be lots of other little children around. These are very community-based projects. Lots of families living together."

"But you'll be moving from place to place."

"Yes." For a moment it seemed as if Eva was going to qualify this. But under Kim's steely gaze, she said nothing.

"Do you want my opinion?"

"Of course." Although, looking at Eva's face, it seemed more likely that she'd rather be buried up to her neck in a pit of scorpions.

"I think you're being completely irresponsible. You've got a child to consider."

"But I am considering him. I think he'll have a good time."

"Being dragged from place to place, surrounded by people he doesn't know—strange food, strange beds, different weather, different languages . . ."

"I'll be there. I'm not abandoning him."

"You're putting yourself first. You're doing what you want and making him fit in."

"Like our own mother did you mean."

Kim shifted uncomfortably. "I'm not saying that."

"But it's what you're thinking."

As usual, Kim was growing hot with indignation while Eva stayed perfectly calm. It made her even angrier. "Well, maybe there's some truth in it. Maybe you think that having a child shouldn't make any difference to your life. That Otis doesn't need stability and security. That it's OK to swan off and expect him to put up with whatever happens."

"He's happy with any kind of change as long as I'm there. You know that. He's really easygoing."

Kim glared at her. She wanted to cry.

"He's fine as long as I'm with him. And I will be with him. All the time."

In her mind, Kim saw Otis packed into a rucksack, his little soft head sticking out from the drawstring at the top.

Eva said, "Can't you see? There's a crucial difference between taking Otis traveling with me and doing what our mother did.

She left us. It wasn't right. And I would never do that to my son."

A little voice inside Kim's head was shouting, But what about me? You're abandoning me, too.

"It won't be forever. A year. Maybe two. And then we'll be back." Eva smiled. "A bit older. A bit wiser. But otherwise just the same."

Kim found her voice. "I won't see Otis for months."

"You can come and see us whenever you want. It's only Europe. And there's emails and Skype and Facebook—"

"But you're going to ecovillages."

Eva was puzzled. "But they all have Internet connections. I can show you the websites." Realization dawned. "You didn't actually believe all Harry's propaganda, did you? About them being stuck in the Middle Ages?"

Harry, thought Kim, with a tug of grief. If Harry were here, he'd stop her. He'd make her see that this is mad and dangerous and wrong. "Have you told him?"

"Harry?" Eva nodded. "Yes, he knows."

The surprise was so sharp that it felt like a shard of ice in her stomach. "So you're still in touch with him?"

"Of course."

"I thought you didn't speak to him anymore."

"Did you?"

Kim stared at her. There was something that Eva wasn't saying. Kim knew from experience that it would be pointless to try to worm it out of her. But she gave it one last try. "I thought it was a clean break."

"Oh no," said Eva. "I'll always have Harry."

Which was so ambiguous as to be utterly useless.

≈2010≈

So you're back." Leon swung his leg over the back of the chair and sat down. He looked just the same. But Harry was surprised to see the depth of the slashed scar on Leon's cheek. In his mind, it had faded to nothing. "For good?"

"Who knows?" Harry smiled. "It's a different world."

"I thought of you. Each time I saw the news. All those bankers on TV."

"It was a mess. Complete meltdown."

"You know everybody hates you? People talk about bankers and spit."

"Don't hold back. Tell it like it is."

Leon laughed. "So why did you come back?"

An offer I couldn't refuse, thought Harry. Top investment bank. Bigger salary. Bigger bonus. Bigger team. "I missed you."

Leon laughed again, running his hand over his smooth, shaved head. "Been doing any training?"

"Some." In New York, Harry's boxing gloves had stayed zipped up in his sports bag under the bed for the first year. But he'd carved out time eventually—found a good gym and a friendly coach. No one like Leon, though. Harry leant back against the painted brick wall. "So what's been happening here?"

"How long were you away?"

"Nearly three years."

"Rent went up. Roof fell in."

Harry smiled. "It's like I never left."

Leon gave him a long, steady look. "So we'll be seeing a lot more of you."

"As often as I can make it."

You could hazard a guess that Leon was pleased.

Harry picked up his sports bag and swung it over his shoulder. "Happy New Year."

"Have a good one."

Talking to Leon was like texting—communication reduced to essentials.

Outside, the streets were hard with frost. It had been a strange Christmas. Harry had come home, but he felt displaced, a stranger in alien surroundings. His new employers had rented him a temporary flat in Mile End, an area of London east of the City that he didn't know well. Eva was still away traveling—he'd spent several weeks with her and Otis in Portugal after leaving New York—and wasn't planning to come back to the UK for at least another year. And Harry hadn't known how to contact Kim. Even if he'd wanted to.

London had subtly changed while he'd been away, like a friend who'd had a haircut or a colleague who'd lost weight. Some of the streets had grown shabby as businesses went under, the windows boarded up and covered with peeling flyers. Woolworths had disappeared. But there was new building, too. Glass and steel architecture had shot up in the City like random stalagmites. By London Bridge, the cranes were beginning construction of the Shard. At the Elephant and Castle, a strange and spectacularly ugly tower block had risen up near the Walworth Road, ruining the skyline for miles around.

In some ways it was good to be back. He'd already visited the CEOs and finance directors of some of the newer companies in his sector. Michael Adewale, the CEO of Medway—which designed and manufactured high-tech medical equipment—had turned the company from a modest start-up into one of the leading innovators in the field in just ten years. Medway hadn't been affected by the recession at all. "It's win-win," said Michael, pacing round the office punching the fist of one hand into the palm of the other. "We make money. And we save lives. What's not to like?"

I never managed to explain that to Kim, thought Harry as he walked home afterwards—how investing in companies like Medway can benefit everyone. Capitalism can wear a benign face. The City doesn't always unleash the dark forces of Sauron.

But as Christmas approached, and the parties dwindled away, and people in the office kept disappearing to buy presents for nieces, and nephews, and boyfriends, and wives, Harry started to feel lonely. He called Syed, who now worked for one of the bigger hedge funds, but his friend sounded distracted.

"It's the fuckwit brother-in-law. He's done it again."

"Again?"

"Lost a fucking fortune. And I'm expected to bail him out. Just like that. My mother says, I trust you. You know what to do." He sighed. "They say family is a blessing. Not for me, it isn't."

"Can I help?"

"No. It's Christmas. You go and enjoy yourself. I'll see you in the New Year."

Harry tried to enjoy himself. He decided to be a tourist and get to know his new surroundings. He wandered the narrow streets of the East End, imagining the slums of Dickensian London. He found Spitalfields Market, admired the arts and crafts exterior of the Whitechapel Gallery, and studied the Huguenot simplicity of the Brick Lane mosque. He ate jellied eels and Bangladeshi fish curry. Nothing worked. The harder he tried to distract himself, the more desolate he felt. He tried to be rational. You can't just disappear for a few years and expect everyone to jump up and down with excitement when you return. People get on with their lives, fill the hole you left with new faces, new interests. It takes time to build up a circle of friends again.

But deep down, Harry was worried. Tactically, from a career point of view, coming back to London had been a good move. Since the crash, no job was safe—and, as an outsider from Europe, he had been particularly vulnerable in the US. His new employers in the UK had offered him more money, more responsibility, and a bigger department. They were so keen to have him, they'd even guaranteed the bonus he would have earned if he'd stayed put.

But, thought Harry, sitting alone on a park bench in the cold East End, I loved New York. In England, you don't admit to being happy. You take pleasure in the kind of humor that goes with gray skies and perpetual rain—self-deprecation, slagging off other people's success, and gloomily predicting the worst. It's clever. It's funny. It's a very British way of seeing the world. But he'd been surprised by how much he'd enjoyed trying out a different attitude. In New York, everyone is optimistic. Smiles are dazzling. Achievements are celebrated. You not only set bold targets but assume that you, and the people around you, will reach them.

"You always look like this is the best day ever," his new boss had said to him one morning as they stood waiting for the elevator.

"It is," said Harry, grinning.

It had taken a while to adjust to the work ethic. In New York there was no distinction between private and professional. Harry was on duty 24/7. Even going out to a bar or a restaurant or a club was all about networking. But this suited him. He didn't want complicated relationships. He didn't want any woman to get too close. Hinting at some kind of aristocratic background, he modeled himself on all the rom-com parts that Hugh Grant had ever played. Fuck, he said. Fuck. I'm so awfully sorry. Fuck. He blamed a fictional boarding school upbringing—somewhere between Hogwarts and Gordonstoun—for what he called his emotional repression. You're so full of life, he'd say. You deserve better. You need so much more than I can possibly give.

Sometimes he was so busy giving an Oscar-winning performance that he didn't realize he was in the wrong film.

"You're full of shit, Harry." She worked at the same bank, on the same floor. Curvy, dark, sweet face. They'd been eyeing each other in the corridors for weeks.

Harry, sitting up against the pillows, redoubled his efforts. "I'd promise to change. But there's no point. I'd just slide back into my old ways. I'm not good enough for you."

"You don't want commitment."

He sighed deeply. "I'd better go. The longer I stay, the worse it gets for both of us." He leant forward to the muddle of clothes he'd thrown onto the floor the night before. "I'm terribly sorry. I just don't feel the way other people do. Sometimes I think there's a piece of me missing."

"Harry?" He turned round. She was lying on her stomach, looking up at him. He took in her naked brown back, the dip of her waist, the rise of her buttocks. Her eyes were full of light. She was laughing at him. "Would you like me to help you find it?"

Most of the time, life was so busy that he didn't have time to think about what he'd left behind. Sometimes he remembered. There would be a girl with white-gold hair. Or nude wood under peeling bark, like the plane trees on Peckham Rye. Then, briefly, his head would be crowded with images of southeast London—the red buses toiling to the Elephant and Castle, the dingy pubs, the endless terraces of small Victorian houses under a wide gray sky.

Manhattan was vertical. You looked upwards, through a funnel of brick and glass, to a tiny patch of blue right at the very top. It was a different way of seeing.

At the last minute, on Christmas Eve, unable to stand one more minute of isolation among the crowds of London commuters, Harry cracked. He rang Titania on her mobile. "How are you?"

"Well, fine, except for the terrible problems."

Harry's heart sank. "What's been happening?"

"You tell me. There are parts of Manhattan that have been cut off for years. No phone signal. No Internet. It must have been so difficult for you doing business. In fact, come to think about it, was that the reason for the whole financial crisis? People in New York completely unable to contact anyone else in the entire world?"

"I'm sorry. I just thought you might not want to talk to me for a while."

"It might have been nice to ask me. Rather than making the decision for me."

"Would you have wanted to talk to me?"

"No."

"Do you want to talk to me now?"

"Possibly. I'm not sure. I'll have a think about it."

"What are you doing tonight?"

"Oh, for God's sake, Harry."

"What?"

"It's Christmas Eve. I'm not going to drop everything and rush out to see you just because you ring me for the first time in over two years."

"I just thought, if you weren't busy—"

"Besides which, I'm six months pregnant."

There was a tiny pause. "Congratulations."

"You sound shocked."

"No. Not at all. Surprised, maybe."

"You didn't think I was the motherly type?"

"I just didn't think you wanted children this soon."

"No, well." Titania sounded resigned. "Life has a habit of turning out differently than you expected."

"And is there . . . ?"

"A man involved?" She hesitated. "You won't like it. It's Giles."

No, thought Harry. No. He had a vivid mental picture of the clay-pigeon shoot in Wales, with Giles, red-faced, potbellied, prematurely balding, exploding with excitement. "I always liked Giles."

"Liar."

Harry cleared his throat. "So have you got some lovely moated manor house in Suffolk?"

"Sevenoaks," said Titania. "We thought Kent was an easier commute."

Harry suddenly felt overwhelmed by misery. "Well, it's been lovely to catch up. Send my best wishes to Giles."

"So that's it then, is it?"

He knew what she meant. He had rung up to reestablish contact. But he'd wanted the old relationship. Not some awkward, strangled friendship between a loved-up couple and the old boyfriend.

Titania said, in a quiet voice, "Happy Christmas, Harry."

Unlikely, he thought, ending the call.

.   .   .

Jake liked to pretend he could cook. What this meant, in practice, was that he would invite people round to supper and then find a complicated recipe that he thought would impress them. Because he never experimented with the same national cuisine twice, the cupboards in the kitchen were full of unlikely companions—nam pla, turmeric, pesto, allspice—like a suburban train coming into London on a Saturday afternoon. Kim looked at it all with a degree of suspicion. She liked wandering round Borough Market and had been known to splurge on goat cheese. But she found food snobbery irritating. What was wrong with a plain roast chicken?

"If you have to ask," said Jake, "we're not really on the same page."

Kim wondered whether Jake's guests were secretly as unimpressed as she was. One Saturday night he finished off a duck mousse by wafting it with wood smoke, a technique he claimed was used in all the best restaurants. (Although whether top chefs lit damp twigs, blackened them to cinders, and set off the smoke alarm was open to debate.) Everyone applauded. But no one ate more than a mouthful.

"Colombian," said Jake. "Chorizo, arepa, and chicharrón."

"What about simple Italian," said Kim, "like risotto? You could get everything you need from La Dolce Vita round the corner."

"Or something from the Kakheti region of Georgia. Followed by churchkhela. Washed down by a superb Saperavi."

I give up, thought Kim.

Early in February, Jake invited some of his political contacts round for supper. It was a group of people whose opinion mattered. He was almost nervous. Wanting to make some kind of statement, he created a clearing in the middle of the flat and set the table with antique cutlery and silver candelabra. Because of the dust and cobwebs, the effect was slightly spooky—more Miss Havisham than English stately home. But at least the flickering light from the candles meant that most of the rubbish was hidden in shadow.

Jake was now the charity's head of campaigns. (Kim had taken over research and development, and had her own intern working with her in the cubbyhole.) He enjoyed his new role. He said it had great political significance. He particularly liked hobnobbing with the lobbyists, bloggers, and journalists who hung around Westminster. It was, as far as Kim could see, a world that thrived on gossip. A vague rumor in the morning could become a major scandal by teatime. Watching it grow made observers feel busy and important, like someone whose tweets are retweeted.

But by the time the guests had sat down and were halfway through the first course (shredded rabbit and smoked haddock with puréed fennel in a blackcurrant jus), Kim was feeling completely out of her depth. The rules of the game seemed to be that you had to shout about how important you were ("Well, of course, that's what I predicted weeks before it actually happened"), name-drop ("Gordon was only saying the other day . . ."), or outdo everyone else with aggressive banter ("So I said to him, I hope you get cancer"). She tried pinning on various expressions, ranging from awed admiration to intense interest. But everyone ignored her. She was outside the bubble. Her only function was to collect the plates.

Towards the end of the evening, one of the guests broke ranks.

"So what is it that you do, Kim?" said a woman with gold-rimmed spectacles and short gray hair dressed in a sort of purple tunic.

"I head up research. At the charity."

"My old job," said Jake.

"Ah," said the woman. "Following in the master's footsteps."

"Jake likes his trainees," said the middle-aged man at the end of the table. He had red-rimmed eyes and jowls like a bloodhound.

"Whoops," said the gray-haired woman, her eyes glittering behind her glasses.

Kim looked at Jake.

"The last intern," said Jake, "your predecessor, is working at the House of Commons now. A political researcher."

Kim still stared. But Jake was looking down at his fingers, peeling the shell off a prawn with immense slowness, as if one tiny, pearly fragment would choke him.

Much later, when the last dinner guest had finally left after raucous good-byes in the hallway, Jake sauntered back into the shadowy living room and sat down. He picked up his phone. "Went well, I think. A few favors returned."

Kim said nothing.

"Interesting conversation about Elliot Morley and the MPs' expenses scandal."

Still, Kim said nothing.

Jake put down his phone. "Come on then." He seemed sad but resigned. "Out with it."

"Do you sleep with all your interns?"

Jake looked completely relaxed. "They're poisonous. You know that. They like stirring things up."

"So it's not true?"

"Not the way you've put it, no."

"So what way should I have put it?"

He shrugged. "She was my girlfriend. For a while."

"For how long?"

"Kim, I don't like this. It feels like you're accusing me of something."

Until this moment, that tone of boredom would have been

enough to silence her. Again and again, over the past two years, he had made her realize how little she knew. He was there to instruct her. To help her. To support her in her slow progress up the career ladder. Sometimes, when she was being particularly naïve, he couldn't help sighing. Betraying a little weariness at her lack of experience. But he didn't do it often. Most of the time, like a kindly uncle, he waited until she'd caught up. A generous man. A good teacher.

Kim had been careful not to try his patience. She had bitten her tongue on so many occasions. But now she needed an answer. "How long were you together?"

"I've told you. I don't like the implication that I've done something wrong."

Kim thought about this. Then she stood up and reached for her coat.

Jake looked surprised. "Where are you going?"

"I don't know."

"You can't just walk off into the night. It's not safe."

"So tell me what I want to know."

"If you promise to sit down."

Kim sat.

Jake said, "We were together for a year or so."

Kim stared at him.

"Three years. We were together for three years. We broke up when she got her new job."

"Just before I started working for you."

"Yes. It was a time of major reorganization in the charity, as you know. She decided her future was elsewhere."

"And you never told me."

Jake smiled as if she was sweet but foolish. "You never asked."

"You didn't think it was important?"

"I thought we'd agreed that the past was the past. We said we wouldn't pry into each other's lives. You seemed happy with that."

Kim felt muddled and anxious. Did we? Did we agree to that? After a while, she said, "But don't you think it's strange that you went out with two interns one after the other?"

"I think you get to know someone when you work together. Especially work like ours. When you're committed. Passionate. Putting in long hours. I don't think it's that surprising."

Maybe it isn't, thought Kim, his patient tone of voice making her feel, as usual, that she was making a fuss about nothing.

Jake said, "I'll tell you everything about her. Anything you want to know. Just ask me questions. I would have told you before. But I didn't know it was important."

"It isn't important."

Jake's expression cleared. "Good. I'm relieved. That's what I thought our understanding was. So let's forget all about it. Let's draw a line under it and move on."

Kim, in her mind, saw Jake painting a thick black line across a piece of white paper. She felt outmaneuvered. What's wrong with me? Why do I let him walk all over me?

Jake stifled a yawn. "Do you need a hand with the clearing up? Or can I go to bed?"

· · ·

A few days after he'd signed the lease on a brand-new riverside apartment near London Bridge, Harry realized that he didn't have any furniture. The flat in Mile End had come completely kitted out, right down to the espresso machine, as had the apartment in Manhattan. But this one was empty. Walking through the big, open-plan living area with its floor-to-ceiling windows overlooking the Thames, Harry was tempted to keep it all completely minimalist. Just a bed, he thought. And a laptop. I don't need anything else. But late the following evening, sitting in his office under the pool of light from the desk lamp, Harry realized he wasn't being practical. It was a hard job. You got tired. You needed a few home comforts. A sofa, at least.

So the following Saturday, Harry headed for Tottenham Court Road. He felt uneasy. This was all new to him. Obviously, he'd done a bit of background research online—Harry never went into any situation unprepared if he could possibly help it—and buying a sofa didn't look too difficult. Size, fabric, comfort, style—not that different from buying a suit. Which he was good at. How hard could it be?

But Harry had a nagging suspicion that he was being naïve. Since living in New York, where he'd learned how to play the part of a British toff (tortured but basically decent), he'd become even more sensitive to tiny clues about class and status. Back in the UK, he realized just how much he still had to learn. Recently, on one of the bank's dress-down Fridays, a fellow analyst—an old Etonian—had turned up at the bank wearing salmon-pink cords. Harry had only just managed to wipe the look of astonishment from his face before anyone noticed.

Maybe, thought Harry, the perfect sofa—the equivalent of salmon-pink trousers—will be right in front of my nose, and I won't even see it. Perhaps I should have paid someone else to do the buying. An interior designer. A stylist. Some kind of concierge service.

"Can I help you, sir?" The young man had shaved so fiercely that his cheek was raw. The skin, outraged, was one great burning rash.

Harry shook his head with what he hoped was a forbidding frown. The young man backed off, terrified.

There were sofas everywhere, as far as the eye could see. Plain ones, flowery ones, checked ones, leather ones. There were two-seaters, three-seaters, five-seaters, seven-seaters. Some had curved arms, some had square arms, some had no arms. Some had giant puffed-up cushions like clouds. Others had thin understated cushions, as if the new fashion was to sit on cardboard. In between them were chairs, footstools, occasional tables, side tables, and coffee tables. For a moment, Harry fantasized about walking out and buying a macchiato. But he squared his shoulders. I can do this, he thought. I can buy the kind of sofa that will mark me out as cultured, educated, and full of natural good taste.

Somewhere at the end of the first showroom, Harry caught sight of a squashy sofa that was so vast it seemed to disappear round the corner. L-shaped, he thought, his heart sinking. So there are geometrical options, too?

He sat down heavily. The sofa gave a small squeak of delight and hugged him closely. Harry shut his eyes. Maybe something like this, he thought. You wouldn't even need to go to bed. You'd get home from work, sit down, and drift off. It was like being in a warm bath. Or wrapped in a duvet. Distantly, from the room he couldn't see, from somewhere at the other end of the L shape, he heard a phone ring. An impatient voice said, "Yes?"

His eyes flew open. Every muscle in his body tensed.

"I told you. I'm looking at sofas . . . We talked about this . . . No, I'm not trying to be . . . One sofa, Jake. One single piece of furniture that isn't old and dusty . . . It isn't the Sistine Chapel. It's not going to be desecrated by a . . . I explained this to you. It would mean such a lot to have some say in the way we furnish . . . Blue? You've always liked blue, haven't you? I'm sure they can get it up one flight of stairs . . . No, I haven't forgotten . . . OK . . . Yes . . . Good-bye. Good-bye."

There was a pause.

"It's just a sofa," the voice muttered to itself in a tone of outraged misery.

Kim, thought Harry. He struggled to get to his feet but was somehow wedged. Violent movement did nothing but set up a crescendo of squealing from somewhere deep inside the cushions, like guinea pigs calling for cucumber. He felt either side of him with his hands, hoping to find something solid to push against, but his forearms just disappeared up to the elbows in soft, feathery nothingness.

"Kim?" he said.

There was a long pause. Then the voice said, "Harry?"

"I would get up," said Harry, "but I can't."

"Neither can I."

Maybe it's inflated with something, thought Harry. I could find something sharp and jab a hole in it.

From round the corner, Kim said, "This is weird."

"Tell me about it."

"No, I meant, both of us being here. I thought you were in New York."

"I was."

"So why are you in London?"

"I work in London."

"Since when?"

"Since last December."

"Oh."

Harry rocked back and forward. The guinea pigs set up a frenzied chorus.

"I tried that," said Kim's disembodied voice. "I think it makes it worse."

"This is ridiculous. How are you supposed to get out of this thing?"

"I don't know."

"Isn't there a salesman around somewhere?"

"I think he's on his break. I haven't seen him for a while."

Harry, defeated, leant his head back. "So how are you?"

"OK."

"I did think about giving you a ring."

"But you didn't." Kim's voice was neutral.

"No." Harry looked out over the sea of sofas. Apart from a few customers far away on the other side of the showroom, the place was deserted. It was August. People were probably waiting for the summer sale.

"Eva's in Spain."

"I know," said Harry.

"She said that Otis can ask for ice cream in five languages now."

"He must have changed so much."

"Taller, probably," said Kim.

With a sudden burst of irritation, Harry kicked both feet upwards and grabbed his ankles. The guinea pigs, with frenzied alarm, burst into chorus again. Now what? Harry felt worse than if he'd done nothing at all. He was curled up like a baby in a cot, holding his own feet. He took a deep breath, tucked his head into his knees and, with a sort of roar, rolled over onto his side. The momentum, as he'd hoped, bounced him upwards. Thrown off balance, he fell back onto the hard showroom floor, cracking his skull.

"Ow," he said.

"Harry?"

"Hold on." He pushed himself up to sitting and felt the back of his head. Nothing. Just a bruise. Very slowly, Harry stood up. Then he limped round the corner.

And there she was.

His first thought, before he'd had time to consider anything rationally—before he'd even got ready for the inevitable duel of wits—took his breath away. She's beautiful. Of course he'd always known that. Right from the very beginning. But for a moment, it was as if he'd never seen her before. He took in her short blond hair, her fine cheekbones, her determined chin, and it was like looking at a photograph of someone he didn't know. It was like being presented with evidence of something that was obvious but that he'd always chosen to ignore. Against the billowing octopus of a sofa, with her knees in their black jeans drawn up to her chin, she looked like a small child stuck in a wastepaper basket. But her expression was just as he'd remembered— defiant, questioning, ready for a fight. All the time I've been away, thought Harry, I've never met anyone like her.

"What?" said Kim.

"Nothing."

"You're staring at me."

"Am I?"

"Is my face dirty or something?"

"No." But Harry just stood there motionless.

After a while, Kim said, "So are you going to help me?"

"Yes. Sorry." Harry held out his hand so that she could hold on while he pulled. She raised her eyebrows. Of course, he thought. That's not going to work. She's buried way too deep.

"Harry," she said, "you're going to have to lift me out."

This was, for some reason, a frightening prospect. Harry took a deep breath, bent forward, and pushed his arms down into the marshmallow puffiness, trying to find Kim's waist. Then he hesitated. If he wasn't careful, he'd lean in too far and the sofa would swallow him up again. So he dropped his weight down through his legs, splaying his thighs like a sumo wrestler, and reached behind her ribs. His head was against her shoulder. "On my count."

"What are you," she said, "a paramedic?"

He ignored her. "Focus. All your energy. One, two, three—"

Once again, taken by surprise, Harry found himself flat on his back on the showroom floor. But this time, Kim was on top of him. For one charged moment, they stared at each other, nose to nose. He felt her breath on his face. Then, with a sudden movement, she rolled off. They lay side by side, stunned, like lovers who'd just completed a sexual marathon.

There was a small, nervous cough.

Harry looked up. There, just in his field of vision, was a shaving rash.

"Can I help at all, sir?" said the salesman. "Or are you just browsing?"

.   .   .

Kim stirred her coffee. This was a completely pointless exercise, as the coffee was black and she didn't take sugar. But she felt agitated. She had to have something to do.

Opposite her, on the other side of the tiny table, was Harry. She hadn't seen him for three and a half years. He seemed, at the same time, both familiar and a complete stranger. It was like bumping into a TV personality in Covent Garden, saying hello, and then realizing (oh, the shame) that you've never met. He sort of looks the same, she thought. But he seems taller, and possibly wider, as if his shoulders have got bigger. Or perhaps he was always this huge, but I just shrank him in my mind to make him seem less important.

The café was crowded and noisy. Something by the Pretenders was playing in the background. People were pressing in all around them, and Harry had so little room that he'd positioned his long legs either side of her chair. This was embarrassing. She kept her knees very still.

But what embarrassed her even more, and made her keep dropping her eyes to her small white cup, was that she could see he was good-looking. This was the man she'd hated for years— ever since he'd first blocked the sun in the garden in Nunhead. She'd got so used to thinking of him with loathing that she wouldn't have been surprised if he'd turned up today with cloven hoofs, horns, and a forked red tail. But the real Harry, this

Harry, looked normal. He looked like someone she could talk to. He looked like someone she might even like.

Kim was choked with confusion. It was as if the time they'd been apart had put them into a sort of no man's land. Somehow they'd both put down their weapons, and it felt all wrong. It wasn't what they did. I can even see what Izzie meant all those years ago, thought Kim. She said he was a catch. That any woman would want him. At the time, I thought she was mad. But of course he's attractive. Anyone can see that. Especially when he smiles. He's got the kind of grin that makes the whole world seem a better place.

Bewildered, Kim stirred her coffee again.

"So tell me. What's been happening?"

Kim shrugged, trying to look casual. "Nothing much."

"Still in housing?"

"Still at the charity."

"Same job?"

"A promotion. I'm head of research and development."

He looked genuinely impressed. "You must have worked really hard."

I don't know, thought Kim miserably. Maybe it was just because I slept with the boss.

"Still with . . . who was it? Jack?"

For a moment, she was suspicious. But he didn't look as if he was trying to score points. "Jake."

"Jake. Are you still together?"

Kim nodded. She didn't want to talk about Jake. "And what about you?"

"No one special."

Kim realized she didn't want to talk about that, either. "Where are you living?"

"I've just got a new flat. Near London Bridge. You must come and see it sometime."

You say that, thought Kim, in the way that polite people say, You must come to dinner sometime. Which means, I'm never ever going to invite you. "Have you been out to see Eva?"

"Only once. A year ago, when I left New York. I don't have the kind of job that gives you much time off."

"Still in the City?"

"Different bank. But the same kind of work. Which shows a complete lack of initiative on my part."

"I expect it has its compensations."

"You could say that."

"Massive bonuses."

Harry grinned. "People hate us."

She wouldn't be charmed. "Are you surprised, after what happened? Ordinary taxpayers had to buy up a whole bank to stop it going under."

"Are you sure you want to talk about this?"

"One of the reasons the crash happened was that no one was willing to talk about it. Even quite clever people just shrugged and thought it would sort itself out. But it couldn't, could it? Because bankers had gambled on assets worth nothing. So now we're in a recession. Deep public spending cuts. Which means the bankers got away with it. They got richer and more power-ful, while the poor got crushed."

She expected him to laugh. But he didn't. "There are a lot of people like you who are angry about what happened."

"But not enough of them."

He nodded.

She stared at him, astonished. Was this Harry? The man who had always jumped down her throat if ever she made the smallest criticism of the City?

Harry said, "There have been changes. More regulation. The same thing couldn't happen again."

"Maybe not exactly the same thing. But it's like putting an obstacle in a river. The water will just find another way. Nothing's really been done to stop the banks being too big to fail."

"I know you won't believe this," said Harry, "but I don't like greed either. What makes me happy is finding investors for companies that need money to grow."

Kim raised her eyebrows.

"I said you wouldn't believe me."

"It just sounds a bit saintly. You're in it for the money, aren't you? Like everyone else."

Harry smiled. "Of course I am."

Now I don't know if he's being serious, thought Kim.

The music had stopped. They sat listening to the sounds all around them—the shouting and laughing, the rush of the machine frothing milk, the crash of cups and cutlery.

Harry said, "What about you? Did you go out and visit Eva?"

"Lots of times. Germany twice, and then Lithuania. Italy. Spain a few months ago. That was amazing. A medieval village in the mountains that had been abandoned. They got together and rebuilt all the old houses, and set up a bakery, and grew vegetables, and now they're completely self-sufficient. Living off the land. It's so beautiful up there. I can see why they wanted to do it."

"But you didn't want to stay?"

"Part of me did. But part of me wanted to get back."

"To the job."

Again, she couldn't tell if he was laughing at her. "It's important, the research I do."

"And Jake?"

The change of subject was so fast it caught her unawares. "What about him?"

"Was that another reason to come back?"

They held each other's eyes. "Of course."

"He was the person you were talking to on the phone. In the shop."

"I can't remember."

"You didn't sound happy."

"It's always hard to tell exactly what's happening, isn't it," said Kim, "when you listen in on other people's conversations."

"So you are happy."

Kim felt hot and uncomfortable. "Yes."

Harry smiled. But it was one of the old smiles, empty and insincere, that didn't reach his eyes.

"I'd better get back," said Kim. "I didn't mean to be out this long. We're having some friends to supper tonight."

"What are you cooking?"

"I don't cook. Jake does."

"He sounds perfect."

Kim dropped her eyes.

"I'll get this," said Harry, reaching to pick up the bill.

"Are you sure?"

"Don't you remember? I'm the rich banker. The one who pays."

Oh, she thought wearily. So we're back here again. She had a picture in her mind of a soldier in filthy battle dress bending down to pick up his gun.

. . .

"What do you mean he didn't talk about Eva?"

"Well, he talked about her a bit. Asked how she was when I went to Spain."

"Nothing else?"

"No."

Grace's exaggerated sigh down the phone was so huge that Kim felt as if a gale was blowing in her ear.

"Well, that's it then, isn't it? Nothing's going to happen now."

"Eva's coming back next year. I'm sure they'll see more of each other then."

"It's not some *friendship*, Kim. Not some kind of vague *social arrangement* that they can pick up whenever they feel like it. They have a *child* together. Who's now three and a half. Practically at *school*. Who doesn't even know what his father *looks* like these days."

"We don't know for certain—"

"They forget so quickly, you know, children. Unless you see them regularly."

"When did you last—"

"I really think you could have done more. It sounds from what you've said that you were quite sharp with him in the café. Confrontational, almost."

"It was about the—"

"Men don't like talking shop, you know, on social occasions. They don't want to feel they're at work all the time. They expect us to be gracious and charming and to lead them into different avenues from the ones they're used to. Infinite variety. That's the whole point of art and literature. Monet, Manet, Virginia Woolf. It's a diversion from the ugly necessity of making money."

Kim was silenced.

"Well, what's done is done," said Grace. "It doesn't do to dwell on what might have been. There are two things that ruin the complexion—the sun, and regret. Disappointment is so aging. All I wish is that you'd taken the whole thing more seriously years ago when he first went to New York. That would have been the time to act. As it is, everything's ruined. I don't like to say this, Kim. It's hard for me to criticize my own daughter. But this whole miserable situation is all completely your fault."

. . .

Jake directed Kim's career very carefully. He made sure she kept the CEO of the charity informed of all her achievements ("It's not enough to do it—you have to tell her you've done it, and done it well") and helped Kim revise her goals and objectives every six months ("Know where you're going, and keep reviewing how far you've got"). To succeed, he said, you have to be both nimble and flexible, taking advantage of opportunities before others notice them and being willing to adapt to new circumstances as they arise. "It's a cutthroat world," he said. "Make sure you're prepared."

Kim was constantly amazed that someone so clear-thinking could live in such a muddle at home. At least, she thought, plumping up a cushion on the new blue sofa, Jake has got somewhere comfortable to sit now.

At the beginning of September, when London was smiling in late summer sunshine, Jake came home in a state of suppressed excitement. "They're opening up a new role." He unplugged himself from his phone. "Regional development manager. Responsible for raising the charity's profile all over the UK. It's a secret, of course. No one knows about it yet. It's not even on the internal website."

Kim didn't bother asking how he knew about it. Sometimes she thought Jake must have supersensory hearing that worked through office walls and over the sound of the office kettle. Or perhaps he just hacked into the CEO's emails.

"So will you go for it?"

Jake looked puzzled. "Why would I go for it?"

"But I thought—"

"No, it's way below my pay grade. Much too junior. I was thinking of you."

"Me?"

"Why not?"

"Well"—as usual, talking to Jake, she felt wrong-footed—"well, because I like what I'm doing at the moment, I suppose."

"Research."

"Yes. I think we're doing a good job."

"And how many staff do you have working for you?"

"You know that."

"Humor me."

"Just Rhodri. My intern."

Jake shook his head. "So it can't really be described as a management position, can it?"

I didn't say it was, thought Kim. But that doesn't stop it being useful.

Jake, still holding his briefcase, sat down on the arm of the new sofa, rucking up the fabric. "We've talked about this before. Slow and steady progress. Managing more and more staff. You have to show leadership potential. Or you'll get left behind."

He had the hypnotic tone of voice he always used when stating the obvious. Kim, attentive, nodded.

"And, of course, it's a fantastic way of seeing how the charity works at the grassroots level. It'll give you a three-sixty view of what homelessness looks like across the UK. Once you've got that experience, you could pick up any job in this sector anywhere in the country. So you're increasing your marketability. Becoming, if you like, more desirable."

Kim swallowed. She felt ashamed that he'd had to spell it out. "Would they consider me, do you think?"

He smiled. "Why do you think I've always been so insistent about emphasizing your achievements to the CEO? You're in a perfect position. Of course, they'll have to advertise externally. But there's nothing to stop them offering the post to an internal candidate if she's the best. Which you will be."

Jake sounded so certain of this that Kim felt a small frisson of alarm. She had a vision of a horse's head in the CEO's bed.

"Are there any drawbacks?"

"To the job? None."

"But will it involve traveling?"

"Oh yes," said Jake. "All the regional centers. Week here, week there. But you'll get expenses. For meals and hotels."

Kim imagined sitting alone in a poorly lit dining room.

Jake bent down and opened his briefcase. "I've downloaded the application form for you. It's a long one. Because it has to be scrupulously fair to all candidates. I've filled in the sections on 'Capabilities and Experience' and 'What Skills Can You Bring to This Job?' And I've drafted the 'Additional Information' section. It'll probably only take you a couple of hours to finish it. And then as soon as it's publicly advertised, you can whack it in, way ahead of the game."

Kim looked down at the neat stack of typed sheets.

"Will you be my reference?"

Jake frowned. "I don't think that would be very ethical, would it?"

It wasn't easy carrying on as normal in the cubbyhole. Cooped up all day with her intern, she felt guilty. Rhodri was one of the few people at work she really cared about. Brought up in a tiny village in Anglesey, he'd spent his whole life in north Wales—including three years at Bangor University—before coming to London. He was bright, hardworking, and idealistic, with the kind of open expression she associated with choirboys in cathedrals. Was she letting him down? Would he be ready to take over as head of research if she got promoted? He was only twenty-three. And he didn't seem to have a thick enough skin for the kind of office politics she was used to. If she wasn't there to protect him, Jake would probably have him for breakfast.

Anxiety gnawed away at her. Apart from anything else, she wasn't sure she was ready for promotion, herself. This was, she was well aware, a stereotypically female response to the chance of a leap up the career ladder. Men think, I've got fifty percent of what they're looking for—I can fudge it. Women think, I don't know, I only tick ninety-nine percent of the boxes—am I good enough?

But after serious reflection, she decided that what was really bothering her was the thought of spending so much time away from home. She was used to leaning on Jake when she needed coolheaded advice about problems at work. Most evenings, she sat at the kitchen table while he filled the sink with dirty pots and pans and told her exactly how she should respond to tricky situations. Of course there are any number of ways to have conversations when you can't be in the same room. But would he be able to direct her quite so efficiently by text, Skype, or email?

A few days after the job was made public and she'd sent in her application, Kim realized that she was also sad about the timing. Eva might be home by Christmas. So if Kim did get the regional development officer job, she'd be heading off for Leeds and Newcastle and Manchester and Bristol just as Eva and Otis were finally back in London.

Because of all this mental turmoil, Kim was very glad that she wasn't in Rhodri's line of sight for most of the day. Because the big flat computer screens formed a barrier between them, they had become used to interacting as disembodied voices. Luckily, like most Welsh-speakers, Rhodri articulated each consonant very clearly, so Kim never had to ask him to repeat himself.

"Are you going to the Labour Party conference?"

"No," said Kim absently. "Why?"

"I don't know, really. Because Jake's going, I suppose. I thought you might make a week of it."

"Living it up with party activists in Manchester."

"Well, maybe not, if you put it like that."

"It doesn't even sound like you get time to see the city."

"I've never been to Manchester," said Rhodri. "Although I haven't really been anywhere much. Apart from Dublin." He added, after a pause, "And Corfu. Although to be really honest, we were so mangled most nights, I don't remember a lot of it."

Kim moved her head from side to side, feeling the tension in her shoulders. "There aren't many people from here going to the conference, are there?"

"No, I don't think so. Just Jake and Zofia."

"I didn't know Zofia was going."

"Well it makes sense, doesn't it? They're probably thinking it would be more efficient to work as a team. And give her more experience as an intern. I mean, if you were going, you wouldn't not take me, would you?"

This was so full of possible misunderstandings that Kim wasn't sure how to answer.

"Of course they'll have the results of the leadership election at the conference, won't they? Miliband versus Miliband. My money's on David. But I don't think either of them will be the winner, really, will they? They're both going to lose in a situation like this."

Later, in the kitchen, as Jake burnt chicken in a wok, Kim said, "I didn't know Zofia was going with you to the conference."

"It's quite exciting for her," said Jake, adding spring onions, which spat back at him. "Coming from Gdańsk. Home of Lech Wałesa. Solidarity. And finally elected president of Poland in 1990."

The pungent smell of fish sauce filled the room.

. . .

Each time Harry saw Syed, he was struck by how sleek and shiny his friend looked. It was as if wealth was polishing his skin. Working for a hedge fund suited Syed. He liked gambling, he enjoyed split-second trades on stock worth millions, and he had the arrogant self-confidence that made him a winning player.

He'd ditched the suits. People who work for hedge funds don't have to try that hard. They dress down every day.

"So how's the brother-in-law?" Harry said, leaning back in one of the chairs in Syed's Mayfair office. On the wall opposite was a Lichtenstein print in yellow, red, and blue. Or maybe it was a Lichtenstein original.

Syed, like a conductor bringing a symphony to a close, made a gesture with both hands to show it was all over. "I am a genius. I find solutions to all problems."

"And what if he does it again?"

"Even a businessman as bad as my brother-in-law can't fuck it up a third time."

"The triumph of hope over experience."

"What are you trying to do? Drive me to drink?" Syed stood up. "Come on. I've booked a table round the corner. The ceviche is incredible."

Outside in the brilliant October sunshine—ice-cold wind, bright blue sky—Harry looked around at the gracious town houses, the parked Jaguars, the whole spruce prosperity of one of the most expensive residential areas in the world, and felt a small surge of pleasure. Wealth cocooned him. He felt safe.

"I'm hearing good things about you."

"Are you?" Harry tried to sound casual.

"One of the sharpest analysts in the City. So sharp you might cut yourself."

"But you still don't rate us."

Syed smiled. "You do your job. We do ours." He stepped back with a flourish to make more room on the pavement for a blonde with dark glasses and thigh-high black boots. "Do you still miss New York?"

"Sometimes. But I think if I was in New York, I'd miss London."

Syed laughed. "The human condition. Perpetual dissatisfaction." He glanced up at Harry. "She had a son, I hear."

"Yes," said Harry, wondering how Syed had heard about Otis.

"Of course he's not good enough for her. I never liked him."

Harry was lost.

"It's the Old Etonian charm. They fall for it every time."

They walked on in silence. Harry had just worked out that Syed was talking about Titania when Syed said, "Of course that's the trouble with the work we do. No time for relationships. It's all so shallow. Luxury holidays, fine dining, fast cars—but we'd give it all up in an instant if we thought we had a real chance of enduring love."

"Would we?"

Syed's eyes were bright. "No."

Harry laughed. "Although you're—what? Thirty-two? Thirty-three? It might be time to find a good woman and settle down."

Syed's smile disappeared. "You sound like my mother," he said gloomily.

* * *

"Where are you?"

"In France. In a rather beautiful villa near Nice."

"You're at Mum's?"

"At Jean-Marc's house. He insisted. Otis is a bit shy. He's never seen so much marble."

"Is Jean-Marc really rich, then?"

"Faded grandeur. Old aristocracy. I don't know if he's actually got any money. But Mum's happy. She's wafting about in white linen trying to pretend she doesn't find three-year-olds annoying."

"So when are you coming back?"

"That's why I'm ringing. Just in time for Christmas."

"When?"

"The fifteenth."

"Oh, Eva! That's so exciting! Shall I come and meet you? Is it Gatwick or Heathrow?"

"We're coming by train. St. Pancras."

"I'll be there. I promise. Help you with all your luggage. Will you come back and stay here? Jake would love it. He could show Otis his Matchbox collection."

"There wouldn't be room, though, would there? In a one-bedroomed flat."

"I'd have to tidy up a bit. But it would be fine."

"I'm really grateful. Really. But I don't think it's a good idea. Three-year-olds are a bit manic. It's bad enough here. Although Mum can't really complain because everything's all cracked and chipped already. But Jake collects things. Valuable things. Otis would destroy it all in five minutes."

"But—"

"I just think we'd really piss Jake off if we stayed. And I wouldn't be able to relax for a second. I'd be running around after Otis trying to stop him killing himself with ceremonial daggers."

"So where will you stay?"

"Harry's offered to put us up."

"Harry?"

"He hasn't got round to buying much furniture. So it's just an empty space. Which is perfect. Otis can run around screaming as much as he likes. Kim?"

"What?"

"You don't mind, do you?"

"No."

"You sound like you do."

"You're my sister."

"It'll only be for a couple of months. Until we've worked out where we want to be. Ideally, I want to join some kind of community. But not too far away. Kim? Say something."

"I got that job."

"Regional development manager? Oh, you're so clever! That's such good news!"

"I suppose so."

"What's wrong?"

"I'll never be in London. You come back and I leave."

"It'll settle down once you've got it all organized. When do you start?"

"February."

"So there's a bit of time before then."

"Except you'll be at Harry's."

"He says you're welcome anytime."

"Oh, does he?"

"You're not still feuding, are you?"

"I've got no idea. I never see him."

"But over Christmas?"

"I don't know. Jake and I might be going away."

"Kim? Please?"

≈2011≈

The wedding was fixed for June. The best time of year, Grace insisted, when the rough winds have blown away and summer is just beginning. Eva was talking about wild flowers from the country. But roses are always so elegant, don't you think? So very English.

"I'm impressed," said Izzie. "I thought you'd be frothing at the mouth."

"I've turned over a new leaf," said Kim. "From now on, I'm going to be calm and serene."

"I'll believe it when I see it."

"It's true. I've been reading books about mindfulness. I've decided that getting angry is bad for my health."

Izzie put her head on one side. "I thought you'd say the whole thing was ridiculous. Especially as they're already living together."

"They should do whatever makes them happy."

Izzie laughed.

"What?" said Kim.

"You look as if you've just sucked a lemon."

Kim hastily rearranged her expression.

"And you're going to be a bridesmaid?" said Izzie.

Kim forgot about being calm and serene. "Why would I want to be a bridesmaid?"

"Did you know," said Izzie, "that you puff up like a pink toad when you're cross?"

Kim took a deep breath. "I just meant that I don't think I'd be very good at it."

"You don't have to wear layers of tulle with a ribbon round your waist."

"It won't be that kind of wedding. She says she wants to keep it simple."

"They all say that. How many guests are coming?"

Kim slumped, defeated. "I've lost count."

"Well, I suppose he can afford it."

Kim looked even more depressed.

"What about your father? Will she ask him?"

"Why would she do that? She hasn't seen him for years."

"I don't know. As a way of saying that all the bad things are in the past and we're all making a new beginning."

"You watch too many rom-coms."

Izzie laughed. "Look at it this way. At least you're getting a holiday in the South of France."

Kim fixed her with a baleful stare. "I can assure you that being around my mother while she plans her wedding to Jean-Marc is not going to be a holiday."

"Is Jake going?"

The question hung in the air. Kim didn't know. When she'd asked him at the weekend, he'd said, "Why would your mother want me there?"

"Because you're my partner?"

"But your mother doesn't really know me."

You spent Christmas Day together, Kim thought miserably. It was still vivid in her memory, like a bright red scar. Harry's vast white apartment overlooking the Thames. Lunch from Harrods Food Hall, with carefully chosen additions from Fortnum & Mason. Several bottles of champagne. The floor covered in crumpled silver wrapping paper. The sky outside pale blue.

It was years since they'd had Christmas in the Nunhead house with all the old decorations—the bald angel with the missing tiara, the papier-mâché reindeer with three legs and a squint, the red paper chains that fell from the ceiling because Dad never put them up properly. But the tasteful opulence of Harry's version of Christmas made Kim miss all the festive rubbish from her childhood with fierce longing. Christmas shouldn't be delivered in a wicker hamper, she thought. What will Otis remember from today? How the icing on a shop-bought Christmas cake is so neat it looks like decorative cornicing in a stately home?

"Will it snow tomorrow?"

Lunch was over. The Christmas pudding had been eaten. They were all lying around on the brand-new sofas, almost too full to move. Harry, the benevolent host, was nursing a small brandy.

"It might do," said Eva.

Otis tried again. He turned to Harry, his brown eyes serious. "Will it snow tomorrow?"

"Maybe."

Otis looked over to Jake but thought better of it. He turned to Kim. "Will it snow tomorrow?"

"Do you want it to?"

Otis nodded.

"So we have to hope it'll get very cold," said Kim. "Zero degrees."

"Although, in fact, that's a common misperception," said Jake. "The air temperature needs to be below two degrees, not zero. And of course above two degrees, you get sleet or rain."

Harry seemed to be trying not to laugh.

"Oh, not rain, please," said Grace, wide-eyed and appalled. "London is so desolate when it rains." She shivered, a rose petal buffeted by the wind.

"Gam-ma," said Otis.

"Oh call me Grace, darling. 'Grandma' is so aging."

"Gam-ma, will it snow tomorrow?"

"I do hope not. I've got my flight back booked for the twenty-seventh. I can't leave Jean-Marc to fend for himself for much longer. You know, I was very lucky to get here at all. With all the blizzards. Heathrow was practically closed."

"I heard," said Harry, "that they had to shut the Eiffel Tower earlier in the month. Because of the snow."

"Oh, Harry," said Eva with affection, as if he was being very silly.

Harry looked offended. "It's true. I read it in the *Telegraph*."

"The weather gets more and more extreme," said Kim. "You have to wonder why."

"And there was that earthquake in the Lake District," said Harry. "Scary. That's never happened before."

"Hasn't it?" said Eva.

"Well, maybe," said Harry. "Quite a few times. Every year,

in fact. You often get earthquakes that size in the UK. But I still think we should be really, really worried."

"You think climate change is funny, don't you?" said Kim.

"So, Jake," said Eva, "Kim tells me you used to restore windmills."

Harry's whole face lit up with delight. He swung one long leg over the other—the brandy nearly slopping over the edge of the glass—and leant towards Jake with an expression of rapt interest.

"Used to," said Kim loudly. "Used to restore windmills. You don't really have time anymore, do you? Now that you're head of campaigns."

"What can you do?" said Jake. "It's full-on. Twenty-four/seven."

"Like an emergency plumber," said Harry.

It was excruciating. Kim escaped to the ultramodern white-and-chrome bathroom and rested her forehead against the mirrored cupboard above the sink. Beneath her, three toothbrushes were lined up in the stainless steel holder—one blue, one pink, and a little red one with a Mickey Mouse face. Harry's enjoying every minute of Christmas Day, she thought. But the more he laughs, the more I die inside. I feel like a withered old prune.

"It becomes quite addictive, working at the heart of government," Jake was saying as she walked back into the room. "They'll do anything to stay in power. The main policy objective of any politician is to get reelected."

"Absolutely," said Harry. "What an amazing insight."

"What about the Queen?" said Grace.

"Well, if we're talking about power," said Jake, "she doesn't really have a place in this discussion. Because she's a figurehead. More of a ceremonial role, really."

"I meant the Queen's Christmas message," said Grace, looking at Jake as if he were stupid. "Three o'clock. We're all avid royalists in Nice, you know. Often gather round the TV waving our Union Jacks."

"I'm more of a republican myself," said Jake.

"How interesting," said Grace.

Kim cringed with embarrassment.

"Talking of royalty," said Grace," I see that Princess Anne's daughter has got herself engaged to that rugby player."

"Mike Tindall," said Eva.

"I do think she has to be careful. Standards are so important."

"What standards?" said Kim.

"Standards of behavior."

"Absolutely," said Harry, grinning. "I couldn't agree more. Where would we be without standards of behavior?"

It was one snide remark too many. All day, it had been building up—that feeling that Harry was laughing at them, that they were toys in a nursery lined up for his entertainment. Kim, like a warm fizzy drink, suddenly exploded. "What would you know," she said loudly, her voice shaking with dislike, "about standards of behavior? You don't have any. All you care about is yourself."

There was a shocked silence. Kim looked round the circle of stricken faces. Her mother had her hand to her forehead as if she was about to faint. Eva looked upset. Even Jake couldn't meet her eyes, staring down at the floor between his thighs.

That night, lying next to a gently snoring Jake, she thought,

Enough. This has got to stop. As Christine always says, what's important is family. And I seem set on destroying it.

There was one silver lining. According to Grace, Jean-Marc was so overcome with horror when she told him about the appalling outburst (*the ultimate incivility, being rude to your host*), he insisted they get married straightaway so that he could protect her from future eruptions.

"Kim?"

Kim, whose heart was beating fast at the unwelcome memories of Christmas, blinked.

Izzie said again, "So is Jake going? To your mother's wedding?"

Kim took a deep breath. "He's not sure. Whether he can get time off work."

Izzie frowned.

"It's true," said Kim. "He's very busy."

"Very busy."

"What are you trying to say?" said Kim, raising her voice.

Izzie opened her eyes wide, pretending to be shocked. "I thought you'd turned over a new leaf. I thought from now on you were going to be all calm and serene."

Kim opened her mouth to protest. And then shut it again in a thin, tight line.

•　•　•

Watching the kids' class in Tommy's Gym, Harry didn't recognize Ethan straightaway. A lot had changed in four years. Ethan now had a shaved head, which made his neck look bare and vulnerable, and his face was more angular. But he was still small. He hadn't yet started that adolescent growth that turns boys into pieces of string. You must be at secondary school now, thought Harry. You must be one of the youngest, stunned by the giants with stubble who look way too old to be sitting in classrooms.

Ethan still didn't look you in the eye—just the odd quick glance when he thought no one could see.

Harry ran through his usual workout—jump rope, squats, push-ups, crunches, heavy bag work—and then, breathing hard, wandered over to where Leon was sitting in his usual place, legs astride a chair that had been turned the wrong way round, arms resting on the wooden back. The kids' class was just finishing. The coach was taking them through some basic stretches while they cooled down.

"Good Christmas?" said Leon.

"Full of comfort and joy," said Harry.

Leon laughed.

One of the other coaches came up to ask a question about the staff rota, so Leon turned away and didn't see what happened next.

When Ethan bent over from the waist, arms reaching for the floor, his shirt fell down towards his ears, exposing his back.

It was covered in dark bruises.

The kind of bruises, as Harry knew well, that you get from being pushed against a wall, or kicked so hard that you fall downstairs.

• • •

When Kim suggested an outing to the winter ice rink at the Tower of London to celebrate Otis's fourth birthday, she had imagined herself gliding about in the twinkly frost of New Year like Kate Beckinsale in *Serendipity*. The reality was very different. Clinging desperately to the side, she hobbled round the edge like someone recovering from abdominal surgery. Harry, meanwhile, sailed past with a cheery wave. Typical, she thought. Typical. He has to show off even on the ice rink.

Just in time, she caught herself and quickly erased the thought. I will not drift back into negative thinking. I will change the way I view Harry, and everything he does, by emphasizing his kindness and generosity. Like the fact that he has now taken hold of both of Otis's hands and is skating backwards, *backwards*, very slowly so that Otis can enjoy sliding along in the cold January air. It's *lovely* that Harry bought the tickets and refused to let anyone pay. It's so *exciting* to be here, on a bright clear day, surrounded by the sounds of happy laughter, with pretty tinkling music on the loudspeakers. So *awe-inspiring* to stand here in the shadow of the Tower of London, where King Henry, his eyes on a better wife, decapitated Anne Boleyn. Kim, holding tight to the side, watched as Eva—tentative but perfectly balanced—joined Harry and took one of Otis's hands. To the outside world, she thought, they look like the perfect family. But it's a lie. He has all the *benefits* but none of the *responsibilities*. He plays a part, like an actor onstage, but his arrogant, self-serving, self-centered life carries on as usual.

Kim screwed her eyes tight shut and made herself wipe her mind clean. Yes, they have an unconventional setup, all living in the same flat even though Eva still insists they're not together. But who am I to judge? I should be glad that Eva and Otis have a roof over their heads. I should be delighted that they have no money worries because Harry's so rich he could use £50 notes as toilet paper. I should be happy that he always makes me welcome—insists I can call in at any time, stay for supper, spend the whole weekend with them if I want to. Which is completely ridiculous. I can't do that. What about Jake?

"You're always saying how busy he is. I thought you'd rather be with Eva and Otis. Instead of cooped up waiting for him."

The worst thing, thought Kim, is that Jake is always in meetings where he has to turn his phone off, so I can't even text him to find out what's happening. "I don't just sit around waiting for him. I get on with things if he's not there. Work. Reading. Answering emails."

Harry nodded. "Sorry. Yes, of course."

He was trying hard these days. Kim could see that. Every time Kim suggested an outing together that Otis might enjoy—the Natural History Museum to see the dinosaurs, or Covent Garden to see the street performers—Harry was always enthusiastic. Maybe he hadn't enjoyed her mad outburst at Christmas either.

Although none of them had mentioned it since. It had been kindly forgotten, like a teenage misdemeanor.

With a sudden sound of scything ice, Harry came to a neat stop in front of her. "Need any help?"

"What?" said Kim, surprised out of her thoughts. "No, I'm fine. Just taking it slowly."

Far away on the other side of the rink, Eva and Otis, hand in hand, were part of the great circular motion of skaters, sweeping round and round under the battlements.

Harry grinned. "There's taking it slowly. And there's being completely stationary."

"Really. There's no problem."

"You've never done this before?"

She shook her head.

"You need to find your feet," said Harry. "It's like riding a bike. The only way to learn is to do it."

Behind her, other equally terrified novices had come to a dead halt, like sleepwalkers stumbling into a wall. She looked over to the middle of the ice. A long-limbed boy with a gray woolly hat was scrabbling about like an emu trying the splits.

"Kim?"

For a moment, she thought Harry was going to put his arm round her and whisk her off into the crowd of skaters. She shrank back against the side. "I'm fine. Go and help Otis."

He looked at her with that same unreadable expression she knew of old. For some reason, she felt ashamed.

"OK," he said.

And then he was gone.

In the queue behind her, among all the people clutching on to the side, she heard an exaggerated sigh. "Excuse me," said a young man in a bored, supercilious voice, "but are you ever going to move?"

"No," said Kim. "I want to stand here and watch you skate past me."

•   •   •

Michael Adewale was in his early forties. He had the kind of engaging expression—attentive and amused—that suggested he didn't take life too seriously. Despite being CEO of a company that was growing so fast it had recently opened new offices and doubled its workforce, he looked fit, healthy, and relaxed—clear eyes, a very white smile, and a conspicuous lack of any kind of middle-aged paunch. Harry had once asked him the secret of his success. Michael laughed. "I'm not going to tell you that, am I? Or they'll all be doing it."

The restaurant had been empty when Harry arrived. Michael didn't like waiting for anything—meals, taxis, company audits—and always suggested meeting before the lunchtime rush. Perhaps that's the secret, thought Harry, watching him greet the maître d' and stride past all the tables. He packs more into twenty-four hours than most people manage in a week.

"Ten point eight million pounds," said Michael, waving a copy of the *Telegraph*. "Christie's lucked out. But then, Andy Warhol. And it covers a lot of wall. Red and white. I could go for it."

"I didn't know you were an art collector."

"I'm not." Michael grinned. "I just like showing off."

Michael's interests were broad and varied. For the next hour, the conversation ranged over President Obama's proposed budget, David Cameron's Big Society, Colin Firth being tipped to win Best Actor for *The King's Speech*, and Downing Street's new cat, Larry.

"Pest control," said Michael, filling his glass with water.

"You'd think they'd use poison."

"Ah, but you're forgetting the British love of hunting."

Michael had four sons. His eyes lit up when he talked about them. He pretended to be outraged by the chaos they caused—the noise, the confusion, the expense—but it was easy to see that he thrived on it. I bet you're a good father, thought Harry.

Kind, generous, supportive. He felt a small stab of loss. Which, of course, made no sense. You can't lose what you've never had.

Over coffee, they discussed Medway's most recent trading update and press reports about the new factory in Rochester. Michael said, "I can't tell you anything specific, obviously, because there hasn't yet been a public announcement, but research and development is going well. We're focusing on diagnostic equipment for cervical cancer. That's where I see Medway going. Cheap, affordable tools that can be used anywhere—from NHS clinics to field hospitals in Uganda."

"You'll end up with a knighthood."

Michael smiled. "Why else would I be doing it?" He glanced at his watch. It was precisely one thirty p.m. "I must go. Thanks for lunch."

"It's a pleasure."

"I'll send you that Shapiro book." As he stood up, Michael said, "Have you ever thought of going into business yourself? I know you're up for MD this year, so you probably won't want to move. But I think you'd like it."

Was that an invitation? But before Harry could answer, Michael had put on his jacket, raised his hand in farewell, and set off through the restaurant, striding past all the diners who would end up eating too much and staying too long.

He moved fast, the CEO of Medway.

Harry signaled for the bill. I like my job, he thought. But it's people like Michael who set the pace. The rest of us just hold tight and hang on.

. . .

As winter turned to spring, Kim stuck to her resolve and made herself see Harry in a new light. It wasn't just to keep the peace. Sometimes, on rainy Sunday afternoons, all Otis wanted to do was lie on his stomach playing with his train set. Otis lived in Harry's riverside apartment. So if she wanted to see Otis, she had to get used to spending time with Harry.

One weekend in March, Kim turned up at the flat to find Harry and Otis painting large pictures on the dining room table. Otis seemed to be going for something in the style of Jackson Pollock, and there was a lot of red paint on the floor. Harry didn't seem to mind, or hadn't noticed.

The old Kim would have seen this as evidence of Harry's extreme wealth. He obviously didn't have to look after his possessions. (Don't bother mending it—just throw it out and buy a new one.) Reformed Kim decided that Harry was more concerned about Otis having a good time than whether there was the odd splash of scarlet on the floorboards.

"Look at my lion," said Harry.

Kim opened her mouth to say that it looked more like a tortoise and then remembered her resolution to be nice. "It looks very fierce."

"What noise do lions make?" said Otis.

"They roar," said Kim.

"Can you roar?"

"She roars all the time," said Harry, but he was smiling in a friendly kind of way, so she decided not to bristle with indignation.

Eva was lying on the sofa, facing away from them, Harry's

laptop open in front of her. "There's a farm in Devon," she said, "with apple trees and a cider press."

Eva still hadn't decided where she and Otis were going to live. She'd visited various communities in Essex, Kent, and Dorset. She'd talked on the phone to big groups managing acres of farmland and to small cooperatives living near Leeds and Oxford. Everything sounded good. But nothing was nudging her towards a final choice.

Kim took off her coat and draped it over the back of the sofa. "That's quite a long way from London."

Eva looked up at her. "I know. But everywhere seems to have something wrong with it." She pulled a face. "I don't know why I'm making it so complicated. We moved around all over Europe without any of this fuss."

"But you weren't thinking about putting down roots," said Kim. "This is a bigger decision."

"You just like being a kept woman," said Harry.

Eva picked up a small blue cushion and threw it backwards over her head in his general direction. "Says the man who comes home to a cooked meal every night."

Sometimes, looking at them both, Kim wondered whether Eva had been telling her the truth all along. Eva and Harry didn't behave like lovers or even ex-lovers. They were close. They teased each other, and wound each other up about politics, musical taste, and disgusting personal habits. But it was like the banter between brother and sister. They had huge respect for each other. But there didn't seem to be any passion between them.

Although you can never tell with Harry, thought Kim, looking at him as he added the finishing touches to his lion-tortoise. He's a manipulator. He plays games. He could be keeping everything light and casual just to make sure that Eva doesn't leave.

"Maybe it's not the right time," said Eva. "Maybe I should stop trying to force it."

Perhaps Eva can't decide where to go because, deep down, she wants things to stay as they are, thought Kim. She likes living as a family with Harry and Otis. Which is deeply depressing. There's one tiny sliver of hope: Maybe Eva isn't actively choosing to be with Harry. Maybe she's just hanging around until her options become clearer. She's never been good at making up her mind about anything.

"Are the stars not aligned?" said Harry.

"I don't mean in some kind of mystical sense. I mean, maybe there's something holding me back."

"Like the thought of paying rent?"

"You may mock." Eva shut the laptop with an air of finality. "But we don't always know why things happen when they happen. Right now I feel as if I'm leaning against a locked door trying to push it open. Maybe I should just give up and let fate take over."

Kim shivered.

"It is cold, isn't it?" said Eva. She swung her legs down and stood up. "It's Harry's guilty little secret. It's nearly summer. So he keeps turning down the thermostat."

.　.　.

You wouldn't know from a quick glance that anything was wrong. Any casual observer would have noticed nothing unusual—just

two old friends having a drink after work. You would have had
to know Harry quite well to see that he wasn't relaxed at all. He
was leaning back in his chair, smiling at Syed on the opposite
side of the table. But his eyes were blank. It was as if someone
had drawn down a blackout blind and cut out the light.

His glass of wine was untouched.

The pub, an old coaching inn in the City, stretched all the
way from the street to a tiny courtyard at the back. It was a war-
ren of interconnecting rooms, lit by lamps with red shades that
turned everything the color of old blood. Cracked oil paintings
in gilt frames hung from the dark wood paneling. The floorboards underfoot were sticky with spilled beer. Harry and Syed
were sitting in an alcove underneath a vast portrait of the Duke
of Wellington. The duke wore a scarlet military jacket with
fringed gold epaulets and a white cravat bandaged all the way
up to his chin like a sort of neck brace.

Syed was drunk. He'd been drinking all afternoon. Harry
hadn't noticed at first. Syed had seemed his usual boisterous
self—a little louder, perhaps, the jokes a bit cruder. But now, in
the hour they'd been together, Syed was sinking into a dark pool
of serious inebriation. "No one will suspect a thing. Happens all
the time. Up and down faster than a whore's drawers."

Harry said nothing.

"What?"

"You need me to tell you?"

Syed looked belligerent. "I need the money."

Syed's brother-in-law, true to form, had once again crashed
into debt. (It's not possible, said Harry. Not again. Syed looked
gloomy. It's the only thing he's any good at, he said.) The night

before, the family home had been ringing with wailing and re-crimination. Syed had tried to stick to his guns. What's the point of bailing him out again? He'll just lose it. It's like throw-ing a match in a pile of £50 notes. But his mother wouldn't lis-ten. You must put it right. Think of your sister. I trust you.

He probably doesn't mean a word of it, thought Harry, try-ing to push down his mounting irritation. He'll have forgotten all about it tomorrow. He wouldn't be stupid enough to risk his whole career.

"Your sector's a good one," said Syed, stumbling over the syllables like someone blundering about on a pebble beach. "Health care."

"You think so?"

"I say something won't get FDA approval. And that's it. Nosedive."

Harry shook his head. "It takes more than that."

"Depends who you tell. They trust me. Syed has the magic touch. Syed can't fail." He tried to tap his nose but missed.

I should change the subject, thought Harry, before my op-position makes him more determined.

"I know the market," said Syed. "If I say it's true, they'll be-lieve me."

"Why don't we go and get something to eat?"

"That's all it takes."

"There's a restaurant round the corner."

"Just a word in the right ear."

Harry lost patience. "You're not serious."

"Of course I'm fucking serious."

"It's illegal. It's immoral. And you'll get found out."

Syed waved his hands around, as if shooing a cluster of kittens. "Happens all the time."

"If someone finds out you've spread false information in order to influence a share price, you'll be prosecuted. You know that."

"What I need is a bright new company. Brilliant prospects. Growing fast."

"This is a joke, right?"

"Sell high. Buy low. Job done."

Harry imagined himself at work, staring at the screens. The share price in Medway was falling. A couple of big pension funds had sold off their stakes. He saw himself putting in calls to old colleagues in New York. Yes, they'd heard rumors. Nothing concrete. Doubts about FDA approval. But it was enough to get people nervous. He imagined Michael Adewale pacing up and down in his brand-new office. He thought about Medway's research and development into innovative, affordable medical equipment that could be used across the world.

Harry leant forwards. "Don't do this. I'm telling you, as your friend, that this is a bad idea."

"You're telling me no one ever breaks the rules?"

Harry fantasized about upending the table, grabbing hold of Syed, and pinning him to the wall. Shouting into his face until he saw sense. This is not a victimless crime. You will affect thousands of lives—from the elderly investor in Halifax to the woman with cancer in Nairobi. You'll end up in prison. You'll never work in the City again. All for the sake of a relative who's got himself into debt. "I'm telling you not to do it."

"What you don't seem to understand," said Syed, "is that I have no choice."

"Of course you have a choice."

Syed focused with great difficulty. "It's too late."

Harry stared.

"I've already done it."

·   ·   ·

Kim was in the quiet carriage on the train back from Bristol. She had booked it on purpose because she assumed she'd be using the time to write up her notes. The new job was complicated. It wasn't just about raising the charity's profile in the regions. She'd also been asked to streamline operations and cut costs. Jake said that unless the charity became a leaner organization, it wouldn't be able to survive.

But now that she was sitting here, in total silence, Kim didn't feel like working. She wanted to ring Eva and discuss final plans for the wedding. She wanted to chat to Otis. She wanted to play silly clips on YouTube. I'd quite like to talk to Jake, she thought, staring out of the window at the open green countryside. Because it doesn't feel like we've said anything to each other for weeks. Maybe ringing or texting is the only way to communicate these days. He doesn't seem to think anything's worth listening to unless it comes out of an iPhone.

"Yeah, I'm on the train," said a voice from the next bay.

Kim looked up, surprised.

"Only just. Few seconds to spare."

He doesn't realize, thought Kim. He doesn't realize he's in the quiet coach.

"Got no idea. Around seven, maybe."

Oh, thought Kim. It's just a quick call home. To say what time he's getting in. He'll stop in a minute.

"Oh, you're an angel, babe. I'm fucking knackered."

Although you would have thought he'd have seen all the signs.

"Did he bollocks. Came out with the whole fucking history. Couldn't shut him up."

Kim got out her phone and scrolled down her messages. I could always text Eva, she thought. That's a quiet activity. I'm sure you're allowed to text people. That doesn't disturb anyone.

"No fucking thought for anyone else."

Kim shut her eyes.

"You would have thought he'd have learnt by now. But once he started, he couldn't fucking stop. No one else could get a word in."

Does he realize he's shouting?

"I know, babe. I know. Fucking unbelievable."

It's like he's trying to tell the whole train.

"I tried. I said, Listen, mate, I'm not interested. It's gone on long enough."

At full volume.

"But he said, You're forgetting where this started. What you—"

Kim stood up. In the next bay, spread-eagled on the seat, was a man of about thirty, clean shaven, with slicked-back dark hair. He was wearing a navy-blue suit, a white shirt, and a thin red tie. Quite professional looking, thought Kim with surprise. "Excuse me."

"Sorry, baby, hold on." The man cupped his hand over the phone. "Can I help you?"

"You probably didn't realize, but this is a quiet carriage."

"So?"

"That means you're not supposed to be using a mobile phone."

"It's disturbing you, is it?"

"Yes."

"I'm not going to be long."

"Yes, I appreciate that. But I'm trying to work."

"Trying to work."

"Yes. That's why I chose the quiet carriage."

"Fair enough."

Kim sat down. There, you see? she said to herself. No fuss. No drama. Just a polite request, a reasonable conversation, and a rapid resolution.

"Babe? Yeah, sorry, got to move. Someone complaining about my mobile. Hold on." Kim could see the man reaching up to the luggage rack above his head to pull down a briefcase. She tried not to stare. Grace in victory, after all.

Passing the end of Kim's bay, the man paused, the phone still held to his ear. "Haven't got a fucking clue. Some sad old cow wants to sit in silence."

•   •   •

Constantly moving. Heart pounding. Head slipping, head ducking. Beat the crap out of it. Till your ears are singing.

When Harry eventually stopped, unable to breathe, the pressure in his ears had got so extreme he was deaf—as if the heavy bag, swinging, had walloped him in the head. His legs were tired. His arms were trembling. Sweat was blinding him.

He wanted to sit down. But his body, in shock, could only wonder that it was still alive.

"You OK?" said Leon.

Harry nodded. He leant back against the wall, fighting for breath.

Leon stood watching him. Gradually, Harry heard the sounds of the gym again—shouts and thuds, the thwack of the jumping rope, a body falling to the floor. Blood was pumping round his body, making his skin feel fat. His shirt stuck to his chest like plastic wrap.

Leon said, "You want a few rounds?"

Harry nodded.

Much later, outside the gym, Harry stopped to check his phone. The entrance was busy because the kids' class had just finished, so Harry moved off down the road, away from the streetlamp, and stood in the shadow of the railway arch. The boxing had left him weightless, as if his bones had melted to air.

He'd beaten down the shock. All the fear and anger and grief had gone. Harry felt empty.

It was a fine May evening. There was a gentle warmth in the air. When a car pulled to a halt outside the gym, Harry looked up. It was a battered blue Toyota. Now, for the first time, he saw Ethan, standing against the wall. There was no one else around. All the parents had collected their kids. The street was empty.

A man got out of the car. He was shouting. Ethan began to

sidestep with small movements as if he were about to run. But the man closed the distance between them in just a few strides. It happened so fast. Ethan was lifted and thrown back against the wall. There was another push, a slap to the side of the head, and then the boy was on the ground, curled up, raising his arms to defend himself.

For a moment, Harry stared. Then he put his phone back in his pocket. He lifted up his sports bag, slung it over his shoulder, and strolled back to the gym entrance. Ethan had got to his feet and was stumbling behind the man to the car, hunched over as if he was trying to make himself as small as possible.

As Ethan was about to get into the backseat, Harry tapped on the driver's window. Ethan, holding the door—half in, half out—looked at him in terror.

The man wound the window down.

Anyone watching would have seen two mates exchanging a friendly greeting outside a neighborhood boxing club. A normal south London conversation. Harry bent down, relaxed and smiling, his arm resting on top of the car above the open window. He waited, allowing the man to assess him—his height, the bulk of his shoulders and arms, the expression in his eyes. He waited just long enough to make the point. Then he said, clearly and slowly, "So now I've seen you. I know who you are. And I'm telling you this once. If I ever see another bruise on him—a mark, anywhere—I will come and find you. And I will beat you to a pulp."

There was a long moment when time stood still.

It was only when the car sped off, tires grinding into the tarmac, that it all came back.

That afternoon. Sitting with Eva. Everything that was said. But Harry—like someone stepping back from a cliff edge, horrified by the fall—blanked the thought from his mind. He wouldn't let himself remember.

This isn't happening. This can't be happening.

.   .   .

Izzie sat back on her heels. "You're not going to forgive him, are you?"

No, thought Kim, I'm not. Sitting there smugly at the wedding, knowing secrets that didn't belong to him. He must have felt so powerful. Like a god. Like the center of the universe.

"Eva told him in confidence."

"I know."

"She didn't want to tell you before the wedding."

But she told Harry. I can't forgive him for knowing before I did. Kim closed her eyes. Pictures of the wedding crowded in. She remembered the cavalcade of cars covered with flowers, balloons, and streamers, all sounding their horns as they wove their way through the sunlit streets of the village near Nice. She remembered the pretty restaurant with its pink-and-white awning hosting the *vin d'honneur*—the celebration after the civil ceremony—with champagne and tiny canapés, and fresh lemonade for Jean-Marc's grandchildren.

How hard it was not to feel intimidated by the neat tailoring and high heels and perfect manicures all around her. For once, Kim had made a huge effort with her appearance. She'd had a haircut. She'd even polished her shoes. But the casual elegance of the French guests had made her feel clumsy and unfinished.

Eva had said her navy dress, a silk shift, brought out the blue of her eyes. But Harry looked taken aback when he saw her, which said it all, really.

Grace shone like a film star, elegant and demure in a white lace dress with a high neck and long sleeves. Her white-blond hair was swept back from her face, showing off her beautiful bone structure. She's Princess Grace, thought Kim. She has become the woman she always wanted to be.

Jean-Marc, to Kim's surprise—because Grace had described him as impossibly good-looking—turned out to be small, with brown hair speckled with gray, a hooked nose, and a slight stoop. He made Kim think of a hooded falcon hunched against the wind. Grace had insisted he stay with his eldest daughter in the days before the wedding (*There is simply too much to do. Men just get in the way*), so there had been no chance to get to know him at all. After the ceremony, conversation was hard going because Jean-Marc spoke no English, and Kim spoke no French. Harry, who had never met Jean-Marc before either, came out with a few formal sentences that he'd painstakingly learnt, and Jean-Marc inclined his head, as if to show he was pleased that Harry had made the effort.

But it was Otis who saved the day. His face lit up when he saw Jean-Marc. He remembered staying with him the year before. "*Hola*," he said, holding out his hand. "*Bom dia. Buon giorno. Guten Tag. Sveikas.*"

They all laughed, and Eva hugged him. "Nearly."

Jean-Marc bent down low and took Otis's hand, looking right into his eyes. "Hello."

Oh, thought Kim, seeing how Jean-Marc's face had softened

and been made younger by his smile, I think I can see what my mother means.

After the formal reception, they got back into the noisy procession of cars, and the select few—family and close friends— were driven to Jean-Marc's grand old villa in the hills. One long table had been set up in the shade of a pergola twisted with vines. They had course after course—melon, then scallops, chicken with fresh thyme, a green salad, local cheeses on a wicker platter, and then a *croquembouche*, a great pyramid of choux pastry puffs threaded with caramel and decorated with sugared almonds. The wineglasses were filled and refilled.

Somewhere at the bottom of her third glass of peachy Bellet rosé, Kim, who was beginning to feel drowsy and happy, found herself wondering how her mother had managed to make it all happen. Jean-Marc may not be a Grimaldi, she thought, looking out at the bright blue sky beyond the olive trees. But this is pretty close to the Palace of Monaco.

"So what do you think?" Harry sat down on the empty chair next to her. It was that time of the meal when people were changing places to catch up with gossip. Later, the children might swim in the pool behind its hedge of oleander, or play hide-and-seek in the formal gardens planted with lemon and olive trees.

"I think she'll be really happy."

"Jean-Marc seems OK."

"I like him." She frowned. "Because he likes Otis. I like everyone who likes Otis."

Harry smiled as if she'd said something funny.

"What?"

"I like Otis," said Harry. "But you've never liked me."

Kim was about to say, Yes, but I'm trying really hard these days not to hate you, but realized that might sound rude. So she took a sip of water instead. "I've been wondering whether my mother deserves it."

"Deserves what?"

"All this. She's been so supremely selfish the whole of her life. But now all her dreams have come true."

Harry looked amused. "So you think good things should only happen to nice people?"

Kim felt a flash of irritation. Trust him to talk to her as if she were a child. "Don't you?"

"It's completely random. Bad things happen to good people. And good things happen to people who shit on everyone else."

Well, you would know, thought Kim.

"Not that Eva would agree, of course," said Harry. "She believes in karma. Good deeds mean future happiness."

They sat in silence for a moment. Then Harry said, "I'm sorry Jake couldn't be here."

Kim shot him a quick look. But the remark seemed genuine. "It's the job."

"Busy?"

"Very busy."

Harry leant forwards, hesitated, and then sat back in his chair.

"What?" said Kim.

"It's none of my business. But I just wondered if you and Jake were OK. You haven't talked about him much recently."

Is it that obvious? Kim was about to say something off-puttingly neutral and change the subject but the words wouldn't come. She was suddenly tired of lying. "He's moved on. To the next one."

"The next one?"

"The next intern."

Harry looked shocked. "I'm sorry."

Kim was surprised. He sounded as if he meant it—as if he cared how she felt. "I should have seen it coming. It's all part of a pattern. It's what he does."

"When did you find out?"

"Oh"—Kim's voice trembled, despite herself—"three weeks ago. When I got back from Bristol."

"You don't have to say—"

"No, it's OK. There was a letter waiting for me. Telling me it had been a real struggle to decide between us. In the end, he'd had to write down both our names, and list all the pros and cons under each one. And my cons went all the way down to the bottom of the page. So there was no contest really."

Harry looked down at his feet.

"Damaris was really angry when I told her. She said he sounded like her consultant at the hospital. All decisions must be evidence-based."

Still Harry said nothing.

"I don't know why I'm telling you all this." I really don't, thought Kim. It must be the rosé.

Harry said, "So you've moved out?"

Kim nodded.

"Where are you living now?"

"With Izzie."

"Does Eva know?"

Kim shook her head, looking over at Eva on the other side of the table. "And you mustn't tell her. She'll be upset. So I'm not going to say anything until we get back to London. This is Mum's time. Her wedding. I don't want anything to spoil it."

"You're not the only one."

"What do you mean?"

"Nothing. Just that it's what we all want. Your mum to have a perfect day."

But he had that blank, shut-in look in his eyes again. So Kim knew he was hiding something. She was about to ask more, to get to the bottom of what was going on, when Otis came up with a shiny green shield bug cupped in his hands, saying he wanted to build it a bungalow and call it Charlie.

So the moment was lost. But I should have listened more carefully, thought Kim, self-recrimination howling in her head as her memories of the wedding faded away. I should have worked it out for myself. Harry was telling me that someone else had a secret. And of course that person was Eva—Eva, who had taken him into her confidence. Who had chosen Harry, not me. Again.

"You did the same, in a way," said Izzie.

Izzie's flat was always full of sunlight. From the bay window at the front, you could see right over Sydenham to the bright green leaves of ancient oak trees, last remnants of the Great North Wood. "I did the same?"

"You kept something to yourself. You didn't tell Eva about splitting up with Jake because you wanted your mum to have her big day without anyone being upset."

But breaking up with someone, thought Kim, isn't the same as finding out you've got cancer.

My sister has cancer.

In her mind, as usual, she heard Grace's voice. *Of course they have such marvelous treatments these days.*

"He went to the oncologist with her. Her first appointment."

"You were in Bristol."

Kim fought back tears. "I could have cut it short."

"I think she just wanted to get it out of the way."

That's not the point. It should have been me. I should have been sitting with Eva, asking questions, taking notes. Not Harry. Not Harry.

The important thing is to stay positive.

"And I don't think," said Izzie carefully, as if she was talking to a child, "that Eva gave him much choice."

That's what Harry does. Gets people on his side. Gets a whole army of supporters fighting his corner. Kim felt angry and outmaneuvered. "So what are you saying—I should move on?" And then, using Jake's favorite phrase because she hated it, and it still hurt her, and somehow flinging it out into the conversation made her feel she was able to hurt other people, too, "Draw a line under it?"

Izzie looked down at the pleats of her red skirt. "She'll get better, Kim. It's not like the old days."

Although of course she has the most aggressive kind. With the worst survival rates.

"And Harry's done a lot of research. He understands what the treatment involves."

Cancer is the rampant growth of unregulated cells. Like the banking industry. I'm sure Harry understands it perfectly.

"Don't shut him out. He wants to do anything he can to help."

Harry had made her trust him. He had even made her tell him about Jake. And all the while, like a miser hugging gold, he had kept Eva's cancer a secret.

She couldn't forgive him.

•   •   •

Harry stood in front of St. Paul's Cathedral, looking at the multicolored tents huddled on the cobbles like upturned teacups. Occupy London. Numbers were growing day by day. According to the papers, people were mystified. What do they want, these people camping outdoors in late October in central London? What are their demands? They don't know yet, Eva had said the night before. They're working it out. All they know at the moment is that they don't like the way the world's organized. Everything we do dominated by money and led by people who have money. They want something different. They want us all to think how things could change. Sometimes that's where you have to start. It's enough to say no.

It sounds like the Summer of Love, Harry had said, grinning. A whole load of hippies drifting about, trying to change the world.

I think they're angrier than they were in the 1960s, said Eva, her blue eyes serious.

It must be cold here at night, thought Harry, looking at the white stone façade of the cathedral. And noisy, with the traffic and the clock bell marking the hours. You wouldn't get much sleep. A gust of wind would probably blow the tents away. Maybe they don't sleep, he thought. Maybe they operate in shifts, taking it in turns to organize new arrivals and talk to the press. It was just before seven a.m., but already there were people moving round the camp. Someone was carrying a kettle. Of course, thought Harry. That's how the British protest against global capitalism. They make tea.

Eva had wanted to come. I could cook, she said. Or sing. There are mothers with children sitting on the steps of St. Paul's.

You need to rest, he said.

There's more to life than resting, she said.

Across the entrance to the camp was a huge green banner with pink letters spelling out CAPITALISM IS CRISIS.

"I keep forgetting things," said Eva.

"No change there, then."

She gave him a small push on the shoulder. "It's a recognized side effect. Chemo brain."

"Maybe it is," said Harry. "But I don't think you can blame the drugs. You've always had a brain like a sieve."

"Were you always this rude?"

Harry raised his eyebrows. "You can't remember?"

Eva laughed. She still laughed a lot.

But there were days when she was so tired that he put them to bed one after the other, Otis, then Eva.

And then he sat on the sofa in the dark, looking at the lights on the Thames.

"Promise me you won't talk about fighting. Or battles. Ever." Eva's manifesto, right at the beginning. Sitting in the sunshine, the light in her white-blond hair.

Harry smiled. "Make love, not war."

"When have I ever wanted to fight anything? And anyway it's not a battle. It just is. Like rain. Or mold."

It's Kim and I who fight, thought Harry. Every step of the way.

"You've got to help me. I don't think she's got the right attitude." A pub near Paddington, one Tuesday evening before Kim got the train back to Bristol. She was angry, on edge, her face set. "I don't mind all the homeopathy and essential oils if it makes her feel better. But no one seriously thinks any of that makes any difference. Exercise, maybe. Nutrition. There are studies pointing to the advantages of a vegan diet. But the most important thing is attitude. She's got to make a commitment. She's got to be determined to beat it."

"I'm not sure she sees it that way."

"This isn't about you, Harry. This isn't about what you think. This is about Eva."

It was the same clipped tone she always used whenever she spoke to him these days. But what did he expect? That's how she coped under pressure, with extreme efficiency. Whenever Kim came round to the flat, her arms were always full of books, leaflets, and box files bursting with information. Harry could see that the words made Eva tired. But she never showed it. She sat with Kim on the sofa—the sofa that looked so tiny in the corner of Harry's vast apartment—and listened carefully as Kim explained the latest treatments, the ongoing trials, the papers published in academic journals.

Sometimes, when Kim was talking, Otis would come and stand next to Eva, and she would put her arm round him and pull him close. They weren't even looking at each other, but you could see that they had taken refuge, as usual, in the silent communication that excluded everyone else.

Otis had just started school. He liked it. He had a blue sweat-shirt with a line drawing of the school building picked out in white on the front. His book bag was blue, too. The school was only ten minutes' walk from the flat. Most of the time Eva managed it. But sometimes Harry went in late. Or a friend—another parent—picked Otis up and brought him back at the end of the afternoon.

It seemed strange to think that Eva had ever contemplated moving away. This was her home now. She had found her community in the fug and dirt of central London.

Great Tom, the bell in the southwest tower, chimed the hour.

At least I can tell her about this now, thought Harry, looking out over the tents. Eva had liked the idea of a peaceful protest against capitalism. Gentle resistance. I can describe what I've seen, the encampment on the steps of St. Paul's.

He turned to make his way to work.

A jogger ran past in skintight Lycra—red-and-blue leggings and a long-sleeved white top. He started threading his way through the tents, using the camp as an obstacle course, pausing just long enough to shout, "Why don't you all get fucking jobs!"

No one responded. No one even looked at him.

She's had the surgery. Halfway through chemo. Radiotherapy in December. All over by Christmas.

Next spring I'll take her to Monterey. I want her to see the place where they sang. Jimi Hendrix, Otis Redding, the Mamas and the Papas.

．　．　．

Kim stood in the bay window of Izzie's flat in Sydenham. She had offered to look after Otis for the whole day. We'll have a great time, she said. We might go to Crystal Palace Park. Go and see the Victorian dinosaurs—great green models looming out of the bluebells. No one ever seems that surprised to see them there. Let's go to the park, have an ice cream, and see some extinct animals! But then this is southeast London. There are billionaires stepping over beggars. Why would anyone be surprised by a stegosaurus?

I'm really grateful, said Eva.

Polite, thought Kim. As if I was a friend doing her a favor.

Kim leant her forehead against the glass. Behind her, Otis, who had emptied his rucksack onto the carpet, was already managing a fictional world in which a badger grappled with a giant octopus, a sea lion rode a fire engine, and a space rocket landed upside down in a farmyard, scattering the sheep.

Below her, in the street, Harry and Eva were getting into the Porsche. The roof was down. Kim, the all-seeing eye, the secret camera, felt like a spy. A Peeping Tom. She saw Harry speak. But she was too high up to hear the words. Harry had given Eva a silver charm bracelet that morning—antique, heavy, jangling like wind chimes whenever she moved. But up here, high above, Kim couldn't hear that either.

Eva had a long gauzy scarf tied round her head. It was pale blue and white. You couldn't see she was bald.

Then Harry started the engine, and there was a rumble, like the roar in the throat of a big cat. Harry didn't move off straightaway. They just sat there, talking and laughing, as if they had all the time in the world. Then Harry pulled out of the parking space, and the car built up speed—fast, streamlined, racing

down the dull suburban street—until all Kim could see was
Eva's scarf fluttering, like bunting, in the wind.

. . .

Rooftop bars in London get very crowded on a Friday night.
People like the contrast. All week they've been ground down by
pressure and deadlines. Released from the bunker of work, they
want to get as high as possible, physically and metaphorically.
The taller the City grows, thought Harry, the more important it
is to be way up in the clouds. Otherwise you can end up feeling
like an ant. Busy but easy to crush.

Normally, if you want to enjoy stunning views over London,
you have to book. Or queue. But the waiter just nodded them
through.

"They know me here," said Syed.

Harry didn't realize he was joking until they got the other
side of the glass doors. It was November. The roof terrace—
open to the elements, slightly shiny with rain—was cold and deserted. A few months ago, Harry would have said, What are we
doing out here? Bad idea. Let's go in. But their old easy relationship had disappeared. The row in the pub had cut deep. Nowa-
days, whenever Harry heard rumors in the health care sector,
or saw shares unexpectedly plummet, or watched as companies
scrambled to make statements about price-sensitive information that had somehow been leaked, he wondered whether Syed
was behind it.

You need to be able to trust your friends. It doesn't work if
you're suspicious of what they're doing behind your back.

For a few minutes, they didn't talk at all—just stood there with their bottles of beer, looking out over the waist-high barrier onto the darkening City. They could see the Tower of London, St. Paul's, the Shard, the Gherkin. All the office buildings had horizontal stripes of yellow light like deck chair fabric. If I leant right over and peered round the edge, thought Harry, I could probably wave at Otis. Or at least in his general direction.

"I thought you might not come," said Syed.

I nearly didn't, thought Harry, staring out over the gray skyline.

"I thought you might have written me off as someone you didn't want to associate with."

Harry took a mouthful of beer. He felt Syed watching him.

Syed said, "I didn't do it. And I'm not going to."

Harry looked at him properly for the first time. "You said it was too late."

"I was lying."

Harry thought about this. "Why?"

"So you'd think there was nothing you could do."

I should have known, thought Harry. Typical bravado. "What happened to the brother-in-law?"

"An uncle. An interest-free loan. So he's fine."

They stood in silence. Harry said, "Would you have done it?"

"Spread false information? Probably."

It goes on all the time, thought Harry. It seems like a game. A bit of light law-breaking. You forget all the victims at the end of the process. All the little people investing their money.

Syed said, "The family is angry."

"With you?"

"They think I'm rich. They think there's no reason not to pay my brother-in-law's debts. I'm being selfish. Unreasonable."

"I'm sorry."

"Don't be. It had to happen." Syed took a deep breath and let it out in a sigh. "I couldn't carry him forever."

They stood side by side contemplating the horizon. Syed said, "And anyway I'm glad it happened. It made me stand up to my mother. She loves me. I'm her world. I can do no wrong. But that's a hard burden to carry. Being someone's pride and joy. She has a picture in her head of who she thinks I am. And every day I feel I'm failing, because I don't match up. However hard I work, however successful I am, I'm not the perfect son she carries around in her mind every minute of every day. So when I said I wouldn't give him the money, and she couldn't shame me into changing my mind, something shifted. I had disappointed her. I was no longer perfect. I felt free. She kept saying, 'What's wrong? What's happened to you, Syed? Are you ill?' And I said, 'No. I'm just not going to do it.'" Syed was silent for a moment. Then he said, "And you know what? It feels good."

Harry said, "You could feel even better."

"How?"

"Tell her about the gambling. And the strip clubs."

Syed laughed. The atmosphere between them was suddenly lighter. He said, "Why did you do it?"

"Do what?"

"Warn me off. Stop me doing it. Most people would have just let me go ahead and make a complete dick of myself."

Because I wanted to do something right for once. "I didn't think you'd like the food in prison."

"Seriously."

Harry said, "My friend Christine says you should look after your friends. And I always do what Christine says."

"Christine?"

"Not your type."

Syed smiled. A gust of wind ruffled the large red cordyline at the corner of the terrace. He shivered and turned up the lapels of his jacket. "It's fucking freezing. Shall we go in?"

"I thought you wanted to suffer," said Harry. "I thought that's why we were out here."

"I just wanted you to see the view." Syed took one last look at the London skyline. "The City. Cause of jubilation and despair."

The only thing, thought Harry, over which I have any control at all.

. . .

Most of the time, Kim managed to forget that she and Jake worked for the same organization. He, after all, was based in the head office in Vauxhall—and busy in the Palace of Westminster—while she trailed around the regions, causing distress in Bristol, Leeds, Birmingham, and Cardiff. Even if she was called in for a meeting with the CEO, she was unlikely to bump into him. Jake was always out. He was that kind of person. Too busy to sit at a desk.

Rhodri hadn't been promoted to head of research, but he seemed remarkably unconcerned. "It wasn't my time, was it?" he said. "That's what I always think. Sometimes you're lucky. Sometimes you're not."

"When did you become so wise?"

"I don't know if it's wise. It's just the way it is."

"So what will you do?"

"Well, I can't carry on working for nothing. Which is all that's on offer here—another internship. So I'll have to look for something else."

Kim, now part of the management team, was shamed into silence.

Back in her office—having slipped through the fire exit and up the concrete stairs to avoid walking past Zofia's desk—Kim checked her phone, plowed her way through the outstanding emails, and sorted her desk into some semblance of order. She didn't like leaving things in a mess when she was away—it looked so unprofessional—and she was due back in Bristol in the morning. Her heart was heavy at the thought. Her restructuring plan had boiled down to slashing the hours of part-time employees who needed the work (paying them less) and increasing the hours of full-time employees who already had too much to do (paying them the same). And tomorrow, she thought, I have to make two people redundant. Tony and Catherine. Who both have families. And mortgages. Bills they can't pay and credit cards stretched to the limit.

You should never make people redundant on Fridays, in case they're going back to an empty flat and end up alone and suicidal. But you do it all the time. So you don't have to witness the fallout. So the workforce doesn't get upset.

Oh, thought Kim, suddenly desolate. I always used to comfort myself that I was the best person for the job. I followed the rules. I handled the process properly to minimize pain and shock. Now I'm not so sure. Now I hide behind words like consolidation and staff surplus.

She looked up. There in the doorway was Jake.

"So," he said, as if they'd seen each other a few minutes before and were resuming the conversation, "you're off home, are you?"

How strange to see him standing there, she thought, the man I lived with for three years. I know the feel of your hair, the smell of your skin, the blotchy rash on your neck after sex. I know the way you sleep, kicking out at imaginary chihuahuas. I know the sound you make drinking tea. I know, if we were in a room full of people, that you would be furtively assessing who's who, ranking importance, reviewing worth. Constantly checking your phone. Texting when you think no one's looking. Working on those clever put-downs disguised as compliments. Impatience repackaged as charm.

You stand there clothed, with your thick thighs in your baggy chinos, but I see you naked.

He smiled. "Drink?"

Brutal verbal editing, she thought. He must be spending too much time on Twitter. "No thanks. I need to get back."

Jake leant against the door frame. It looked like a casual move. But it's never casual with Jake, thought Kim. He's blocking my exit.

"Shame. I wanted to catch up." A look of concern. "Ask about Eva."

It felt to Kim as if he'd grabbed her round the throat, squeezing hard.

"I was talking to Rhodri. Tragic news. It must be so hard for you and your mother."

I find illness so draining, of course.

"Particularly hard that she's so young." He shook his head. "It doesn't seem fair, does it? Her whole life ahead of her. And a small child, too."

"It's all fine. The treatment's going really well. We're all looking forward to Christmas."

"You can't help thinking, Why? Why has this happened? Why her?" Jake sighed. "On a happier note, I wanted to offer my congratulations."

Kim stared. "On what?"

"On the excellent job you're doing in Bristol. I was chatting to Lulu"—it took Kim a moment to realize he was talking about the CEO, who, as far as she knew, only ever used the name Louisa—"and she told me you'd cut back all the dead wood. In record time. Textbook right-sizing. Managing reduction. Ramping down resources. Of course, I don't want to take all the credit. That wouldn't be fair. You've worked hard." He smiled. "But since you learned so much from me, I think I have just a small understanding of how George Osborne's maths teacher must feel."

The silence grew just long enough to become awkward.

Jake glanced down at his phone and raised his eyebrows. Kim could see his mind moving off to great and important events involving influential people she didn't know and would never meet. "Well," he said, making an effort, but obviously itching to be elsewhere, "I'll leave you to your evening. Perhaps next time you're in London, we can try to organize things a bit better. I know Zofia would love to see you." Staring at his phone, not even looking at her, he raised his hand in a general gesture of farewell. "*Ciao.*"

The doorway was suddenly empty.

Kim stayed quite still until she was sure it was safe enough to breathe.

2012

t's like he wants to pretend it's not happening."

"What's wrong with that?"

Kim couldn't think where to start. "It's not real."

"I'm not sure," said Grace, on the other end of the phone from the South of France, "that dinner at Le Caprice is any less real than the inside of a cancer ward."

Kim was so angry she thought she might explode. Eva had been through months of grueling treatment. She was tired. Her body was battered and bruised. She didn't need Marilyn Monroe at the National Portrait Gallery, Jane Birkin at the Barbican. She didn't need ice-cream sundaes at Fortnum & Mason, afternoon tea at the Ritz, an outing to Regent's Park zoo. Rushing from Harrods to Buckingham Palace to the London Eye. Gallivanting round London like a tourist. It had been going on for weeks. And it was completely unnecessary. Superficial frippery. What was Harry playing at?

What Eva needed was rest. Time to recover. Sleep.

Damaris said, I think he's just trying to cheer her up.

She doesn't need cheering up, Kim said. She needs to concentrate on getting better.

Damaris looked as if she was about to say something and then stopped. They're all on his side, thought Kim. They've all

225

been completely taken in. They're charmed when Harry zooms up in his Porsche, grinning like an idiot, throwing money around, offering yet another stupid surprise. Eva's not a child. She's a grown woman who needs to concentrate on her health.

Sometimes, looking at Harry, Kim wondered if he realized quite how ill Eva had been.

And my mother's no better. Kim imagined Grace drifting round the ancient splendor of the villa in Nice, looking out onto the formal gardens, the swimming pool, the lemon and olive trees. It's easy to ignore reality, she thought, gripping the phone, if you're never required to face it. So far, throughout Eva's months of chemo and radiotherapy, Grace had visited London only once. *People like me find illness depressing. We're so sensitive.* Kim said, "And now he wants to take her to Monterey."

"To where?"

"Monterey. Near San Francisco."

Grace sounded puzzled. "Why would he want to do that?"

"The music festival in 1967. Otis Redding. The Mamas and the Papas."

"Oh," said Grace, sounding vague, "her hippie phase."

The night before, Eva had talked again about going to Black Bear Ranch, north of San Francisco. In the spring of 1968, a group of hippies had set up a community in an abandoned gold mine at the end of nine miles of dirt track. A remote canyon, with eighty acres of forest, orchards, creeks, and meadows, it was an idyllic setting for a whole new way of life. But it was hard going. None of them knew how to chop wood or cook. They were surrounded by black bears, cougars, and lynx. That first winter, there was four feet of snow.

"But the community survived," said Eva. "And over the years, people have come and gone. Children were born there. Families grew up there. There's a whole gathering every year to celebrate the summer solstice. They welcome visitors. I'd love to go and see it."

A brave new world on the surface, thought Kim. But from what I've heard, it wasn't all flowers and butterflies. Free love. Happy drug trips. Communal possessions. But also sexual jealousy, petty arguments, and disillusionment. Most people gave up and went back to the city. But Kim didn't say any of this. Over Eva's shoulder, she had admired the website, looked at pictures of the ranch, and read Peter Coyote's *Free-Fall Chronicles*. She wanted her sister to be happy.

But she was still dead set against a trip to the States. Eva's oncologist had said it was OK. But Kim knew it was too risky. What if there was a medical emergency?

"It's too far," said Kim to her mother. "She'll be exhausted."

"But Harry will go with her, won't he?"

As if that's going to help, with his insistence on constant activity. "I don't think it's sensible. She's been very ill."

"I think," said Grace, "that it's up to her."

Kim made one last attempt to yank the conversation in the direction she wanted it to go. "She should be recuperating. Building up her strength." She took a deep breath. "Convalescing somewhere warm."

"As should we all," said Grace. "I've never known a spring this cold. It may be the South of France, but I'm sitting here in this drafty old villa in layers of cashmere. Shivering. Wondering if the sun will ever shine again."

.   .   .

"I've done something bad."

"No you haven't."

"I have. Really bad. Really, really, really bad."

Kim shook her head. "I don't believe it."

"It's true." But Damaris didn't look distressed. She looked, if anything, excited. Unwinding a purple scarf from round her neck, she dropped her coat and bag on the floor in a heap. Kim was astonished. Damaris was normally so careful about neatness and order.

"So what is it?"

"Tea," said Damaris. "I need a cup of tea."

It was a Sunday morning in late March. They were in Izzie's flat in Sydenham. Kim felt guilty that she was still living there. There was only one bedroom, so whenever Izzie was in London, Kim had to sleep on a blow-up mattress in the living room. But it wasn't just the practical difficulties. Years ago, Kim had abandoned Izzie in New Cross. Because she herself found it hard to forgive anybody for anything, Kim felt Izzie should still be bearing a grudge. She should have said, Sorry, Kim, this is my flat so you can bugger off. But she hadn't. She'd said, Stay as long as you like. It's fine. I'm often away anyway. You're doing me a favor. Keeping the flat occupied so I don't get burgled. Which was, of course, rubbish. But extremely kind.

Kim liked Sydenham. It was so high up. Sometimes you came across a view over London that made you catch your breath with surprise.

This weekend, Izzie was in Manchester. She said she didn't

mind being away from London. But she had developed a deep-seated hatred of trains.

"Why?" Kim had said, expecting Izzie to talk about rude station staff, dirt, and delays.

"They're so boring," said Izzie. "Either going straight there, or coming straight back."

Damaris—sitting at the kitchen table in Izzie's flat, watching as Kim filled the kettle—was working at Accident & Emergency in King's College Hospital in Camberwell. Kim had been surprised at her choice of specialism. Medical emergencies, from what she'd seen on TV, were all about panic and snap decisions. Surely Damaris, with her love of detailed and thorough analysis, should have gone for something more sedate, like research? No, Damaris said, you don't understand. It's like being Sherlock Holmes. Not the accidents, obviously, or the heart attacks. You just deal with them quickly as possible and get the patients admitted. But the weird, random symptoms that come on so suddenly that people call an ambulance—you have to stay calm and think. It might be nothing. Or it might be life-threatening. Analysis is crucial.

I wish her hours weren't so long, though, thought Kim, reaching up for the bright blue teapot. Whenever I get worried about Eva, Damaris explains what's going on. All through her treatment, Damaris has found the words that help me understand. I don't get that panic that rises up whenever I take Eva to hospital. Panic makes you deaf. All you can hear is the pressure in your ears.

"So go on, then," said Kim, pulling out a chair and sitting down. "What have you done that's so terrible?"

Damaris took a deep breath. "Jake came into A&E."

Kim's heart missed a beat. "Did he?" she said, trying to sound casual.

"He didn't recognize me," said Damaris. "At all."

Kim thought back. How many times had they met? There was the disastrous supper in Eva's flat when Otis was a few months old. And they'd sat side by side in the audience for Izzie's first big stand-up in Deptford. Kim also had a vague recollection of a group outing to see *Shutter Island* in the cinema because Damaris loved Leonardo DiCaprio. But she couldn't remember their ever actually talking to each other. Jake had tended to hold himself aloof from all her friends because, she suspected, he found them young and boring. Which I suppose, thought Kim miserably, we are.

"So I walked into the cubicle, and there he was, sitting there, looking all tragic. I was smiling, because I thought he was going to say, Oh hello, Damaris. And feeling a bit embarrassed, because it's awkward bumping into your friend's ex, especially when he's been a complete prick and dumped her in the cruelest way possible, so that you hate him and think you might make an effigy out of plaster of Paris and stick pins in it. But you know you've got to be grown-up about it all. So you're all ready to look pleasant and say, in a mature and professional way, Hello, Jake, how can I help? Do you want to talk to me, or would you prefer a doctor you don't know? But he just looks at me like he's never seen me before. Like I'm nothing. And I think, You bastard. All those times we met, I was so beneath your radar that you didn't even see me. And I start feeling really angry. So the smile disappears, and I sit down at the computer and look up the notes they took in triage. And it says he's come because he's got a bit of pain in his thumbs. Which is so incredibly irritating, because it's clearly something he should take to his GP, not clog up emergency appointments on a Saturday night in the middle of inner London. But I don't say any of this, obviously. I nod and ask all the usual questions, and check the range of movement and ask when it started, and what makes it hurt, and it doesn't take long to work out what's happening. He spends all day on his phone. It's some kind of repetitive strain injury. OK, I understand he's concerned. He's someone who thinks the world will come to an end if he's not texting. Normally I'd be sympathetic and explain that it's not an acute injury so he needs to go to his normal doctor and let us be. But I'm tired. It's been a long night. He behaved like a bastard to you. And he's still looking at me like he's never seen me before. Not a glimmer of recognition. So something snaps. It's never happened before. It's like someone else is doing the talking—some other Damaris from an alternative universe. I say, I'm really sorry, it's not good news. He looks taken aback. He wasn't expecting this. Why would he? He's only come in with a pain in his thumbs. I say, This is a very rare symptom. I've only seen it a few times before. It's an STI. A what? he says. A symptom, I say, of a sexually transmitted infection. Do you have a lot of sexual partners? A generally promiscuous lifestyle? He just sits there, looking as if I've thrown a bucket of cold water over him. And then I laugh. I'm just joking, I say. He carries on staring, his face white. I pretend to be puzzled. You've just been texting too much. Put the phone down for a couple of days and it'll probably get better by itself. He carries on staring. I lean forwards. I'm so sorry, I say. You do recognize me, don't you, Jake? Damaris.

Kim's friend. It was just a joke. I apologize. And suddenly his face is bright red, and he says, Damaris! Yes, of course. Yes. And he gives a little strangled laugh. Yes, of course I recognize you! And I say, Go and see your GP on Monday. But I don't think it's serious. Nothing a bit of a break from instant messaging can't cure. And I carry on smiling, and he gets up from the chair and turns round and somehow trips and falls through the curtain. Straight into a walking frame that someone's left outside. So I help him up from the floor, and he's saying, Oh sorry, sorry, and coming out with that same strangled laugh. And then he says, And how's Kim? Never see her these days. And I say, She's having an affair with Leonardo DiCaprio. Spends most of her time in LA. But I'm sure she could fit you in somehow if you got in touch. And then I wag my finger at him and say, But don't do it by text. Or those thumbs will never get better! And he's in such a hurry to leave that he walks into an instrument trolley and there's a huge crash. And then he's gone."

Kim, who had been staring at Damaris openmouthed during the whole long tirade, found her voice.

"Can you tell me all that again, please?" she said. "From the very beginning?"

·   ·   ·

The club, in Soho, was in the cellar of a pub. It smelt of beer, cold brickwork, and damp. From time to time you could hear the distant rumble of trains on the Northern Line way down below. There weren't enough chairs, so people were standing against the walls all the way round, like a decorative Greek frieze. It was dark except for the spotlights. Billy Swan's "I Can Help" was playing.

Kim took a mouthful of bitter. It was weak and sweet.

These days she was two people. There was the Kim that everybody saw—walking around, going to work in Vauxhall, planning a trip to the Cardiff office, admonishing Eva for not eating properly, criticizing Harry for making Eva so tired. And then there was the other Kim, a clear, gelatinous jellyfish that floated about to no apparent purpose. Jellyfish Kim—drifting about in a trailing, dangling sort of way—seemed to be waiting for something.

You turn into a jellyfish, thought Kim, when your brain isn't working properly anymore. You become colorless from confusion. It's like sucking all the sugar and additives from an ice lolly and being left with nothing but water. Seeing Eva bald, plump from steroids, her skin dotted blue from repeated injections, was shocking enough. But there was also the effort of maintaining that this was all perfectly normal. Positive, even. You had to pretend, week after week, that seeing the person you love turn into someone completely unrecognizable was good news.

You can do anything for five minutes. It's doing it for weeks and months that turns you insane.

Luckily, if you're a round, rubbery jellyfish, you're insulated from shock. You float about in the cold, dark void, and nothing's going to affect you. Eva's last scan was good. But the consultant wasn't happy. Something not quite right. What, exactly? We're not sure. We'll have to wait and see. *Of course she has the most aggressive kind. The kind that affects young women.* But she'll be fine. Of course she will. Eva will beat it. She's having the best treatment. Newest drugs. Top London teaching hospital.

Kim took another sip of her warm, sweet beer.

The warm-up comic ambled onstage like someone's younger brother gatecrashing a girls' night in—not sure of his welcome but determined to stay. His clothes were all a bit too small. Seeing a bony wrist stick out from a frayed sleeve, Kim felt almost sorry for him. She wasn't sure he should be up this late.

The comic may have looked like a little boy lost. But he got people talking. He picked on the cocky ones, the loud ones, the ones who looked too conventional for an underground comedy club. Before they knew what was happening, they were spilling out their guilty secrets—old lies, dirty habits, hidden crimes. The audience had turned itself into one huge joke. By the time it was asked to give it up for the first act, it had been warmed up, ridiculed, and cut down to size.

Izzie was third in the lineup. She came onstage wearing a high-necked white blouse with a lace front, baggy black trousers, red braces, and Doc Martens. Her cloud of frizzy hair was piled on top of her head. As usual, before she started to speak, there was an uneasy silence. No one was quite sure what to make of her. She looked like an old-fashioned schoolmistress ready for a night out in Camden. Or perhaps Emmeline Pankhurst at Glastonbury. Part of you wanted to put her back into a grainy black-and-white photograph with bloomers, a bicycle, and a poster saying VOTES FOR WOMEN. Part of you wondered if she socialized with Agyness Deyn.

But as soon as she started talking, the whole room relaxed. Because she knew what she was doing. And for a moment you saw the world through her eyes, in all its mad, ridiculous glory.

Izzie stepped into imaginary conversations. She had Barclays CEO Bob Diamond talking to Wikileaks founder Julian

Assange about learning to love yourself. She had the Queen and Prince Philip standing on the Thames Jubilee barge, discussing the appeal of One Direction. She had the dean of St. Paul's addressing a flock of pigeons about their illegal occupation of Trafalgar Square. She made the absurd seem normal. She made fiction more comfortable than fact. And that's what public figures do, she said. They tell us the stories we want to hear.

"Because you don't want to think about climate change or the credit crunch or chlamydia, do you? It's just going to make you depressed. That's why David Cameron said he'd bought a hot pasty from a shop in Leeds that didn't exist. Because it was a nice story. Nicer than the truth. Which is that he'd never eaten a pasty. And this was the first time he'd heard of Leeds."

And once you've made it up, you hold on. Defend it to the death. Right to the bitter end. Lance Armstrong. Bill Clinton. Chris Huhne. Like a toddler with chocolate round her mouth. The evidence is there for everyone to see, but still she denies it.

All around Kim in the darkness, people were laughing.

"You can end up with an elephant so big it's filling the whole room. And still you say it's not there."

Don't, Izzie. Don't.

"Dropping great piles of dung. Flattening the carpet. Knocking the ornaments off the mantelpiece. But what do you do?"

Kim couldn't see Izzie anymore. Everything was distorted—just a shifting, shimmering blur of tears.

"You ignore it. That's what you do with the truth. Close your eyes tight. Pretend it's not happening."

.   .   .

London, in terms of area, takes up less than 1 percent of the UK. But it's home to 13 percent of the people. It's something you're aware of all the time if you live here, thought Harry. You can feel the crush of bodies all around you—hot breath on your neck, feet clipping your heels.

The way to cope, as all Londoners know, is to pretend other people don't exist. Own your space. Never make eye contact. Sometimes people take this too far. A total stranger will walk straight at you as if expecting to meet no resistance—as if expecting to dissolve through you, in a slither of liquid metal, like the T-1000 in *Terminator 2*.

But generally, if you convince yourself that the heaving mass of humanity isn't there (despite the elbow in your ribs, the cough in your face, the briefcase in your shins), you can enjoy all the advantages the city has to offer.

And one of the advantages is the likelihood of bumping into an old friend when you least expect it.

Harry was walking next to the river—past the concrete underbelly of the Southbank arts complex, which rang with the skid and clatter of skateboards—when he saw her ahead of him in the crowds. It was a perfect July day, with bright sunshine and a pale blue sky, and tourists were out in force—loitering by the jugglers and jazz musicians, dawdling by stalls of Brazilian street food and Peruvian handicrafts, leaning right over the black iron railings staring at the muddy shallows of the Thames. But even though he could catch only glimpses of her through the throng—just enough to see her long blond hair and beautifully straight back—he knew who it was by the way she walked. As always, she strode purposefully, as if she had somewhere important to go.

It was only when she slowed right down in front of a troop of Gambian drummers that Harry caught up with her. He put his hand on her shoulder and she spun round, catching her breath. Her magnificent chest rose in delight.

"Harry!"

He grinned. It was so good to see her. Titania looked just the same—clear skin with a hint of a blush, pearl earrings, pale pink lipstick. Her skirt, which was ankle-length, seemed almost transparent against the light, making her appear both completely covered up and wantonly seductive.

"But what are you doing here?"

"I live here. On the river." Harry gestured vaguely towards London Bridge.

She raised her eyebrows. "Well," she said, "so we're doing quite well for ourselves, are we?"

Harry smiled. "Still in Kent?"

"Well remembered. I think it would take quite a lot to winkle me out of Sevenoaks these days. There's something so incredibly calming about well-heeled suburbia."

"Coffee?"

"I would have loved to. But I'm just on my way to meet Giles. By Tate Modern. And I'm already late." She smiled. "Come with me. He'd love to say hello, if you've got the time."

They fell into step together, moving slowly through the milling mass of people. Titania said, "So go on, then. Still in banking?"

"Of course. What about you?"

"I'm taking a break."

Harry looked at her, trying to work out from her expression what she meant.

"I went back after maternity leave," said Titania, "but we were all miserable. Me, Emma, and Giles. I could have looked for a bank that had a better commitment to retaining its staff, I suppose. Or one that didn't bully new mothers to the point of exhaustion. But at the time, I just needed to get out. Which I think was the right decision."

"I'm sorry."

"The biggest problem, which I hadn't expected, is that I'm not sure who I am anymore. Emma's mother, obviously. But I never expected to define myself through my family. I miss my job. I was good at it. I still have no idea what to say when someone asks me what I do."

They stood watching as a small boy edged forward to drop a coin at the feet of a street performer with chalk-white skin who stood completely motionless, impersonating a stone statue.

"I think men are very lucky," said Titania. "They don't have to face this. You are who you are. You never have to worry about losing your identity."

"Are you happy with Giles?"

She looked at him, her eyes amused. "That's a very un-Harry-like question."

"Is it?"

"You know it is. The Harry I knew would rather have died than ask a question that mattered."

"Maybe I've changed."

"Maybe you have."

The little boy, right at the statue's feet, put down his coin. The statue burst into life, bowing down with a huge theatrical flourish. The little boy jumped out of his skin.

She said, "The answer is that we suit each other very well. He's what politicians call transparent. Honest. Straightforward. You know where you are."

"Titania—"

"That wasn't a criticism. It was just an explanation."

He felt ashamed. They turned away from the statue and started walking towards the Millennium Bridge—strings of steel across the Thames so that people could walk to St. Paul's. The wobbly bridge, thought Harry, as it was for a while, swaying to the rhythm of footsteps.

"So what about you?"

"What about me?"

"There was always someone very special in your life that you never talked about. Are you still pining for her?"

For a moment, the world felt empty—no people, no noise, nothing but blue sky. Titania disappeared, too. There was nothing inside Harry's head but silence.

He felt Titania's hand on his arm. She was staring up into his face, pulling him close. "Harry, what is it?"

He shook his head.

"Let's find somewhere to sit down. I just meant it as a joke. I'm sorry."

Harry said, "Eva is dying of cancer. And I don't know what to do."

There was a small mechanized truck with a flapping multicolored banner making its way through the crowd. People were standing back, laughing, skipping out of the way. Harry allowed himself to be pulled to the side, and the truck trundled through, taking its time, and now there was a clearing where once there had been people, and the sun was beating down so hard that Harry felt too hot to breathe.

"Harry!"

Harry heard the voice before he recognized its owner. A tall, red-faced man wearing a Hawaiian shirt and khaki shorts, his paunch so huge he appeared to be pregnant, was waving at them from the other side of the sudden space. One hand was holding on to a navy-blue buggy with a great spotted sunshade. In the buggy, clutching on to a glittering pink windmill, was a little blond-haired girl.

Harry turned to Titania with a huge grin. Apart from the fact that his eyes held no expression, like the blackness at the bottom of a well, you wouldn't have guessed there was anything wrong. "Is that Emma? She's beautiful."

"Harry—"

But he ignored her. "Giles!" Harry walked forward, hand outstretched. "Just bumped into Titania and she said she was coming to meet you."

"Look at you!" said Giles. "Same old Harry. Hasn't changed a bit, has he, darling?"

. . .

"You can't see it," said Kim.

Sticking out from Eva's chest, somewhere below the collarbone, was a white silicon tube. It emerged, man-made, from soft tissue, like a drainpipe bursting out of sand. At the end hung two brightly colored bungs, red and blue, like beads in braided hair. A Hickman line. No more needles, thought Kim. No more punctured veins. Now, whatever she needs, whenever she needs it, they pump it straight in. It's a plumbing issue, that's all. Bodies don't have the necessary infrastructure, so you have to add a bit extra. A black mark against evolution. All these veins and arteries rushing around like scribble inside, but not one of them poking out of the skin.

You have no right. You have no right to do this to her.

"I'll have to buy some new clothes," said Eva, "to cover it up. Something with a high neck."

A pussycat bow. A frilled ruff. Kim could see the headline in a women's magazine: "How to disguise your Hickman line." She said, "I could come with you."

Eva nodded. She looked tired.

Outside, London was baking in August sunshine. But Harry's flat, complete with air-conditioning, was hermetically sealed. It was like being zipped up in a freezer bag. You wouldn't know it was summer. And you definitely wouldn't know a five-year-old lived here. All the toys had been tidied away. Harry had a cleaner who came in twice a week to polish the floor and dust behind the fridge.

"So what's new?" said Eva.

She doesn't even look like herself. The lines of her face are blurred and blubbery like someone made up in a film to look fat. Like Gwyneth Paltrow in *Shallow Hal*.

"I haven't been out much," said Eva, "what with all this going on."

The skin around the Hickman line was red and inflamed.

"I'm sorry I wasn't here."

"You didn't need to be."

I shouldn't have gone to Cardiff. I should have postponed

it. What's the point of it all, anyway? As Izzie says, If I keep on getting rid of people, there won't be anyone left to manage. I'll do myself out of a job.

"You clean it out with saline solution once a week," said Eva. "To stop infection."

Kim felt sick. "Do you need help with it?"

Eva smiled. "You?"

Why not me? Am I incapable? Kim took a deep breath.

"It's OK," said Eva. "The nurse does it."

Kim swallowed. "How's Otis?"

"He draws me pictures. To cheer me up. The Macmillan nurse is great. She's spending a lot of time with him. Helping him to understand."

Kim felt suddenly tired and cold, as if she'd been out all night. She looked down at her lap.

"It's what I worry about most," said Eva. "Because he's so little. I don't want him to think it's his fault."

Kim heard a distant hum as if some brand-new appliance had switched itself on. Maybe it'll happen to us all one day. Maybe we'll all have lines going in, plastic tubes delivering energy, sugar, drugs.

"Kim?"

Like *The Matrix* in reverse.

"It's different for everyone. I know that."

Kim wanted to look up, but it was way beyond her.

"Some people don't want to talk about it."

It seemed as if Eva's voice was coming from a long way off, echoing, like a lifeguard shouting from the side of the pool.

Through the tears in her eyes, Kim saw the grain in the fabric of her black jeans magnified to tiny stitches.

"It's fine if you don't want to talk. Really."

Kim said nothing.

"It's OK," said Eva.

Kim's head shot up. She wanted to shout, It's not OK. It's not OK at all. It's evil and ugly and disgusting. Why are you so calm? Why are you just sitting there, accepting it? You should be yelling and screaming and throwing things at the wall. You should be raging and wailing and fighting. But her sister's face was blank, like white paper. It made Kim mean. "It isn't OK for Otis."

Eva didn't flinch. "I was going to ask you."

No. That's not what I meant. I don't want to talk about this.

"I need to know. I need to have it written down."

Kim was in a tunnel, Eva's voice a tiny speck of light.

"Having a child around will change your life."

Please don't ask me.

"It might not be what you want."

Why aren't you asking Harry?

"Will you?"

Kim opened her mouth to say something. But she couldn't speak. She felt as if someone had knotted a rope round her neck. So, after a while, she nodded.

Eva took a deep breath and let it out in a sigh. "When we're a bit nearer, we'll tell him together, so that he knows what's happening."

Kim looked away.

"Whatever you do, however you do it, it will be the right way. I know that. I trust you."

Please stop. Please stop.

"But can I ask one thing?" Eva sounded exhausted. "It's a big thing. Don't cut Harry out of your life."

Kim couldn't help herself. The words rushed out like tiny black spiders from a burst sac. "And what does Harry say?"

"About what?"

Kim lost courage. "About this. About everything."

Eva smiled, her eyelids closing. Sleep was overtaking her. "Harry," she said with difficulty, "says we should all be drinking a lot more wine."

. . .

Kim had never been to Leicester before. She got the one waiting taxi from the station to the street where her father lived. The cab driver had a beard and a turban. He wanted to talk about Michael Schumacher retiring from Formula 1, but Kim couldn't think of anything to say. She didn't like cars much. And she thought driving them fast in a circle until the tires blew, and bits of flappy burnt rubber flew all over the track, was faintly ridiculous.

When the taxi pulled into the street where her father lived, Kim was surprised. The houses were Edwardian and double fronted, well kept, each with a neat garden. Remembering the family home in Nunhead—the yolk-yellow paint of the kitchen, the broken concrete patio at the back, the missing tiles on the roof—Kim wondered whether she'd come to the right address.

Once she'd paid the driver, and the car had sped off down the street, she stood there, unable to move, wishing she hadn't come at all.

The porch of number 62 had been glazed over to protect it from wind and rain. Inside, on the red tiles, Kim could see a line of Wellington boots—two adult pairs in black, and two much smaller ones, a red pair and a blue pair, decreasing in size. His sons, thought Kim. The half brothers I've never met. How old would they be now? Twelve and eight? Jia was pregnant soon after he moved out to live with her. Sealing their relationship before he could change his mind.

Leaning against the wall were two umbrellas, one with turquoise-and-white stripes and one bright scarlet. I wonder what she's like, thought Kim. I wonder if he went for another Hitchcock heroine, with pale blond hair and a tiny waist.

Kim took a deep breath. She rang the bell.

For a long time, she heard nothing. She wanted to laugh. All this fuss and tension, and they're not here. At the cinema, maybe, or doing the supermarket shop. She started to wonder how long she'd wait if no one came to the door. They could be away the whole weekend. Gone to visit Jia's mother, perhaps. The grandparents Kim didn't know would be gathering up the little boys she'd never met in huge enveloping hugs before finding a stash of chocolate in a kitchen cupboard. Don't tell your mother. It's our secret.

Kim felt a tiny drop of rain. She lifted her face. The sky was turning dark gray.

And then the inner door opened and there, in the glass cabinet of the porch, was her father.

When he saw her, he didn't look surprised. Perhaps he didn't recognize her. After all, she'd been fourteen when he left—thinner, straighter, even angrier than she was now. He pulled open the outer door.

"Kim," he said.

He made no move towards her. But then, he'd never been one for physical contact. They might have stayed like that, staring at each other, if it hadn't started to rain in earnest. He stood back, and she walked past him into the high-ceilinged hall, which seemed to be a corridor that ran all the way to the back of the house. She didn't know where to go, so she stood by the foot of the stairs waiting. And then he was by her side again, gesturing for her to go ahead, which is how she found herself in a great square kitchen full of light. At a rectangular wooden table, seated in front of the remains of Sunday lunch, was a woman with a red shirt and long black hair, and two boys who looked away quickly as soon as they saw her.

Her father said, "This is Kim."

To her great credit, the woman pushed away her surprise very quickly and got to her feet, smiling. She was tiny, with dark eyes and high cheekbones. Asian. Very pretty. How does he do it, my father? How does he attract such good-looking women? It seemed, for a moment, such a complete mystery that Kim turned and stared up into his face, examining him carefully. Maybe it's because he looks so serious. A furrowed brow, as if he's thinking great thoughts.

Like a young Gregory Peck. You know Hitchcock's Spellbound?

But if he is thinking great thoughts, he keeps them to himself.

"So would you like some tea?" said Jia. Her accent sounded Chinese.

Kim nodded.

"Your father didn't say you were coming."

Because he didn't know. I didn't want to ring him at home in case Jia answered. I thought about ringing him at work because I had it at the back of my mind that he had a job at the university. In the library. Special collections. Ancient books on insects and Roman remains. But I wasn't sure. Not sure enough to make investigations. Not sure enough to track him down.

The younger boy was staring at her. He had his mother's high cheekbones and black hair. Kim thought her father might introduce them. But he didn't. He just stood there.

Jia was by the sink, filling up the kettle. "So you've come from London?"

"Yes."

"And how is your mother?"

"Fine, thank you." She glanced at her father. "She got married again."

"That's nice," said Jia.

The older boy said, "Dad, can I be excused?"

Kim's father just looked at him.

Jia came back to the table with a tray. "Sit down, Kim. Boys, you can go and watch TV."

He does nothing, thought Kim. He just allows himself to be waited on. Kim sat down in the nearest chair, and her father settled himself opposite, and they both watched as Jia set down mugs of tea and a plate of pink sugary cookies on the table, and then rapidly refilled the tray with the detritus of lunch, piling up plates and glasses, scooping a clatter of cutlery onto the top. Eventually, like a solo violin player against the background percussion of a full orchestra, her father said, "On the train?"

"What?" said Kim.

"You came on the train?"

"Yes."

"You didn't drive?"

"No."

"Why?"

"I don't have a car."

Her father thought about this. "Have you got a job?"

"Yes."

"What kind of job?"

"I'm regional development manager for a housing charity."

"I would have thought," said her father, frowning, "that you'd need a car for that kind of job."

"No," said Kim. "You don't."

I suppose, thought Kim, he might have looked like a film star once. Years ago. If you squint and stare really hard, and take away the gray hair round the temples, you can sort of see bruised and smoldering. Like Eddie Redmayne. Or Adrien Brody.

Her father said, "Where do you live in London?"

"In Sydenham."

"Pissarro."

"What?"

"Camille Pissarro. French impressionist. There's a famous painting in the National Gallery. Called *The Avenue, Sydenham*."

Small, disjointed scenes were struggling to play in Kim's mind. Her mother and father standing in the yellow kitchen in

Nunhead, both tense, her mother tearful, her father bewildered, her mother shouting, "What's wrong with you? Why do you never understand?" Her father's habit of coming home with useful things he'd found in Dumpsters—antique window stays, broken chairs, wicker cat baskets—which, because her mother refused to have them in the house, heaped themselves up outside like abandoned toys. His inability to pass up a bargain, even if he had no use for a mop, a garden hose, or a five-pack of golfing socks. His insistence on keeping all forms of documentation—old passports, used train tickets, guarantees for kettles long since thrown away—as if life was only real if you had a receipt.

"So, Kim, would you like a cookie?" said Jia.

I didn't realize, thought Kim, when I was fourteen, how strange this all was. How completely ill matched they were. It was as if my father was trying to make sense of random objects while my mother was trying to make sense of him. She wanted him to notice her. She was constantly flirting with him, eyes huge as if he was her only focus. Dancing round the living room, her 1950s skirts lifting in a perfect circle. That little laugh in her voice as she teased him. Look at me, look at me, look at me. And all the time, that same expression on his face—anxious, preoccupied, as if he couldn't really work out what was going on.

No wonder they couldn't stay together.

Jia said, "So how long are you in Leicester?"

Kim turned to her father. "I need to tell you about Eva."

His expression didn't change.

"Your sister," said Jia. "Who had the baby."

"A little boy," said Kim, still looking at her father and finding, to her distress, that her voice was trembling.

"I said he should see his grandson," said Jia. "But he doesn't want to go to London."

"Is that true? You didn't want to see him?"

Still, her father said nothing.

"I think maybe he wasn't sure he would be welcome."

Kim whipped round, staring at Jia with furious eyes. "Do you always speak for him?"

"Most of the time. He's not good with people."

Kim realized, to her intense surprise, that Jia wasn't trying to score points. She was just telling Kim what she thought was the truth.

"That's the thing with your father," said Jia. "He's good at his job. He knows all the books in the library. But people confuse him. He doesn't know what they mean. So I tell him. I tell him what they mean."

Kim swallowed. Her father was mute, like someone who doesn't speak the language.

"He earns the money. I do the rest." Jia smiled. "When I can. Because he is very stubborn, your father. I remember when your sister wrote him a letter saying she was having a baby. And I said to him, So don't sell the house now. Because she needs somewhere to live. London is expensive. Help her. We don't need the money. But he wouldn't listen, because he said she was grown-up. She has to be responsible. And I said, But this is your daughter. And your grandchild. But he doesn't pay attention. Because he believes he is right."

Kim's head was blank, like an empty wall.

"So," said Jia briskly, "is that why you come today? Does

she need some money, your sister? Because I think your father should give her some money. For his grandson."

Kim shook her head.

Jia studied her carefully. After a while, she said, in a quiet voice, "So there is something wrong."

Kim, holding her mug of tea, looked down at the table.

There was a long silence.

"Kim," said her father, speaking for the first time, "what is it?"

She was aware of a small flurry of movement to her right. When she next looked up, through a blur of tears, Jia had gone, shutting the door behind her.

.   .   .

Kim had bought a new black suit. Damaris had gone with her to the West End. They found it in Selfridges—a slim-fitting sleeveless shift dress with a black jacket over the top. The jacket had three mother-of-pearl buttons. The whole effect was classic and understated. Kim stared at her reflection in the mirror.

"That's the one," said Damaris.

When the assistant was carefully folding it all away in crackling white tissue paper, Kim wanted to say, It's for my sister's funeral. She didn't know why she wanted to say that. Maybe to make it real. Because nothing much else was real these days. Outside the shop, on Oxford Street, Kim stood on the pavement and stared at the big red bus getting closer and closer until Damaris put her arm round Kim's shoulders and tugged her away.

They bought new dark-blue corduroy trousers for Otis. They

had to guess the size because he wasn't with them. He was with Izzie in Sydenham, playing with his train set. When they got back, he didn't want to try them on, and Kim didn't have the energy to insist. But on the day of the funeral, when Otis got dressed in his new clothes, Kim said, "Oh look. They're the right length." And then she saw Damaris and Izzie exchange glances and she realized there was a story behind it somewhere—the trousers had been exchanged, or taken up, or made longer.

But she was glad no one had told her. Because she didn't really care.

Her father hadn't brought Jia or his sons. When he saw Otis, he said, "And how old are you?" But Otis just looked at him with blank eyes.

Grace was crying.

At the crematorium, which was packed, the music was too loud. Otis sat on the wooden bench and his legs swung like a puppet's in empty space. There were white flowers. The coffin was covered in a red velvet cloth. Something was hurting in Kim's head like an old hangover, but she knew it would pass if she didn't think about it and concentrated instead on the blue hymn books and the November light flooding through the big tall window.

Harry was on the other side of the aisle. He had his head down and his shoulders were shaking.

Outside they looked down at the flowers on the ground. Kim didn't know why the flowers were on the ground, but she didn't really feel she could ask, as she was the one who was supposed to know what was going on. A big man with dreadlocks came up to her and said, in an Irish accent, "I'm so sorry." And she thought, For what? Until she remembered. Someone else, who sounded German, held her hand and said, "Your sister was a wonderful person," which made her cross, because she couldn't think why anyone would want to tell her what she already knew. After a while, she switched off, which made it easier, and people came up and opened and shut their mouths, and she nodded until she was shivering so much that Christine came up and put her arm round her and said, "The car's waiting. It's time to go."

As they left, Kim hesitated, because it felt rude to leave without Eva. But then she remembered that Eva wasn't there.

Damaris guided her into the car as if she was a very old person.

They went back to Christine's. Christine had made little sandwiches, and tiny puffs of pastry filled with cheese, and miniature cakes with sugar icing. There was hot tea, and beer, and sweet sherry. Christine's grandchildren played with Otis under the kitchen table. Conversation was hushed, like the whispering in the waiting room at the doctor's surgery. But then more and more people arrived, all of them carrying plates of food and bottles and cans and glasses, and Christine's house got fuller and fuller and you couldn't breathe, because it was much too hot. And then a woman with long dark hair came over and said, "We wondered if we could play some of the songs she liked?" And after that it was better because Kim could see musicians bent over their big pale guitars, and the air was full of the music she had heard all her life, by the Mamas and the Papas, and Bob Dylan, and the Byrds.

And there it was, King Solomon's song. To every thing there is a season, and a time to every purpose under heaven. A time to be born and a time to die. A time to weep and a time to laugh. A time to love, and a time to hate. A time of war and a time of peace.

Kim bent her head and wept. She said to Damaris, "She's the wrong age. You don't die at thirty-one."

"I know. I know. She was too young."

No, I meant it should have been me. I'm twenty-seven. Like Jimi Hendrix and Janis Joplin and Amy Winehouse and Kurt Cobain. That's the danger age. The Twenty-Seven Club. That's the age you die. Not when you're thirty-one with a five-year-old child. Not when you've worked out what's important. Not when you've realized that all the shit we're meant to believe in—ambition, possessions, wealth—mean nothing at all, and the only thing that matters is love. Eva's death makes no sense. And unless we see that it doesn't, there's no chance for the rest of us. We might as well give up. She so badly wanted to speak, so that people could understand, but her mouth was too full of tears. The pain in her head was getting worse. There was too much noise in the room.

The light was blocked. It was Harry, towering over her. He was in shadow. She couldn't see his face. "I've got to go."

She nodded, impatient. You're not wanted here anyway. You made her worse. You made her tired. Didn't you see how hard it was for her to smile? Day after day, forcing herself to look happy when she felt so ill. All you cared about was yourself. Treating it all as a joke. Harry said, "Tell me if there's anything I can do."

She wanted him to go, to stop blocking the light.

"If there's anything you need."

"Harry," said Damaris, "I think—"

Kim struggled to her feet. Damaris reached up and put a hand on her back to steady her.

"It doesn't make sense," said Kim.

For a moment, their eyes met.

"If you need money—"

It was as if he'd slapped her.

The people nearest to them stopped talking. The music faltered and faded away.

"Get out." Kim's voice rang round the room. She stood there, swaying, deathly white. "Get out. I never want to see you again."

2013

So how are you?"

Kim didn't like it when Jake was sympathetic. It was all wrong.

"It's OK. Worse for Otis."

"Ah yes." Jake shook his head. "And how old is he now?"

"Just had his sixth birthday."

"Tragic."

Kim swallowed hard.

"So"—Jake swung round his chair and tapped hard on the keyboard like someone dealing a fatal blow to a wasp—"your annual appraisal."

"Jake?"

"Hmm?" Jake appeared to be studying the screen intently.

"Why are you doing this? And not Louisa?"

"I volunteered."

Kim frowned. "Can you do that?"

"Well," said Jake, typing quickly, not looking up, "she's so busy."

But this is embarrassing, thought Kim. I don't want to discuss my ongoing personal goals with you. She shifted uncomfortably in her chair. "To be really honest—"

"We could start," said Jake, spinning round to face her, "with an overview of the things you think you've done well this year."

"What about the things I've done badly?"

"We'll come on to that."

"It's just that I'd much rather—"

"Bristol, obviously. A triumph. I would say you handled the whole situation extremely well." Jake leant forward with an expression of concern. "All the more praiseworthy given your difficult family circumstances at the time."

"Thank you."

"And your standards of communication with the team at the head office are always spot-on. There's never a time when I don't know exactly what's going on in the regions. Which is extremely valuable. Especially when I'm planning major campaign initiatives and needing to apply specific and targeted leverage."

Kim let out her breath in one long sigh. "Good. I'm glad."

"Lulu agrees with me by the way. Very impressed."

"So the feedback is positive."

"In that regard," said Jake, "yes."

"Is there another regard?"

"I'm sorry?"

"It's just that you sounded a bit hesitant. As if there was another way of looking at it."

Jake leant back in his chair, put the tips of his fingers together, and stared up at the ceiling. His hair stuck out in bristles like a mop dipped in glue. "I did canvass opinion, obviously, before this meeting. And there was just a tiny hint of criticism from the SMT."

"From Louisa?"

"Not so much from Lulu as from the senior management team collectively."

"Does that mean you?"

"Just a slight anxiety that you haven't always been giving us one hundred percent."

Kim stared. "When?"

"Specifically at the end of last year. Things did tend to slip a little."

"Jake, my sister died."

"Yes." Jake put on an expression of deep sympathy. "Yes, she did."

"I took a fortnight's compassionate leave. There was a lot to sort out. Otis was my priority."

Jake put up his hand. "As was entirely appropriate."

"I had to move him and all his stuff from London Bridge to Sydenham."

From a vast apartment overlooking the river to a tiny one-bedroomed flat where he has to sleep on a blow-up mattress.

"No one on the senior management team would, for a moment, wish to underestimate the severity of the family trauma at that point in your life."

"So what's the problem?"

Jake screwed up his face as if evaluating a particularly complicated piece of modern music. "I think there was a little frisson of concern that, on your return to the office, your work wasn't up to its usual high standard."

"In what way?"

"That's a very challenging tone of voice."

"It's a very challenging criticism."

Jake smiled. "I don't think it's helpful to take this personally."

"What other way is there to take it?"

"And I'm not sure that shouting helps."

"I'm not shouting."

"So hard, I always think, to judge the volume and tone of one's own voice." Jake spread out both hands like a saint offering a blessing. "You must remember that this is a professional evaluation intended to produce specific goals for next year. All of us can learn from the past in order to suggest ways in which work can be improved in the future."

"You're being ridiculous."

Jake raised his eyebrows.

"They were exceptional circumstances. I had lost my sister. If I wasn't concentrating fully at the end of last year, it was because—" Fury grabbed Kim by the throat. Her words tailed out in a sort of rising sob. To her intense shame, her eyes filled with tears.

"It is emotional, isn't it? Would you like a tissue?"

Kim shook her head, unable to speak.

"These kinds of session demand total honesty and a high level of self-awareness. We have to face our true selves. Zofia used to find them particularly difficult. So hard, after all, when you have both a personal and professional relationship with your line manager." Jake leant back in his chair. "While you compose yourself, I'd like to share some important news with you. I'm taking a few weeks off. I won't bore you with the details. Ongoing medical problem. Inflammation of the flexor pollicis longus. Or possibly hypertrophy of the thenar eminence. Stress, obviously. Overwork. Pushing myself to the limit. I'll need tests, X-rays, physio. Possibly even a DEXA scan. On my return, in order to ensure that I don't put myself at risk again, I will be taking on two new interns to deal specifically with social media. Proactive and interactive engagement with supporters. The idea, as I've explained to Lulu, is that the general public will be more likely to donate if they can identify with the human face of homelessness."

Kim nodded. She was finding it hard to concentrate.

"But before we launch the new strategy, I must get fully fit. In order to nuance my strategic role. So the charity will have to do without me for a while." Jake gave her a thoughtful glance. "And without you, too, of course."

Kim was confused. "Without me?"

"Well, that's the other reason for our little session here today. And why I volunteered, in fact. I said, She's already been through so much. The death of a beloved sister. Her life turned upside down by the sudden responsibility of supporting a young child—not only financially, obviously, but emotionally as well. I felt you would be better able to hear the news from me."

Her heart beat faster. "The news?"

Jake looked at her with mournful eyes. "I'm afraid we're letting you go."

"Letting me go?"

"Making you redundant. As an organization, due to internal efficiencies, rationalization, and downsizing, we no longer need a regional development manager."

Kim stared.

"Which, of course, given the major de-hiring program you undertook over the past few months, you will have realized already."

"You can't do it like this, Jake. I have rights. There must be a consultation period."

"Obviously, it has nothing to do with the fact that your new caring responsibilities will make you less agile and less flexible. Less useful to the organization, really. That might have been an issue if the charity had still needed a regional development manager. But, as I've explained, due to the general restructuring and consolidation, it doesn't."

I can't lose my job. Not now I've got Otis to look after.

"You'll be paid until the end of March. Which I think's quite generous."

There was a small silence.

Kim said, "So what was the point of the annual evaluation?"

An expression of mild surprise flitted across Jake's face. "Didn't you find it useful?"

●　●　●

"You're not telling me you haven't rung him."

"Why would I ring him?"

"You said you would."

"I said I might."

"It seems to me, Kim, that you are making life unnecessarily difficult. Harry has a duty to support his son. And he is more than willing to take on that responsibility."

"Eva never wanted—"

"Jean-Marc and I have discussed this at some length. Obviously we don't want you to starve. And you are, of course, welcome to come and stay with us at any time. It would be a pleasure to have you here as our guests. For a limited period, of course. But we're not in a position to pay you any kind of allowance. If only we were. Tax in France is a national scandal. Everyone's talking about it. You can own a country home with marble floors and a swimming pool and olive groves and an exquisite formal garden, but you're still struggling to make ends meet. And how we struggle! I can hardly afford a weekly manicure."

"I've never asked you for—"

"I haven't wanted to bring this up, Kim. But I do feel that your attitude is fundamentally selfish. Surely it would have been better for Otis to stay in London? Of course, it was very kind of Izzie's parents to take you in. But really, Kim. Newcastle. You can't be happy in the north of England. I refuse to accept it."

"I didn't have a—"

"It's not as if it's any kind of long-term solution, being a lodger in someone else's house. You need to put down roots. Think of the future. And I simply can't see why you won't accept Harry's help. He could rent you a nice little flat somewhere charming. Like Primrose Hill. Or Hampstead. Otherwise, Kim, in years to come, Otis may look back and wonder why his aunt deprived him of basic necessities—indeed, of a father's love— just because of some mild dislike on her part. And I hope you have your answer prepared. Because, quite frankly, in your shoes, I wouldn't know what to say."

.   .   .

The worst thing about the playground of Otis's new school was that everyone was so bloody friendly. Kim, in her black jeans and white T-shirt—no makeup, no jewelry, no smile—put her head down, avoided eye contact, and headed for the exit as soon as she'd dropped Otis off. But people kept stopping her, asking polite questions, and inviting her to things she didn't care about.

It was all so meaningless, all this friendliness. All these people milling about, their mouths opening and shutting like letterboxes.

"It takes time, pet," said Izzie's mum. "There's no rush."

Kim felt as if she was looking at the world from inside a glass case. She couldn't feel anything—rain, or cold, or the softness of fabric. She couldn't smell anything. Sounds were strangely muffled. But she got through the days. Meetings at school. Targets at work. Reading aloud to Otis and trying to be prepared in advance for words to do with love and family because they got stuck in her throat and choked her.

Sometimes, like a thief stealing in through the window, the thought of Harry came into her head. But she always pushed it out. She had to focus on practicalities—the present, not the past. Otherwise she'd go under. Even so, Kim worried about having ripped Otis from everything that was familiar. She watched him carefully. At the beginning, he talked about London a lot—his friends, Harry's flat, Harry himself. But then it all just faded away.

"So how's the job?" said Izzie, on a lightning visit to Newcastle. She was living in Liverpool these days with her friend Hannah—a fellow comic she'd met on the stand-up circuit. They were writing a sitcom together. For the BBC, said Izzie, her face lit up with excitement. Kim couldn't stop staring. Hannah, vivid against the faded chintz of the living room, had the brilliance of a painting by Georgia O'Keeffe. Her orange T-shirt glowed like fire against her dark brown skin. She had a soft brown Afro, bright-blue nails, a short silvery skirt, and long legs splayed over the arm of the sofa like a crane fly spilling out of a matchbox.

"It's OK." What else can I say? thought Kim. It's a job. Badly paid. In housing. The only one I was offered. Now, weeks later, Kim didn't find this surprising. After Eva died, all the passion, fire, and commitment had just vanished. I would stare in the mirror, she thought, and see a face so wiped of any expression that it looked like a lump of raw dough. And people could see that. You couldn't really blame them. It was obvious that I didn't give a shit. About anything. And if I'd been hiring staff, I wouldn't have given me a job either. I'd have put me right at the back of the queue.

"And Otis likes his new school?"

"We've bought him a present," said Hannah. "A purple Furby. You can teach it to talk."

Kim usually let Izzie's parents handle all the difficult questions ("It's early days, pet"). But that afternoon they had taken Otis to see an ancient aunt in Prudhoe, leaving her undefended. The truth was, the school was worried about a whole long list of things. Kim had been in to see Miss Carter twice in the past month. Otis isn't paying attention. Or listening to instructions. It's possible he has hearing difficulties. Or language delay. But we think it would be a good idea to see the educational psychologist. And of course the school counselor. There may be bereavement issues. And how are things at home?

"You know what?" said Hannah when the silence got too long. "I think you're working too hard. We need a night out in Liverpool."

Kim couldn't imagine a night out anywhere. "I thought I might take Otis back to see Christine one weekend."

"You can stay in Sydenham if you like," said Izzie. "The flat's just sitting there empty most of the time."

Early in May, on a morning so full of spring promise that the sun was blindly flashing off bits of metal like an overenthusiastic press photographer, Kim was rushing out of the school gates when a woman with red hair fell into step beside her.

"Would Otis like to come round one day?" She had a London accent. "Victor keeps asking."

Victor? Who the hell is Victor?

"I'm Emily. We live near each other, I think. Are you going back now?"

"I'm going to work."

"I'll walk with you for a bit, shall I?"

Oh great, thought Kim gloomily. Company.

"You're a woman of mystery, you know. Everyone keeps talking about you."

Kim looked up, furious. "Why?"

"Because they can't find out anything about you. It's intriguing."

"There's nothing to find out."

Emily laughed. She had the creamy skin that sometimes goes with red hair and freckles. "You're just making it worse. Now I'm curious, too."

Kim took a deep breath. "I got made redundant. I couldn't find a job in London so I came up here. I live with my friend's parents. Otis is my nephew. I was made his guardian when my sister died."

"I'm sorry." Emily looked genuinely sad. "They told us about your sister when Otis started at the school. When did she die?"

"Last November."

"How old was she?"

"Thirty-one. Breast cancer."

"God, that's shit."

Kim nodded.

"I used to work with someone whose best friend died of breast cancer. Same age. It's like some kind of plague, isn't it? Taking out all the women."

They walked on in silence. Emily said, "I was at an investment bank. In the City. But then my husband got a job here. At the hospital. Consultant cardiologist."

Kim said nothing.

At the end of the street, Emily came to a halt and nodded back at a grand three-story house with wisteria all round the front door. "This is me." She hesitated. "Look, I know you want to be left alone. And I understand that. Harry's the same. My old friend from work. He looks like shit, but he'd rather die than talk about it. It's the English disease, isn't it? Keeping it all bottled up. But at least let me help with Otis sometimes. It must be really hard on your own." She stopped and looked at Kim more closely. "Are you OK?"

But Kim didn't answer. She just stood there in the sunshine feeling as if someone had punched her.

.   .   .

One Sunday afternoon in June when Izzie's parents had dragged a silent Otis to the park, the doorbell rang. Kim frowned. She didn't want visitors. She wanted to be alone.

On the doorstep in front of her was a small man with brown

skin, black hair, and dark eyes—probably somewhere in his early thirties, but way too shiny and wealthy to be one of the dads from school. She glared at him.

"Kim?"

"Do I know you?"

He held out his hand. "My name is Syed."

She just stood there, holding on to the edge of the door. "And?"

"Can I come in?"

"No."

Syed nodded. "I don't blame you. I wouldn't let me in either."

"Are you selling something?"

Syed smiled. "Do I look like I'm selling something?"

Kim considered this. He didn't. No clipboard. No leaflets. "So what do you want?"

"The trouble is," said Syed, "that if I tell you why I'm here, you'll shut the door in my face."

"You'd better tell me then," said Kim, "before I do it anyway."

"Just five minutes?"

"No."

"Would it help if I said I knew Christine?"

"How?"

"I might need to come in to tell you that."

Kim started shutting the door.

He said, speaking quickly, "She gave me your address."

Kim stood there, eyes narrowed.

"I said I was like Ban Ki-moon trying to broker a peace settlement. Although, to be fair, I think she was more impressed by the fact that I liked her mango chutney."

"You're not making any sense."

"I know," he said, beaming.

"Are you always this irritating?"

"Always."

Oh, fuck it, thought Kim. She opened the door wider. "Come on, then. But it had better be good."

She led Syed through to the living room. Even now she couldn't believe people made so many different fabrics printed with cabbage roses.

Syed smiled. "She said I might have a wasted journey. Five hours in the car from London, and you wouldn't let me in."

"But that didn't bother you."

"I believe in living dangerously."

She looked at him suspiciously. "So how do you know Christine?"

Syed's smile faded. "You're not going to like it."

Kim, bored, waited.

"Harry had her number in his phone."

Her heart banged unpleasantly.

"Your number wasn't there, unfortunately. It would have made life a lot easier. But I rang Christine and told her why I needed help and she invited me round. And gave me your address. She said you'd be more likely to listen if I came in person."

"Because you're so charming."

"She's worried about you. Says you're still in shock."

Kim ignored that. "If this has got something to do with Harry, I'm not interested. We don't see each other anymore."

"I know. He told me. Although it took all night. You threw him out. Said you never wanted to see him again. And then left

London." Syed took a deep breath. "The trouble is, he promised to make sure you were both OK."

Kim was furious. "Is this any of your business?"

"Eva asked him to. That's what's cracking him up. He's breaking his promise to her."

Kim stood up. "I think you'd better go."

"Hear me out."

"It's just going to be a whole load of lies."

"You think Harry put me up to this."

Kim was scornful. "You're saying he didn't?"

"He didn't."

She shrugged. But something in Syed's face made her pause. She felt almost frightened.

Syed said, "I'm worried about him."

Kim wanted to say, Why should I care? But even as the words rushed into her head, she felt childish and stupid for thinking them.

"I've never seen him like this before. You know what he's like. Never shows what he's feeling. Keeps it all hidden. But he promised Eva that he would look out for you. And he can't. So he's falling apart." Syed paused, his eyes dark with anxiety. "He's a good man. My best friend. Way more honest than the rest of us. He wants to do the right thing."

Something was struggling to surface—anger, outrage, panic. "Tell him he needn't worry. We're fine."

"Both of you?"

Kim took a deep breath. "We have a different life now. Things have moved on."

Syed looked sad. "And that's it?"

"Yes," said Kim. "That's it."

After Syed had gone, Kim couldn't stop shaking. She put on an extra sweater and even wrapped herself in a blanket. But nothing worked. It was like her bones were made of ice.

. . .

The kitchen in Nunhead was full of steam and the smell of fried onions. Christine was out shopping. Her eldest—the IT consultant—was coming over for supper, bringing his wife and three children. Christine had already made two large chicken pies, peeled a whole bag of potatoes, and chopped up carrots, cabbage, beans, and broccoli. But she'd decided at the last minute that they didn't have enough bread.

Kim, sitting at the kitchen table, was so slumped in misery she looked like a pile of dirty washing. "Australia?"

Damaris nodded.

Kim stared at her. "Why?"

"Because they know how to treat A&E doctors there. There are proper resources. Work-life balance. As in, you do your job, and then you have time off to recover."

"When are you going?"

"In a month's time. The first of December."

Everyone was leaving. There was no one left.

"Why don't you come too? For a holiday?"

"How can I? I don't have any money."

"I'll lend you some."

I'd never be able to pay you back, thought Kim. We couldn't even afford the train down from Newcastle. We spent seven hours on a bus.

"Come for Christmas," said Damaris. "It's summer there. Think of all the sunshine."

Kim hung her head. They say you take yourself with you wherever you go. You're the same person, whatever the setting. I'd spend all that money just so that Otis and I could sit in silence in Melbourne.

Damaris leant forward across the kitchen table. "Come on, Kim. We can go sightseeing. Go the beach. You might want to stay on. It's the right age to move Otis. Before he puts down roots."

I can't imagine Otis putting down roots anywhere, thought Kim. He doesn't seem solid enough. It's like he's not even there half the time.

The front door slammed shut. Christine came into the kitchen with a bulging carrier bag and two long baguettes. "Kim!" She stopped and looked round. "But where's Otis?"

"Watching TV with Dad," said Damaris.

"That boy spends too much time indoors," said Christine, unpacking three large round loaves and setting them down on the table next to the baguettes. "He should be outside at his age. Running about in the sunshine. Getting some fresh air in his lungs." She stopped and looked at Kim over the top of her glasses. "You heard about the new job? In Melbourne?"

"I've told her she's got to come with me," said Damaris.

Oh, thought Kim. They're ganging up on me.

"Of course, it's a long way," said Christine, taking off her coat and hanging it on the back of the kitchen door. "And I don't want my daughter on the other side of the world. I want my family all around me." Still wearing her paisley scarf and blue felt hat, she turned round, small, fierce, ready to take on all comers. "But that's what you've got to do when you're young, Kim. Seize your chances. Grab hold of life."

"Make a fresh start," said Damaris.

"I did," said Kim in a small voice. "I went to Newcastle."

Christine shook her head. "You're hiding, Kim. That's what you're doing. You don't want to face it. So you're hiding yourself away."

Kim opened her mouth to protest—stop interfering! leave me alone!—but realized, quite suddenly, that she was on the verge of tears.

"I know you think I worry too much. And I know you don't want Harry to help you. You want to get through this on your own. That's the way you've always been, ever since you were a little girl. Stubborn. Determined. Independent. You used to sit right there, five years old, with the look you're wearing now. Like they could tear you apart, limb from limb, and nothing would make you change your mind." Christine leant forward. "But I'm not going to let you waste your life. You hear me, Kim? You've taken a year out to grieve, you and Otis. But time is passing, and you're still walking around half-asleep. Before you know it, you'll be old and tired, and wondering where it all went. You finish your grieving now. Stand up and face the future. And if you won't take money from Harry or Damaris, you take it from me. Go to Australia. Start your life over again."

· · ·

Dear Kim,

> *I hope you are well.*

> *Jia has asked me to send you the enclosed check. She tells me that you will be facing unforeseen expenses now that you are my grandson's legal guardian.*

> *You may find it sensible to put this towards a deposit if you are thinking of buying property.*

> *However, Jia has insisted that I make it clear that the money is yours to spend in whatever way you think fit.*

> *Best wishes,*

> *Dad*

.   .   .

When you see a shark from underneath it looks like a Boeing 747—white, with a round end, and two arms sticking out. Skates look like children in onesies making angel wings. Shoals of sardines flash silver when they change direction. You can see them all, standing here. Tuna, turtles, sunfish. Jellyfish. Which, of course, thought Kim, watching the frilly pulsing mushrooms shoot through the water like upside-down umbrellas, aren't fish at all. They don't have bones or blood or fins.

But they sting. They have tentacles beaded with toxins. The box jellyfish is the worst. Almost transparent, it floats around off the coast of northern Australia. It can kill you in minutes.

Otis stood very still, looking up at the wall of glass. Moon jellies. Comb jellies. Crown jellies. Dark purple blubber jellies. The flower hat jelly with its brilliant, multicolored tentacles trailing from a pinstriped bell. The flower hat jelly with its vicious sting.

He hadn't said a word since they arrived. Jet lag, probably.

"He's very quiet, your son, isn't he?" They'd sat next to an elderly woman on the way over. She was a grandmother, off to visit her daughter. She'd been brimming with good-natured excitement. As the plane took off, she chatted away to Otis, asking where he went to school, what he liked doing, if he'd ever flown before. At first, she thought he must be shy. Then she decided he was tired. But when he met all her questions with that same empty stare, she began to get uneasy. Then puzzled. Then anxious.

I wish people would just shut up and mind their own business, thought Kim, watching Otis as he stared up at the jellyfish. We'll be fine if everyone just leaves us alone. Maybe we should have hung around the hotel for a day or two. Swum in the pool. Slept in the air-conditioned rooms. But I thought a bit of sightseeing might cheer him up a bit. Take away that blank look on his face.

That blank look worries everybody. "Under the circumstances," said Miss Carter, frowning across her chipped melamine desk, "and since we've nearly reached the end of term, I'm happy for you to take Otis out of school for a holiday."

No one could get through to him these days. It had been bad enough in Newcastle. Communication there had been pretty sparse—down to the level of peanut butter, yes/no, strawberry jam? But here, under bright blue skies, the silence seemed even worse.

"Why California?" said Damaris. "Why not Australia?"

I have no idea, thought Kim. But once I'd thought of it, there was no going back. We had to go to Monterey.

It was a sunny morning. Of course it was. The sun always shines in California. After breakfast, which neither of them wanted, they wandered up and down Fisherman's Wharf. Then Otis stood looking out over the Pacific Ocean, his face, as usual, expressionless.

"We could go whale watching," said Kim in the cheerful voice she always used with Otis these days. Although it didn't make any difference what voice she used.

On Cannery Row, Kim saw the sign for the Monterey Bay Aquarium.

"Is it good?" she said to a woman with brown hair and silver hooped earrings who was just coming out, shepherding two small children in front of her.

"It's really great," said the woman. "Especially the sea otters. They're so cute."

But after the open sea exhibit, with the sardines and the sharks among a forest of waving kelp, Otis had somehow got stuck at the jellies tank. He stared, motionless. Kim tried to chivvy him along. But he didn't look unhappy—just mesmerized. So after a while, in a different time zone, her body clock awry, Kim let her mind drift.

"Don't you love watching them?" said a voice next to her.

It took Kim a moment to wake up to the fact that someone was talking to her. Then, foggily, she realized the woman was talking about children, not jellyfish.

"It's like they're hypnotized? Like they can't stop?"

Kim nodded. Otis was now sandwiched between two blond-haired children, one small, one tall.

"Look at your little boy. He's glued to the glass. How old is he?"

"Six."

"He must take after his dad with all that black hair."

"Maybe," said Kim, struggling not to yawn. "Sorry. We've only just arrived. I haven't caught up with the time difference yet."

"You're English, right?" The woman was blond and blue-eyed with an open, friendly expression. She was wearing a white shirt with red buttons down the front. "On vacation?"

"Two weeks."

"You've come to the best place. Monterey is great for kids. We come most years. You're going to have a really great time."

Kim said, "We're going to see where the festival was, too."

"In September, right?"

"Not the jazz festival. The pop festival."

The woman shook her head.

"A long time ago," said Kim. "Nineteen sixty-seven."

"Oh, right."

"The Summer of Love. All the hippies heading to San Francisco. Flowers in their hair. The first international pop festival." Despite the coolness of the aquarium, Kim was beginning to feel hot and light-headed. I'm talking too much, she thought. Trying too hard to explain. "People like Janis Joplin. Jimi Hendrix. Otis Redding."

Otis had turned round and was looking up at her. You couldn't tell what he was thinking. You never could.

"He sang here," said Kim. "Otis Redding. His breakthrough concert."

He knew, the minute he started singing, that he had the audience hooked. He delivered soul. He sang "Respect," "Satisfaction," "Try a Little Tenderness," his voice cracked with emotion. The crowd was on its feet—they didn't want to let him go. Cheering, clapping, yelling. And then six months later, he was dead. A plane crash. So young. Not even twenty-seven. London loved him. Europe loved him. After Monterey, the world was at his feet. But just when he was going to make it, just when everyone wanted more, he died.

"Are you OK?" said the woman. "You've gone really white."

Hope has gone, thought Kim, standing there, watching the jellyfish fill and float like ever-falling parachutes. When Eva died, she took hope with her. It's disappeared forever.

"You don't look well. Maybe you should sit down."

I can't feel anything. I'm like a jellyfish. Brainless, spineless, heartless.

"I could get you some water."

And I'm not sure, thought Kim, as someone pushed her into a chair, and she felt something cool and damp on the back of her neck, and the voices around her got fainter and more distant, that I can do this anymore.

Much later, Kim and Otis sat in a tiny restaurant on the seafront. The day was beginning to feel slightly surreal, as if bits of dream had got mixed up with Coca-Cola and pizza and fresh tomato salad. Kim ordered a black coffee to keep herself awake. I hope Otis wants to go to bed early, she thought, or I'll never last.

Otis said, "I want to see Harry."

Kim stared, eyes wide open. "What did you say?"

"I want to see Harry."

For a few seconds, she just looked at him. Back in Newcastle, if he'd suddenly spoken like this, out of the blue, it might have been a cause for celebration. She might have run around the restaurant screaming, waving her arms in the air. But here in Monterey the unexpected seemed normal. She felt like Dorothy in *The Wizard of Oz* or Alice in Wonderland—confused but not surprised. She frowned. "You want to see Harry."

He nodded.

But we can't, she thought. Though now, suddenly, she couldn't remember why. It was something to do with the funeral. But while parts of the day were vivid in her mind—the red cloth on the coffin, the white lilies on the ground—she couldn't remember what had made her so angry. And for the first time in a year, for the first time since Eva had died, she began to see that all her recent decisions—leaving London, abandoning everything to do with their old life—hadn't been rational at all. Maybe Christine was right. It was shock. Maybe grief makes people so weird and broken and ugly that they can't think straight. We're like chickens, thought Kim, flapping about after the fox has been in, making a lot of noise in a mess of blood and feathers.

She stirred her black, unsweetened coffee. When she looked up, Otis was still staring at her, waiting for her answer. For a moment, looking at his serious face, Kim felt that Harry was sitting with them, in Monterey, overlooking the bay. She saw Harry's smile. She heard his voice. It wasn't unpleasant. In a strange kind of way, it was almost comforting. If Otis wants to see Harry, would that be so bad? Maybe I could do it, if that's what he really wants. Maybe it wouldn't be the end of the world. And she was hit by a wave of such overwhelming tiredness that she nearly lay her head down on the white tablecloth, closed her eyes, and slept.

Kim put out her hand and touched Otis's smooth brown arm. It was hard to stay upright. So hard to keep her eyes open. She said, very slowly, the words almost too heavy to speak, "We're going to have our holiday. We're going to go on boat rides and eat ice cream and look at all the things that your mummy wanted to see. All the things she dreamed of before she died. And then we'll go home. And when we get back I'll ring Harry and ask if we can see him. OK?"

There was still a look of doubt in his eyes.

"I promise," said Kim. "Do you hear me? I promise."

And then, finally, Otis smiled.

2014

He was tall and black, maybe sixteen or seventeen, with that air of calm that athletes have. All the stress worked out. Happy in his skin. He had a sports bag slung over one shoulder. When he nodded at her, Kim smiled, but she was puzzled. Who was he? Did she know him?

"He's doing all right, you know," he said. "Otis. I watch out for him."

"Oh," she said, glancing at the door of Tommy's Gym across the street. "You mean the boxing."

"It took him a while. It was like he needed permission. But he's OK now."

"He enjoys it," said Kim.

"Harry said you weren't sure. To begin with."

It gave her a shock to hear Harry's name spoken so casually. She still expected a rush of hellfire whenever he was mentioned. "I thought he'd end up with a broken nose."

He laughed.

Kim said, "Are you Leon?"

He looked astonished. "Me? No."

"Sorry," said Kim. "I just heard Harry talk about someone called Leon."

"He's fifty. Sixty. I don't know. I'm Ethan."

"I'm Kim."

"I know."

Kim felt as if she'd drifted onto a film set where everyone except her knew what was going on.

Ethan smiled. "You're his aunt, right?"

Kim nodded.

"Work in a paint shop."

She stared.

"Otis talks a lot. Tells me stuff all the time." He grinned. "You'd better watch out. I know all your secrets."

Kim, who had become completely unused to the kind of everyday conversations that other people have all the time, cringed with embarrassment. "I'd better go in. The kids' class must be over by now."

"Where's Harry?"

"Working."

"You know he saved my life," said Ethan, shifting his bag higher onto his shoulder.

Kim waited, expecting some kind of offhand quip.

"Seriously," said Ethan. "When I was a kid. He looked out for me." He nodded. "That's why I'm looking out for Otis. I'll make sure he's OK. It's like karma, you know? What goes around comes around."

Kim frowned. Harry saved his life? How? But Ethan had raised his hand in farewell and was walking away from her down the street.

.   .   .

It hadn't been easy seeing Harry again. The first meeting, soon after they got back from Monterey, was excruciating. But Otis didn't seem to notice the tension. The minute he saw Harry, his whole body came alive. His eyes shone. He fizzed, all smiles, for the next hour while Kim and Harry limped through polite conversation, gratefully stopping whenever Otis interrupted.

"How's Damaris?"

"She's fine."

"Enjoying Melbourne?"

She has a new boyfriend, thought Kim. Called Michael—another A & E doctor, from Sydney.

"Yes."

"Harry, can we go to the park?" Otis looked up at him, beaming.

"Maybe," said Harry. "If Kim says we can."

They were back in Izzie's flat in Sydenham. (She still refused to let Kim pay rent. "I'm not paying any to Hannah," she said. "So why should you pay any to me?" Which, of course, made no sense at all.) It seemed, in some strange kind of way, as if they'd never been away, as if the year in Newcastle had never happened.

"If you want to," said Kim.

Otis leapt to his feet.

"Let Harry finish his coffee first."

"It's OK," said Harry. "We can go now. I don't mind. Are you coming?"

But Kim shook her head. "I've got stuff to do."

The minute she heard the front door slam, Kim slumped back into her chair, squashed, like a mess of roadkill. It was all so much worse than she'd expected. Harry was different. It was as if he'd been taken over by aliens. When she first saw him, standing on the doorstep, there had been a rush of recognition. Dark skin, dark eyes, black curly hair—the years fell away, and she was thirteen again, flustered and furious. But after that nothing was the same. He was courteous, careful, and polite. No jokes. No teasing. It was as if something had sucked out all his personality and left behind a flat 2-D image, bland and glossy, like a picture in a shopping catalog. Otis still made him smile. But the rest of the time, he didn't seem like Harry at all—just a man in his midthirties with his mind elsewhere.

It's like he doesn't even see me, thought Kim. It makes me wonder if I exist. Maybe it's me who's been taken over by aliens.

"What can you expect?" said Damaris on the phone from Melbourne. "You cut off all contact for months. I don't expect he likes you very much."

"I thought you were on my side."

"I am," said Damaris. "Always. But I still think you were wrong."

Sometimes, in the early hours, Kim stared into the darkness wondering whether she should talk to Harry and try to explain. I went mad for a while. I made you the focus of my grief. I'm sorry. But as daylight returned, she lost courage. They had a fragile truce. It seemed better not to stir up the past.

Harry made it very clear that he didn't want to do anything that might disrupt Kim's normal routine. He usually came round on Saturdays. In the morning, he took Otis to the kids' class at the boxing gym. In the afternoon they went to the Science Museum, or a West End matinée, or the London Aquarium.

To begin with, Kim was grateful. Stan, who owned the hardware shop where she worked—in Peckham, sandwiched between a takeaway selling fried chicken and a small grocer's that smelt of cumin and garam masala—expected her to be there most weekends, and finding child care for Otis on a Saturday had been almost impossible.

"Paint?" said her mother. "You're selling *paint*?"

"It's as close to housing as I can get in this market," said Kim.

That had been the deal she made with herself in Monterey, after all. Come home, back to London. Get a job that fits round school hours. Spend time with Otis. And it wasn't all bad at the hardware shop. They'd even let her mix half a liter of emulsion the other day.

But gradually, as the weeks passed, she was surprised—and irritated—to find herself feeling left out. Harry had somehow made it obvious that he didn't expect her to get involved in what he and Otis were doing. But she wished sometimes that he would suggest an outing they could all enjoy together.

Although she didn't want to go out in the Porsche. Which he still drove. Ostentatiously.

Otis, in Harry's company, became almost chatty. Sometimes Harry came round on a Sunday afternoon. If it was raining, or Otis had a cold, the two of them took over the living room— building complicated models of spaceships from Legos, or towers out of playing cards—and Kim, catching up with emails on her laptop at the kitchen table, eavesdropped as they discussed Formula 1, or how planes fly, or what kind of bees make honey. Once she heard someone picking out chords on the guitar. She thought of Eva and sat for a moment, staring into space.

Money was still an issue. Whenever Harry was around, she was tense all the time, waiting for him to seize an opportunity to show off his extreme wealth. She managed to close her eyes to the cost of theater tickets and meals out at pizza restaurants. Harry always asked her permission beforehand, and she reasoned that she couldn't really expect them to do nothing but wander round London's cold and rainy streets.

But once he went too far. Otis kept asking if it was going to snow and didn't seem happy with any of their explanations. As soon as Otis was out of earshot, Harry said, "I could always take him skiing. At Easter. Kids love it. Just a week somewhere."

"No," she said.

She turned her back so that he couldn't see how that panicked her, the sudden vision of Otis falling down into a crevasse, buried by an avalanche of cold, suffocating snow.

Harry never mentioned it again.

He made her uncomfortable. She could see that he was behaving with tact and consideration—sensitive to her feelings, careful not to make excessive demands—and she hated it. It was like sitting on an unexploded bomb. Were these her rules or his? Who'd made them up? What were the penalties? Most of the time, the only thing Kim could be completely sure about in Harry's company was that she would end up feeling anxious and confused. She'd waste hours after he left going over and over what he'd said and how he'd said it, as if she'd watched a complicated film in a foreign language and couldn't quite be sure of the plot.

This annoyed her. She hardly talked to him and spent no time with him. But he had somehow wound himself back into her life like Japanese knotweed.

"I think you're doing really well," said Izzie, back from Liverpool for the weekend. She'd taken pictures on her phone—Hannah's flat, the Cavern Club where the Beatles first played, Penny Lane, Strawberry Field, Hannah herself.

"You know," said Kim, "she could be a model."

"Six foot one and an Afro," said Izzie. "You can't really miss her."

"How's the sitcom going?"

"It's gone," said Izzie. "The BBC turned it down. They said the sit- bit was all right. But not the -com."

"Oh, Iz," said Kim sadly. "And you worked so hard."

"I think it was the subject matter. People always say you should write about what you know. But I think you should write about what you don't know. There's more chance of making yourself laugh."

"So what now?"

"There's always stand-up." She shrugged. "I'll have just to work on some new material. Something deeply interesting so that the nation takes me to its heart. I'd quite like to be a national treasure. Like Stephen Fry. Or Judi Dench. So they write nice things about me in the *Daily Mail*."

"It's still your flat, you know. You can chuck us out anytime."

"Because you secretly want to live with Harry."

Kim shot her an evil look.

Izzie laughed. "I meant what I said. I think you're doing really well. Both of you. Working really hard to make Otis happy." She stood up, stretching her arms above her head. "You've mellowed in your old age. Just like you always wanted. You used to be all fire and brimstone. And now you're more like a radiator."

Kim's smile was a little taut. She wasn't sure she liked being compared to central heating.

.   .   .

One Tuesday evening at the beginning of June, Kim was just settling down to watch *Working Girl*—she'd found the DVD in an Oxfam shop and had now seen it so many times that she knew most of Melanie Griffith's lines off by heart—when the doorbell rang. As usual, her heart sank. She was slightly more sociable these days. Otis—happy, outgoing, and relaxed—had made so many new friends that Kim had to grit her teeth and talk to their parents. But she still preferred an evening alone in front of the TV. Her job at the hardware store meant she had to be nice to people all day—flirtatious painters in white overalls, taciturn builders covered in a thin layer of plaster dust, anxious house owners with bruised thumbs. She had been promoted to assistant manager, so she could sometimes delegate the jobs she really hated, like serving customers. But she still got home in the evening with her face aching from the effort of smiling all day.

Clattering down the stairs to the main front door, Kim ran through the possibilities. One of the parents from school? Someone collecting for charity? Or maybe a delivery for the flat below.

Never in her wildest imaginings could she have seen herself opening the door to Jake.

"Oh," she said, staring.

He looked exactly the same—fair hair sticking out like thatch on a roof, an intense gaze, and an expression of studious superiority. But the jeans had gone. He was wearing a baggy dark suit with a faint stripe, a white shirt, and a navy blue tie.

Tatty but conservative. You could almost imagine him on the floor of the House of Commons. Maybe he is, she thought. A lot can happen in eighteen months.

"I was just passing," he said.

Liar. No one ever just passes Sydenham. What do you want?

Upstairs in the flat, Kim fought the urge to rush round and pick up newspapers, bits of Legos, and dirty coffee cups. "Would you like something to drink?" Not that I have anything, she thought. "A cup of tea?"

"Chamomile?"

Kim shook her head.

"Shame. So health-giving." Jake smiled. It took Kim a moment to realize that something had changed. His front teeth—which had once stuck out slightly, as if thrown forward by the volume of words—were now straight. Braces? Crowns? "So tell me everything. Life must be so different as a single parent. And my spies tell me you disappeared up north for a year. Where are you working now?"

Kim would have liked to have steered the conversation to somewhere less personal. But this was Jake. Somehow not answering his questions was impossible. "I work in a hardware store."

Jake looked shocked, like a Victorian lady who's just found mouse droppings in her seed cake.

"It's local. And they're very understanding if I need time off," said Kim defensively.

"And do you?"

"What?"

"Need time off?"

"Only if I can't afford child care over half term."

"So they don't pay well."

"Not particularly." Desperate to switch topics before he annihilated her completely, she said, "What about you?"

"Me? Oh, you know." Jake wandered over to the bay window and stood with his back to her, his hands in his trouser pockets. "Bit of a career change. Working in health these days. Still championing the physical and emotional well-being of the British public. But in a slightly different way."

"What kind of way?"

"A sort of government adviser," said Jake, turning round. Oh, thought Kim, I recognize that smirk. He's intensely proud of this. "Providing a framework for the reassessment of hospital care. As it moves, if you like, from local generalism to regional specialism. Investing for the long term."

Kim frowned. "Closing hospitals?"

"That's a little simplistic. There will of course be some closures during the program of rationalization. But the ultimate aim is to commit to excellent service for all UK customers going forward."

I might have tried to argue years ago, thought Kim. But I don't think I've got the energy anymore. Maybe that's the secret to becoming less hotheaded. Work long hours and look after a child.

"Are you still living in Stockwell?"

Jake looked surprised. "Oh no. Moved some time ago. Wandsworth. Between the commons."

"How lovely."

"Quite a lot of work remodeling the house. Not in a bad state when I bought it, of course. But a bit tired."

I know the feeling.

Jake looked at her directly. Those pale blue eyes, thought Kim. I'd forgotten how they pin you to the spot. "I don't want to rush this conversation. It would be delightful if we could talk all night. But I recognize that you are fully committed time-wise on a number of different fronts. So let me come to the point. I came here to find out whether you might consider a career shift."

"A what?"

Jake sighed. "Do you want a job, Kim?"

She stared.

"I have never met someone quite so good at firing people. My plans involve massive redundancies. When I was asked to cost them more fully, I thought of you."

"I've already got a job."

"Oh, come on, Kim. Not this kind of job. Six-figure salary, two-year contract, five weeks' holiday, private medical insurance?"

The numbers pinged about in her brain like balls in a squash court. "So this isn't working for the NHS?"

"The NHS, Kim," said Jake, "but not as we know it."

. . .

For the next few days, Kim wandered round in a dream. She'd pick up a T-shirt shrunk in the wash, the seams so stretched you could see the ladders of stitches, and think, If I took that job I could throw this away. She'd open a kitchen cupboard, stare at the packets of chickpeas and lentils, and think, If I took that job I could fill a whole supermarket trolley with impulse buys—smoked salmon, asparagus, aubergines, mangoes—and not even think about the cost. She imagined hailing a black cab, splashing out on a bunch of flowers, ordering an iPhone, buying a car.

The last of her father's money had disappeared a few weeks ago, swallowed up by the gas bill. She had cleared her overdraft. But she was back to the daily struggle of trying to make ends meet.

I resent the time it takes, she thought. Every waking moment is a calculation. Should I walk or take the bus? Buy shampoo or a bunch of bananas? Can I afford a new pair of shoes for Otis? Tea bags? A newspaper?

Otis is the one who would benefit most. If I took the job, I could start saving for his future. For university fees. So he won't be strangled by debt all his life. I'd be a proper role model. Someone with a career. Someone going out every day and making a difference.

Then she'd remember Jake's penetrating stare and shiver. Why am I even considering working for him again after the way he's treated me?

She was tired of thinking about it. At least, she thought, scouring burnt egg from the bottom of a saucepan, he's the devil I know. I won't be shocked if he tricks me, outwits me, lands me in it, fires me. He's indestructible. One of life's survivors. There's no self-serving, double-crossing maneuver he can come up with that would surprise me at all.

And I don't imagine, she thought, as she stared at the chipped tiles behind the kitchen sink, her hands motionless in the soapy, scummy water, that he has designs on my body anymore.

I am thirty years old. I'm broke. I live in a rented flat with a badly paid job. I'm responsible for the well-being of my sister's child. What choice do I have?

. . .

They could hear the crowd from the dressing room. Restless. Talking. Laughing.

"They've sold out," said Izzie. "Not a seat in the house."

"That's what happens when you go viral." Hannah was sprawled on one of the swivel chairs. She was wearing black army boots, fishnet tights, a pink glittery leotard, and a white tutu. They are so well suited, thought Kim. Every day is a costume drama.

"I haven't forgiven you." Izzie's reflection was framed by old-fashioned lightbulbs all round the edge of the mirror. "I was only mucking about. You weren't supposed to be filming it."

Hannah raised her eyebrows.

"I'm serious. What if Mam sees it?" Izzie dabbed at her cheeks with blusher, her face tragic. "She's got very peculiar since Otis left. Into social media. Using Flickr and Facebook and putting chintz on Pinterest."

"I read somewhere," said Hannah, "that twenty-five percent of the over-fifty-fives are on tablets."

"High blood pressure?"

"Ha ha. Have you ever thought of going into comedy?"

They heard a knock. Hannah stood up and opened the door. A draft of air wafted the smell of old dust into the room. "Two minutes," said a disembodied voice in the corridor.

Kim wasn't the one performing. But her heart skipped a beat all the same. This was a big venue. The biggest so far.

"Right." Izzie stepped back from the mirror. "How do I look?"

She was wearing royal-blue bloomers, a red velvet top, and a huge white lace collar. Her hair fell in tangled curls round her shoulders. She looked like an early-twentieth-century lady cyclist who's just discovered the joys of trousers. Or perhaps a seventeenth-century Cavalier.

"Beautiful," said Hannah.

Izzie and Hannah looked at each other. There was a moment of stillness as if time had stopped. Then Izzie said, "You know what's so strange? I've spent my whole life worrying about the way I look. And I didn't realize the answer until now. If you want an opinion about your looks, or your character, or your career, or the way you live your life, you should always ask someone completely biased in your favor. It's the only truth worth having."

"Well you know what they say," said Hannah. "Love is blind."

They knew when Izzie had reached the stage. The crowd roared, like a lion.

. . .

The final argument with Harry was bad. It came from nowhere, a sudden storm.

Harry had brought Otis back as usual in time for tea on Saturday. Kim, who hadn't been into work that day, opened the front door looking self-conscious. Harry did a double take.

"I know, I know," said Kim. "It's a bit drastic."

Otis looked at her, his eyes anxious.

"It'll grow," said Kim. "In a couple of months' time, it'll be back the way it was."

"It suits you," said Harry. But there was something in his expression she didn't understand.

Otis was still staring. Kim put up her hand to the nape of her neck. She still felt a bit exposed.

"And a new shirt," said Harry. "Special occasion?"

"I was just fed up of wearing black."

But she looked down to avoid his eyes.

Upstairs in the flat, Otis showed her the program from the Cambridge Theatre and talked about how they'd gone to Chinatown to eat dim sum. Then he pottered off to watch TV, and Kim put the kettle on. I don't want Harry to stay too long, she thought. But I can't be unfriendly. There's time for a cup of tea.

Harry said, "He keeps talking about playing guitar."

"Yes."

Neither of them mentioned Eva.

Harry hesitated, choosing his words carefully. "I just wondered if you'd thought about getting someone to teach him. I'd be happy to pay."

Her head shot up.

"I hoped you'd think it was a reasonable suggestion."

The fact that Harry was being so calm and logical made Kim want to behave completely irrationally. "I'm already asking around. At school. For a teacher."

"Oh, right."

"And it's no problem. I can pay."

"Can you?"

His surprise irritated her. "I've got a new job."

"Congratulations." Harry looked genuinely pleased. "What is it?"

"It's in health."

Harry waited for more. The trouble was that Kim was still quite hazy about what she'd actually be doing. So after a while she said vaguely, "Administration."

"Locally?"

"No," said Kim, squirming. "Central London."

Eventually Harry said, "Sounds like a new departure."

"It's Jake," said Kim, angry that he was pushing her. "He wants me to work for him again."

Harry nodded. "Are you sure?"

"Sure about what?"

"Sure about working for Jake."

"Why shouldn't I?"

"Because he wrote you a letter telling you how shit you were when he dumped you."

She shot him a furious look. "That's all in the past."

"Is it?"

"Yes."

The kettle had boiled. Kim found mugs and tea bags, banging around with unnecessary noise.

"You don't have to take the job."

Kim took a deep breath. "I want to. It's a good job. It means that Otis and I can finally afford to eat properly."

"You could have eaten properly a long time ago if you'd let me help."

"I didn't want your help."

"I know. You told me. Often."

The atmosphere was ugly, as if the particles in the air were plumping with rage, ready to burst.

Kim tried to keep her voice calm. "I think we should get this straight. I'm happy for you to see Otis. I've made that clear. But you have absolutely no right to make any comment about anything I choose to do or not do. Either now or in the future." She turned her back to get milk from the fridge. Her hands were shaking. Her heart was beating fast. I knew it couldn't last. I knew the old opinionated Harry was lurking about, just waiting for an opportunity to spring back into action. He's like malaria. Lies dormant for months and then reemerges stronger than ever.

When she next stole a glance in his direction, she caught her breath. He looked angry. She'd never seen Harry look angry before. It shocked her. She carried on making the tea, avoiding looking at him at all, and put both mugs onto the table with immense care.

Harry said, "You're right."

She looked up.

He said, "Really. You're right. I'm sorry."

She swallowed hard. He had that blank look in his eyes again, as if someone had pulled down a blackout blind.

"Very sorry. And I hope you'll forget it happened." Then he said, in a completely different voice, "So does that explain the haircut? And the clothes? Getting ready for a new job?"

She nodded. Her legs felt unsteady, as if she'd been running for miles.

Otis came into the kitchen. "Can I have a drink?"

Kim glanced up at the clock.

"I'd better go in a minute," said Harry, picking up his mug of tea.

The doorbell rang.

"Oh, that'll be Layla," said Kim.

"Girls' night in?"

"Babysitter."

Harry looked up, a question in his eyes.

Kim, flustered, said, "I haven't been out for ages."

"You could have asked me to stay on," said Harry. "I wouldn't have minded."

"You've already done so much."

"Can I let her in?" said Otis.

"Leave both doors open," said Kim, "so I can see you."

She followed Otis out to the hallway. Out of the corner of her eye, she could see that Harry was still sitting at the kitchen table, not moving.

Downstairs, Otis opened the front door. She heard Layla's voice and Otis chatting away, telling her about going to see the musical. Then Harry was at her side, putting on his jacket.

She said, "Thank you for taking him out today. He had a lovely time."

He said, "You're seeing Jake tonight."

They stared at each other. Kim felt herself growing hot.

Harry's eyes weren't blank anymore. He was looking at her with contempt.

~*~ 2015 ~*~

There was no one left but Kim. The women with their Tesco shopping bags had gone. All the rest of the chairs were empty.

She didn't look up when he came in.

Harry set down a cardboard box on the table in the middle of the room. He hadn't known what to buy. She'd said she wasn't hungry. But he thought food might help. So he'd picked a random selection of things in plastic containers—sandwiches, salad, fruit. Dark chocolate. Black coffee—no milk, no sugar.

He'd been gone for an hour. It had been hard wasting the time. He'd stood outside on the shallow stone steps, holding his mobile, watching people come and go. A March evening in south London. Hospital life going on as normal. A boy of about sixteen with his leg in plaster hobbling out to a taxi. A man in a hospital gown, hooked up to a drip, smoking. Damaris? Had she rung Damaris? He couldn't remember the time difference between England and Australia. Or maybe Izzie. She'd want Izzie here. But I don't know where she is, thought Harry. Somewhere on the west coast of Ireland? There had been a postcard pinned up in the kitchen weeks ago. Mists and mountains, blue water, green fields. Houses painted pink and yellow and rust and turquoise.

But I haven't been in the flat since December. That's why it was such a shock when she rang. Her name on my phone out of the blue.

Harry stood outside the hospital entrance, the light fading. But he couldn't stand there forever. Eventually, he had to go back. Even though she didn't want him there.

Kim was sitting opposite the door, underneath the white slatted blinds. Her head was bent, her body turned to one side.

He didn't bother telling her about the coffee. She wouldn't have wanted it anyway.

They sat in silence. After a long time, Harry said, "When did you get here?"

For a while, he thought she hadn't heard. Then she said, "About two."

"This afternoon?"

She turned towards him. He was shocked by the whiteness of her face. "Last night."

Harry stared. "And you've been here ever since?"

"Where else would I be?" She sounded tired. As if she couldn't be bothered to deal with him.

He said, "How did you know?"

"How did I know what?"

"How did you know he had meningitis?"

She closed her eyes and opened them again slowly. "I didn't."

"So what happened?"

There was no reply.

He said, "Can I see him?"

"If you want."

But Harry didn't move. It wasn't exactly an invitation.

Kim said, "He's not conscious."

Harry pushed down panic. He stood up, took off his jacket, hung it over the back of the wooden chair, and sat down again.

Kim said, still looking away, "It might be a long time before he wakes up."

There was a singing scream in his head like the whine of a mosquito. Not Otis. Not Otis, too.

"You don't have to stay. I'll text you if there's any change."

But he didn't move.

From across the room, by the slatted blind, there was a small intake of breath, like the gasp someone makes when they're frightened. Harry, startled, looked up. Kim had turned her whole body towards the wall. But he could see from the way her shoulders were jerking, like she was choking, that she was crying. He watched hopelessly. He knew she wouldn't want comfort. Not from him, anyway. Eventually her body stopped shaking. He could see her pushing at her face with the heel of her hand, wiping away tears. He couldn't bear it anymore. "Kim?"

She didn't answer.

"Kim?"

She whipped round to face him, her eyes so angry that he flinched. They stared at each other. Her cheeks were bright red. Against the whiteness of her skin, it looked as if someone had slapped her. "The one thing I ask you to do, and you won't do it."

He stared at her. What had she asked him to do?

"I want you to go."

"Kim—"

"I don't need your help. If you've got to stay here, find somewhere else to sit. I thought you ought to know Otis was in hospital. But I don't want you here. And I can't leave. Or go back in there."

Her words were ringing round the room, bouncing off the walls. She sounded like she hated him.

He said, "Why?"

"Why?" She looked at him as if he was stupid. "Because I can't stand seeing him like that. Lying there with tubes all over his body. You wouldn't be able to either if you'd been here all night."

He hadn't meant that.

But she wasn't listening. "They're being very kind. Saying there's every chance. But they don't know. Any more than I do. He's eight years old. He might end up brain damaged. Or lose his arms, or legs, or go blind, or deaf—"

"Why did you want me to know?"

"What?"

He kept his eyes on her face, waiting.

"I have no idea." She looked suddenly exhausted. "Because you care about him. It seemed like the right thing to do."

The room was silent. Harry thought about Otis, lying on the white hospital bed. Then he thought about Eva. For a moment, he missed her so acutely that he almost lost control. He gritted his teeth, clamping his jaw shut.

Kim started speaking again. Her voice was so quiet, it was as if she was talking to herself. "He wasn't well all afternoon. But I thought he was OK. I thought it was the start of a cold. He went to bed as normal. I was watching TV. He came into the living room. Saying his head hurt. I gave him Tylenol. But then he was sick. Burning up. So I rang the out-of-hours service at the pediatrician's. They said, It's probably a virus. Cool him down. Ring us back if you're worried. I kept checking on him. Took him a drink. He had a fever. But his hands were so cold. And his eyes were strange, like he couldn't see me. I rang the out-of-hours service again. They said, We'll put you on the list for a home visit. It'll be about an hour. And I sat with him on the bed, and he was moaning and hot, and saying his legs hurt, and I thought, No, I'm not waiting anymore. So I called a cab. The driver said, It's OK, I'm a father too. He ran all the lights. Kept sounding the horn. Jabbing again and again with his fist. But when we got there, Otis wasn't breathing. So I picked him up and ran through A&E screaming. They lay him down and ripped his pajamas off. He had purple blotches on his legs. So they knew straightaway."

He took a deep breath so that he could speak. "What did they do?"

"Antibiotics. Fluids. The tests confirmed it. They spent five hours fighting for him. And then they said, All we can do now is wait."

He felt he had to stay calm even though, inside his head, there was a roaring sound, like someone yelling. "Can I see him?"

She nodded.

"Do you want to come?"

She looked up, and his heart contracted. She was in so much pain.

So he went alone.

.   .   .

After he'd gone, she put her head in her hands. Her fingertips were icy. It was strangely comforting touching her own fore-head. It reminded her that she was real.

Hospitals are so quiet at night. During the day there had been people coming and going all the time. The waiting room had been almost full.

Kim remembered going outside in the corridor to ring her mother. *We'll be thinking of you every minute. But you mustn't worry. Hospitals are so good these days. Although of course it's very serious. Meningitis can be a killer.*

Christine, she thought suddenly. I should ring Christine. Her eyes filled with tears. For a moment, she could almost hear Christine's voice. You hang in there, Kim. You stay strong. For Otis's sake.

And she rocked to and fro, clutching her arms round her body, trying to remember what it felt like to be hugged.

．　．　．

When Harry got back to the waiting room, Kim had leant her head against the wall and appeared to be sleeping. He sat down very quietly on one of the wooden chairs near her.

She said, "How was he?"

He looked up, startled. "No change. Which is good, they say."

"He doesn't look good."

"No." A bloated child in a coma. Harry swallowed.

She sat up. She was a sort of gray color now, like dirty paper. Her eyelids were red. "They said the first twenty-four hours were critical."

"You saved his life."

She looked at him warily.

"That's what the nurse said to me just now. If you'd waited longer at home, he would have died."

"I couldn't have waited."

He didn't say anything for a while. Then he said, "It's good that you're the kind of person you are. That you don't wait for permission."

It's bloody lonely, though, she thought. People get angry with you. She rubbed her eyes.

"I bought sandwiches. If you're hungry."

She shook her head. The idea of chewing seemed exhausting.

"They wanted me to tell you that there's a bed if you need it."

"I know." She looked vague. "But I can't."

They sat in silence. But it was less hostile now. He leant forward, his elbows on his knees, staring at the floor. "I won't stay if it makes it worse. I can go somewhere else." He glanced up. "As long as you promise to ring if there's any change."

She didn't say anything.

Harry was beginning to fold back inside himself—because there was no other way of coping—when he realized she was staring at him.

"Are you his father?"

He shook his head.

"You're not?"

"No."

"How do you know?"

"Because we never slept together."

"Yes, you did."

He said nothing.

"When I was a teenager. You were always in her room."

He shook his head again.

She struggled, out of her depth. "But you were always so close."

"I know. She was my best friend."

The words were dangerous. She could see him clenching his jaw, the muscles working in his cheek. It doesn't take much, she thought. All this time after her death, and we're still in pieces. On the surface we look OK. But it's like a layer of thin ice over deep, dark water.

He said, "She never told me who it was."

She wouldn't tell me either. That's why I thought it was you.

"I said, if she wanted, I could be his father. But she said that wasn't fair on you."

"On me?"

Harry shook his head, as if it was all too complicated to explain.

Because she knew it would be the final straw for me, thought Kim, having Harry in Otis's life forever.

After a while, Harry moved his head towards his shoulders, one side, then the other, stretching his neck like a boxer before a fight. He said, "I never understood why you hated me so much."

It was a shock. Why was he saying this? "I don't hate you."

"Yes, you do."

Kim swallowed. "I don't hate you. I just hate what you stand for."

He smiled. "So it's not personal."

"Private school, rich parents, City banker, flash car . . ." She trailed off. She was sounding petulant, even to herself. "It's about having all the privileges but not doing anything to help other people. Accepting all your advantages and grinding everyone else's face in the dirt."

There was a silence.

Harry said, "It doesn't have much resale value anymore."

"What?"

"The Porsche. It's very old."

She looked away, disgusted. Always, always, turning everything into a joke.

"That's it? That's why you hate me?"

And because you were cheating on Eva. But maybe you weren't. Officially. If you were just friends. Kim's head ached. It was all too difficult to work out. "It's enough, isn't it?"

He stared down at the floor. He said, sounding tired, "There's not much point defending myself. You made up your mind a long time ago."

This made her angry. He was accusing her of prejudice. "So go on, then. Surprise me."

He didn't say anything for a moment. Kim thought perhaps the conversation was over. But then he started speaking again. "I never knew my father. My stepfather hated me. I left home when I was fourteen and lived with foster parents. Finished school, got on a train, and came to London. I met Eva. She was my family after that."

She heard the words, but they made no sense. Eton. Old money. That's what her mother had told her.

"I don't work for a bank anymore. I left a year ago. I work

for a company making medical equipment for the early detection and diagnosis of cancer. Finding investment so the company can grow." He looked up, and for a moment she couldn't breathe. The emotion in his eyes was so raw. "I can go on. I can tell you every single detail of my life. But it won't make any difference, will it? Because it's got nothing to do with what I stand for. It's about me."

She felt cornered. "I don't know what you're talking about."

"You just don't like me."

"Oh, for God's sake, Harry." Her voice was rising. "What are you saying? That this is all my fault? What I feel is completely irrational?" She stood up, furious. "You're the cause of all this. Not me."

He looked up at her, narrowing his eyes against the light.

"You tried to turn Eva against me."

"When?"

"You said I was a fantasist. Insane."

He looked mystified.

"I heard you. In her room. Years ago."

"I was probably talking about your mother."

"Really?" Kim's voice was loud, mocking. "You always seemed to get on with her so well." *Dear Harry. So charming. So kind. So rich.*

"I try to get on with everybody."

Kim was contemptuous. "You've never tried to get on with me."

Again, that blank look in his eyes.

"Oh, come on, Harry." What did this all matter, anyway? Raking up the past. Who cared how it all started? "Be honest.

Admit it. You wanted to be with Eva. And I just got in the way. You've never really liked me, have you? Ever."

"I love you."

She stared at him.

"Ever since I first saw you. I've loved you for years."

The air was ringing in her ears. She had the sensation of things falling all around her. She could see his face, so she knew it was Harry. But at the same time she knew it wasn't him at all. This wasn't real. Any moment now, he would laugh. You believed me? You'll fall for anything. I was just joking. Winding you up.

But he didn't laugh. He just sat there, looking up at her.

She couldn't speak.

"I don't expect you to love me back. I'm just tired of lying. Trying to pretend it's not true."

Still, she couldn't find her voice.

"I'm sorry. I shouldn't have said anything."

She felt for the chair behind her. Her legs wouldn't support her anymore.

"Really. Just forget it. I'm sorry."

They sat in miserable silence.

Eventually, Kim said, "I'll go and see Otis."

He nodded.

"I might sit with him for a bit."

"Yes."

All she knew was that she had to get away. It was too huge, too much.

When she reached the door, she looked back. He was bent right over, his head in his hands.

*   *   *

When Kim got back to the waiting room, Harry was lying down full-length on the chairs against the back wall. Hearing her open the door, he swung himself up to sitting. His face was anxious. "Any news?"

She shook her head. "No change. He's stable."

"Are you OK?"

She sat down. "I'm fine."

There was a pause.

She said, "I was thinking about what you said."

He took a deep breath. "I wish you wouldn't. I'm sorry. I shouldn't have said anything. Especially not now."

"But you did."

They held each other's gaze across the room.

She said, "I don't understand. You always treated me like a child. Like everything I said was stupid."

"Self-defense. So you wouldn't see how I felt."

"Why didn't you want me to know?"

"In case you turned me down."

Round and round in circles. "What about Eva?"

"You mean, did she know?"

Kim nodded.

"She wanted me to tell you. But I couldn't. There was never a right time. Do you remember the earrings? On your eighteenth birthday? I thought about it for months. Something to show you how I felt. That you weren't just Eva's little sister. But it all went wrong. It couldn't have gone worse. I kept hoping that one day something would happen to change your mind. So that you'd see me in a different way. But nothing ever did."

But you were always so arrogant, thought Kim. So sure of yourself. You could have said something. Surely you could have said something.

He said, "I made Eva promise. She wanted to tell you. So many times. She said it drove her mad. She used to say, You've got to find out one way or the other. Otherwise you're just wasting time. Both of you."

Kim sat very still. She thought about Eva and the way she clammed up whenever they talked about Harry. She remembered her graduation from Edinburgh, arguing in the restaurant. The rows when Eva was pregnant. She remembered the terrible Christmas, her mother's wedding, the funeral. It was like trying to read a history book upside down.

Right at the end, Eva had said, Don't cut Harry out of your life. I thought she meant for Otis's sake, thought Kim. But she was trying to give him one last chance.

After a while, she said, "Why?"

"Why?" He looked confused.

But she couldn't say the words.

"Why do I love you?" He looked sad. "I don't know. Do people ever know?"

They try to explain sometimes.

"There's no one else like you. That's all. No one else comes close."

It made no sense.

"I have tried, very hard, not to. But it's like trying not to breathe. It doesn't work."

Kim looked away.

"I'm sorry," said Harry. "Bad timing. Especially now you're back with Jake."

She bit her lip. "I'm not."

"Aren't you?"

"I didn't take the job either."

He looked surprised. "I thought it was definite."

"No." She was shamefaced. "I wanted you to think it was. So when you made assumptions, I didn't correct them."

He smiled. "How devious."

The old Harry. Teasing her. "I felt bad about the whole thing anyway. He's a real shit. A manipulator. And the job was rubbish. I should never have considered it. It just seemed like a good idea at the time."

He didn't say anything.

"I thought you'd be pleased."

"I am."

"So what is it?"

Harry looked down at the floor. When he looked up, his eyes were dark.

She felt frightened. "What?"

He said, slowly, "You haven't said no."

"No?"

" 'No way I'll ever feel the same. Forget it. You must be joking.' "

They stared at each other.

Kim said, in a neutral voice, "I'd really like some coffee."

If he was surprised at the change of subject, he didn't show it. He stood up, reaching for his jacket. "Black? No sugar?"

She nodded.

When he'd gone out, shutting the door behind him, she closed her eyes. This wasn't happening. It couldn't be. This wasn't real.

. . .

All night they took turns to sit with Otis.

Once, when Kim came back and Harry stood up to leave, she said, "Why did you go to New York?"

"Because I couldn't stand it anymore. Waiting for you. Eva said, Put some space between you. See if that helps."

"You were gone so long."

He looked at her. "You were with Jake."

After he'd left the room, she sat there, staring at nothing.

Later, when he came back, he said, "I thought I'd never see you again. Either of you. When you left London."

"Don't."

"It was—"

"I'm sorry. I'm really, really sorry."

He nodded. And they didn't talk again for a while.

Once, in the early hours, she asked about Ethan. Harry was hesitant at first. But he sketched in Ethan's background and then talked about Leon and Tommy's Gym, which somehow led to talking about his own childhood, growing up in Essex with a stepfather who hated him. She watched his face as he remembered. And she thought, When I first met Harry, when he blocked out the light, he seemed so grown-up. But he was just a boy.

"Eva changed everything. Made me see that you have to let go. Move on." He smiled. "She only let me buy the Porsche if I gave a hundred grand to charity."

Kim caught her breath. "And did you?"

"I was going to give some of it to you. But it's all gone now. The homeless. Environmental campaigns. Ecovillages."

She couldn't tell if he was joking.

They talked about the funeral. She wanted to explain why she'd been so angry, but he just touched her hand, and they sat silently instead. He said, "I couldn't stay when they started playing the songs," and she said, "I know, I know."

At the lowest point of the night, the time when it feels that day will never come, Kim said, "Why wouldn't you listen?"

He looked confused. "When?"

"When Eva was ill. She was tired. She needed to rest. But you made her get up, get dressed, go out."

The lines of exhaustion on his face were like scars. "She made me promise. Right at the beginning. She said, There will come a time when I want to give up. Don't let me. It's too precious."

She wept, then, the tears cold on her cheeks.

•   •   •

At dawn, when Kim came back, Harry pulled the cord at the side to open the slats of the white blinds. The sky outside was getting lighter, a blush of rosy pink. There was a little window right at the top. Harry reached up to open it, and they could hear the first birdsong, echoing through the silence.

He said, "It's more than twenty-four hours now."

She nodded.

They weren't talking much anymore. The hours had shifted them to a different place.

Harry switched off the overhead light. The room, which had

been glaring at them all night—officious, bright white—sprang back into the shadows. They both looked over to the window.

Harry said, "It's the end of the night shift. Maybe we should go in together."

His face was dark with stubble. It made him look different—nothing like the Harry she knew. She felt suddenly awkward. She said, "I need to text my mother. Just to tell her that there's no news."

He nodded. "I'll see you in there."

Harry picked up his jacket. His white shirt was crumpled and creased, a mass of tiny lines and folds.

After he'd gone, Kim went to the window and rested her forehead against the glass. Below her, in the street, she could see the lines of cars, neatly parked, belonging to all the staff who'd been keeping the hospital alive all night. She was almost too tired to find her phone. She fantasized, for one wild moment, about telling her mother what Harry had said. *Well, of course I always knew he loved you. It was obvious right from the start.* But she'd be lying, thought Kim. Because nothing is ever that clear. Not when it comes to people. You think you know someone. But you can get it all wrong. And maybe that's what Harry and I have to do now. We have to go right back to the beginning and start all over again.

She stopped, startled. It felt as if Eva was right beside her. There was a lightness in the room, lifting her up. Kim stood there, bemused, her heart beating faster. What's happening? It's because I'm so tired. I'm not thinking straight anymore. But she couldn't shake it off. A rush of joy. A feeling of energy. And something else she didn't recognize, something clear and certain flooding through her like sunlight.

Behind her, the door banged open. Harry was standing there, dark, disheveled, excited. He said, "He's awake. He's calling for you."

Hope, she thought, with wonder. That's what it is. It's hope.

He held out his hand.

Acknowledgments

Thanks to Yvonne Wilcox, Alexandra Fabian, Sally Eden, Stephen Ireton, Pavi Sidhu, Manolo Pedrini, Simon Pinkerton, Eve Zeese, and Tony Williams for all their help with the first draft. Thanks also to the UK charities Meningitis Now and Breast Cancer Care for answering specific queries. Love and thanks to all my family, especially Joe Kavanagh, Ben Kavanagh, and Alice Kavanagh and, as always, my husband, Matt.